Oman Before 1970

Oman Before 1970

the end of an era

IAN SKEET

ff

faber and faber

LONDON · BOSTON

First published as *Muscat and Oman: The End of an Era* in 1974
by Faber and Faber Limited
3 Queen Square London WC1N 3AU
First published in this edition, with new title, in 1985

Printed in Great Britain by
Whitstable Litho Limited, Whitstable, Kent
All rights reserved

© Ian Skeet, 1974, 1985

British Library Cataloguing in Publication Data

Skeet, Ian
Oman before 1970: the end of an era.
1. Oman—History
I. Title
953'.53053   DS247.068
ISBN 0-571-13580-3

for
Elizabeth

Contents

Preface to the Second Edition

Oman has changed so much since 1970 that even the original title of this book has been altered for this new edition. The Sultanate of Oman has well and truly taken over from Muscat and Oman. I have also added a few pages of epilogue which represent little more than a salutation to the passage of time but which may also provide a narrow bridge from old Muscat to new Oman. The rest is unchanged since it is unchangeable and remains as relevant—or irrelevant—now as it was when first written.

October 1984

Eastern Arabia and the Arabian Gulf

Explanation

I was in Muscat and Oman from 1966 to 1968, and finished the draft of this book a few months after leaving. Much has changed since then; even the country has altered its name—it is now the Sultanate of Oman. Every change of any substance has occurred since July 1970 when Said bin Taimur was deposed, and his son Qabus replaced him as Sultan.

It was precisely because the removal of Said bin Taimur, whenever and however it might occur, was certain to precipitate change in everything that was Muscat and Oman, that I decided to write about it. Like Said bin Taimur, I have made no concession to the passing of the years, and have not attempted to bring anything up to date, not even to transpose into the past tense those things that were present and immediate when I wrote, but which no longer are. This is because I feel that, if there is any merit in this book, it is as a sketch, however blurred and impressionistic, of an era that has passed, and that it would be infinitely tedious for the reader to be burdened with footnotes, themselves liable to continual further alteration, telling him that what is written is no longer true.

Because of the peculiar attitude of Said bin Taimur to visitors, progress, change, publicity and the many other concepts to which most of the rest of the world has by now become accustomed, there are, as it so happens, comparatively few people who are able to record what Muscat and Oman was like in those days. It seemed to me that this was a record that ought to exist, and, primarily because I liked the country and its people enormously, I decided to do the job myself. This, then, is my impression of what Muscat and Oman looked and felt like in what turned out to be the fading years of Said bin Taimur's reign.

Glossary

SAF	Sultan's Armed Forces
SOAF	Sultan of Oman's Air Force
P.D.(O.)	Petroleum Development (Oman) Ltd.
I.P.C.	Iraq Petroleum Company
M.T.D.	Maria Theresa dollar

AKHDAR	Green
ASKAR	Guard, soldier
BADAN	A local fishing boat
BEDU	Nomad(s), nomadic
BURASTI	Palm frond
FALAJ	Water channel
FAREEG	A bedu place of encampment
HADHR	Settled (as opposed to nomadic)
HALWA	A sweet
HOURI	A local canoe
HUSN	Fort
KHOR	A saltwater inlet
MAJLIS	Meeting/reception (room)
QADI	Judge
SABKHA	Salt flats
SUQ	Market-place, market
TAMIMA	Senior sheikh of a tribe
WADI	Valley, watercourse
WALI	Governor
WILAYAT	Governorate, Province

You will find that I have used Muscat, Oman, and Muscat and Oman variously to describe the whole country or, as appropriate, parts of it. This is done not to complicate matters, but because, however logically inconsistent it may be, this is how they are generally used.

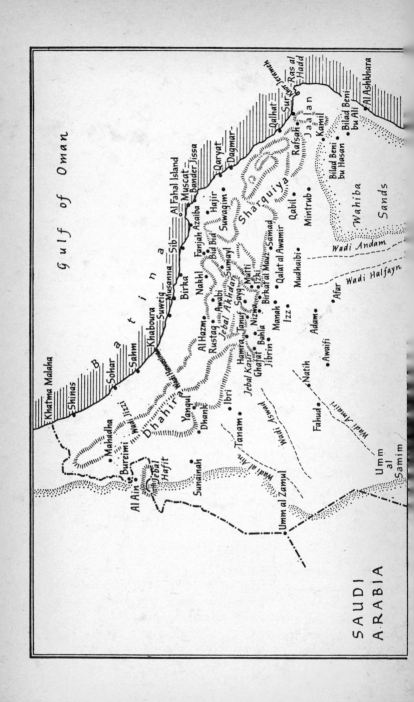

Muscat and Oman

❧ MUSCAT ❧

❧ Muscat ❧

Muscat exhales history. You can sense it in the heavy hot air of summer and the light bright winter mornings, in the dusty alleys and the large crumbling square houses and it's stored up, it must be, in some concentrated distillation in the forts of Merani and Jalali. A whiff is mixed with the breeze daily, but, like the widow's cruse, it will not run out, not at least until the forts, and the houses, and the walls and the towers are torn down to make way for blocks of flats and offices and off-street parking.

The forts are most people's first, and usually most lasting, image of Muscat, an image that is almost tactile, so solid are they. Coming by road up and over the last pass from Muttrah they are angled and merged almost into one, heavy and grey over the faded blue and dirty white wash of the huddled houses. From the sea they stand square in front of you, like two enormous bastions built for a suspension bridge across the harbour; but in place of the bridge there is the front line of the town, dominated by the Sultan's palace and the British Consulate General, both gazing straight out to sea. Very proper too, for much of the history stored up in those forts and pervading the town came in ships from that same post-card blue sea, glittering peacefully in the sunshine of 1967.

Muscat town is built where it is because of its excellent harbour and its equally effective defensive position from landward. Indeed, so ringed is it by steep jagged bare rocks that it is virtually cut off from access by land. There is a road today, but that was hacked out of the coast as a one-lane track only in 1929 by the Royal Engineers; before 1929 you could only approach the town by boat, or by one of two or three footpaths through the encircling hills, each scrupulously enfiladed by solitary watch-towers that stand like eagles, ranged round the back of the town. The place is, or was before wireless, so incommunicado that it's peculiar to find that it was, and could exist as, the capital city. Muttrah, up the coast a few bays to the west, has an equally good harbour, and

with direct access to the interior became the commercial centre—
but never the political capital, for which it seemed to have as good
a claim. To add to Muscat's unsuitability, there is practically no
fresh water within its walls, as various groups of besieged towns-
men have discovered to their cost; and the bare dead grey hills
radiate heat like a grill, which before the days of air-conditioning was further tribulation to those living in the constricted
town.

And indeed, the utter nakedness of those uncompromisingly
spiky hills, and the extremes of heat that can be generated and
thrown off by their stony slopes, has impressed almost every
traveller that has written about Muscat. One comment that I
savour is that of William Francklin, an ensign of the Honourable
Company's Bengal establishment, who arrived on New Year's
Day 1787. 'The whole country round this place', he wrote,[1] 'is one
continued solid rock, without a blade of grass, or any kind of
verdure to be seen; but this barrenness the natives affirm to be
amply recompensed by the fertility and beauty of the inland
country; as indeed', he added, in an aside of deep feeling, 'it ought
to be.'

But, if as a capital city Muscat has its peculiarities, no one can
deny that it's attractive to look at, even though, like J. T. Bent[2]
you are impelled to add 'but detestable to live in', or to agree with
Wellsted[3] that once you land the illusion of beauty disappears.

The town is still walled, and has only three gates: one, the Bab
Saghir, for pedestrians and donkeys; the main gate, the Bab
Kebir, for traffic up to about 15 cwt. capacity; and a third, the
Bab Mathaib, for larger vehicles, which are only permitted to be
driven between Muttrah and Muscat, and into the town of
Muscat, with special dispensation, most infrequently granted. The
Bab Kebir, rebuilt and presented to the town by the present
Sultan in 1354 A.H. (an inscription above it says so, attributing the
building to Said bin Taimur, Sultan of Muscat and Oman and
Dhofar and Gwadur*), is shut three hours after sunset, after
which time vehicles may only be driven in or out with written
permission from the Governor of the Capital. If you walk within

---

* Now no longer. Gwadur was given by the Khan of Kelat to Sultan bin Ahmed
bin Said in 1785, after he had been expelled from Muscat by his nephew, Hamad bin
Said. It was sold by Said bin Taimur to Pakistan in 1958 for three million pounds.

the city walls after this time, you must carry a lantern* (powered by paraffin)—even if you merely get out of your car. To remind you of the time and the guards of their duty, a drum is irregularly beaten from the top of Fort Merani for about twenty minutes before the moment when, on the stroke of sunset plus three hours, three explosions (to take the place of the cannon shots that used to be fired) resound round the town. The gates clang to, lanterns are lit, and the guards search for offenders in the shadows. The ritual of dum-dum is over for another night.

In Muttrah, there is one explosion instead of three, but there are no further regulations, even though the gate, which now stands forlorn and quite detached from its wall in an arch beside the road, is still ceremoniously closed each night for old time's sake.

The guarding of the gates and walls of Muscat was until recently the sole prerogative of the Hawasina and Beni Umr tribes, administered by the Minister of the Interior. More recently, however, the tribesmen have had this easy way of making not much money circumscribed, although the Hawasina are still responsible for the Bab Mathaib and Bab Saghir (for which they provide ten men each) and for the Bab Kebir by day only (one man), and the Beni Umr 'guard' the Muttrah gate and provide askars for the Wali. For the rest, the police have taken over the job and have a guardroom just inside the walls. There you will find one guard standing rather disconsolately outside the police post, and at night a second figure clad in pyjamas will peer at your pass and open the gate for you if he considers it to be in order.

Muscat within the walls is mostly set at right angles to the sea, so that, as in Cape Town, you never know where north is. The town is a warren of crumbling walls, rubble, flaking plaster, padlocked wooden doorways, rickety wooden staircases, barred windows and dusty paths. There are a few open waste areas, and a number of old houses standing four-square and upright, peeling and unkempt. Some are unoccupied, others look unoccupied, and probably should be but aren't. Through this decrepit and dusty conglomeration run two strips of concrete road, one curling along to the British Consulate General, one straight down to Fort

* In 1765 Niebuhr found this rule already in existence.

Merani and the Khor jetty beneath it. At the fork where these roads meet there is a group of new gleaming white houses of rather peculiar design in which live three of the British members of the Sultanate Government. Somewhere in and amongst this disorder, if you can find it, is the suq: narrow paths and shops, mostly raised a few steps above the ground, like square caverns cut out of rock face. Many of these shops are in fairly good repair, and here and there you will see cementing and painting being carried out where a new tenant has taken over. Some are now full of clinical white refrigerators or washing machines, or the latest tape recorders, those symbols of the computer age—Japanese, of course. Most, however, are a queer amalgam of tins, plastic, cloth and wood, places where you might be lucky enough to find just what you are looking for, but far more likely not; where you have the feeling that the beans were baked in the 1940s.

My family and I were lucky enough to live in one of the old genuine Muscat houses, about the only one that looked as if it would withstand the next reverberation from the world outside. To keep a house of this sort properly maintained is, of course, no cheap job. I calculated that the outside wall area of this great cube of a house was 12,000 square feet. A Company could cope with the expense involved in such a house, but few private Muscati citizens could; and certainly not those to whom the houses generally belonged, members of the Sultan's family.

Our house was built, surprisingly, not more than, at the most, 150 years ago; it, and the others like it, look far more ancient, and one likes to feel the presence of the Portuguese in the massive walls, the arched doorways, the wide and tall balcony, the crenellated rim of the roof. It is not easy to establish any date with certainty, for the memories of Muscat are anything but precise, but I ended up with a general consensus that it was built about the same time as two or three other houses of the same design and that mine was constructed to the order of Ghaliya bint Salim bin Sultan. Salim was brother of the great Said bin Sultan who reigned from 1807 to 1856; he was an elder brother, born perhaps about 1785 (he died in Muscat in 1821 of paralysis), so that his daughter Ghaliya could have been born any time from about 1800 to 1815. This would make the likely date of building somewhere around 1820 to 1840.

The design of these houses is a mixture of Arab, Persian, Indian and African, and they are astonishingly small, in modern terms, for their enormous bulk. The ground floor of ours consisted of an entrance hall, a room for guards, and various store rooms, none really suitable for use as living quarters, all built round a central courtyard or well. The walls, even the inside ones, are of massive thickness, up to at least three feet, and this of course acts as a cooling device for the rooms within. The first, and only, floor was about twenty feet up, and the roof another twenty feet above that. The living rooms opened out on to a wide balcony, and although they were of a good size, there were only five of them. Each had a heavy wooden carved door, set beneath a square carved wooden lintel, into which the door could be chained. The tall wooden arches of the verandah were a reminder in silhouette of the Chehel Sutun in Isfahan.

The stairs from ground to first and from first floor to roof were set like a turret into the outside wall of the house and lighted by a few recessed and barred windows. The roof was large and empty, except for another raised wooden platform, like an open arbour, that looked out over a six-foot crenellated rampart which formed a wall right round the roof; the view from here was magnificent, over the roofs of Muscat to the two forts riding at anchor above the sea, and across to the jagged ring of hills that prick the sunset sky behind the town. It was a place for quiet relaxation and rumination during those few evenings of the year when it was neither too hot, nor too humid, nor too cool; there was always plenty to think about Oman.

Years ago the most impressive of these old houses must have been the large one that now squats forlorn and empty just beneath Merani fort, surrounded by nineteen old cannons whose muzzles are sunk insultingly in the dust. It is said to have been inhabited last by the present Sultan's father, and to have belonged to his mother. However, for the last years before she died, his mother lived in the main palace on the waterfront. But for all the signs of activity that emanated from this place she might have been with her son five hundred miles away in Salala. The only movement there, until her death, came from the two sentries who stood at the door day in and day out, and who have replaced two mangy lions that were still installed there in cages even in 1920 when Ronald Wingate was British Agent (Major R. E. L. in those days, later Sir Ronald). Forty-five years earlier, when Admiral Fisher, younger brother of Admiral of the Fleet Fisher, visited Muscat he found a lion, allegedly tame, walking the streets, and also an elephant which would, at the same hour every day, plod round to the Consulate for its allocation of sugar lumps. In between these times, Theodore Bent visited Muscat and learnt about the lions too: 'When we first visited Muscat the Sultan's palace was more interesting than it is now. When the warder opened the huge gate with its massive brass knobs you found yourself alongside the iron cage in which a lion was kept; adjoining the cage was another in which prisoners were put for their first offence. If this offence was repeated the prisoner was lodged in the cage with the lion at the time when his meal was due.'[4] Statistics are not available for the lions' appetites, nor for the frequency of their replacement, but there is no evidence that by the time of Wingate their diet included, even intermittently, prisoners. About this time, however, to add to the generally zoological aspect of Muscat town there could also be seen a tame ostrich ranging the streets.

One day, in April 1967, the Sultan's mother died in the early hours of the morning. The news buzzed round town and it became known, in the way things do become known without ever being made explicit, that she would be buried that same afternoon. The funeral procession would leave the palace at 4 p.m.

I duly presented myself at the palace gates at the appointed time, walking there between crowds of completely silent onlookers; the bier was just inside the gates, and at a signal was lifted and taken out to the accompaniment of wild wailing from women invisible behind the walls. The procession got going, with the Sultan's uncles as chief mourners walking just behind the coffin. The coffin was continuously passed from the shoulders of one person to another, sometimes so dangerously that it seemed it would crash to the ground. We moved in a long, rambling, shuffling crowd, occasionally stopping for a breather or a prayer; silent except for an occasional keening from behind a window on the route, and for the whispered greetings of those who had only just seen a friend. The traditions of greeting, it seems, are second to nothing in their importance and necessity. Once an uncle broke down, and skipped about in an excess of wailing. Otherwise we shuffled on, up a wadi, to the Al bu Said graveyard; there most of us squatted round the inside of the wall where, while the coffin was being tipped into its hole, water was offered to the thirsty walkers; silence, except for the ring of a spade on stone, and a groan from a water well echoing round the hills.

It all took two hours, so it was just as well it was April, not July. A Land-Rover came to pick up the Governor of the Capital, and I retain the memory of the Personal Adviser to the Sultan and the British Consul General being squeezed in with him, the proconsular solar topee and the more up-to-date Foreign Office homburg vanishing bumpily down the wadi behind the wells.

That is all I have seen of the inside of the palace. Its main door is a fine piece of carved wood, with an inscription above to say it was erected by Turki bin Said and opposite stand two old bronze Portuguese cannons, in front of the Treasury, one clearly dated 1606. Further along the waterfront, beyond the customs sheds and offices (where it is incredible to imagine any type of modern business being consistently and successfully completed), is the British Consulate General, a group of buildings in the midst of which is a gravel courtyard and an enormous flagpole which gives a rather faded naval character to it all. The Consulate itself is nearest to, indeed right under, Fort Jalali; from its wide stone-flagged verandah (flagged by Wingate judging from his auto-biography), you can enjoy any breeze there may be in Muscat. It is surely one of the noblest verandahs in the world, looking out over the harbour, the sea to the south through a gap in the hills, the old coaling station of Mukalla behind Fort Merani, and over-looked by the massive story-book fortress of Jalali. It would be cosier if Jalali were a tourist attraction, which one day it probably will be, and not the Sultan's main gaol, stories about which are legion and never comforting.

The Consulate is redolent of the imperial past, from the photographs of former consuls, consuls general, and political agents (depending on the time of their incumbency) lining the staircase, to the fact that there is considerable debate as to whom the building, started in about 1880 at the expense of the Indian Government, belongs. It must sometimes be difficult for a Consul

General, when he is particularly irritated by some action of the Sultanate authorities, to remember that he is a servant of the Foreign Office 1967 and cannot issue an imperial decree to put it right ('Unquestionably', said Bent[5] in 1895, 'our own political agent may be said to be the ruler in Muscat.'). Shades of the India Office, Curzon and Queen Victoria are forever lurking in the corners, ready to mesmerise the unwary; but the place is air-conditioned now, so that wandering minds can always be thermostatically jerked back to twentieth-century realities.

There is only one obvious change in the sea front today from the early photographs, and that is that one of the Consulate buildings has lost a storey. Maybe there is significance in that.

Behind the Consulate, and below the white light that is set into a hill and serves as a bearing for ships approaching the harbour by night, is a part of the town called Sheikh Jabir. It is an area of some more modern and more well-to-do houses that belong to the Baharina merchants. The Baharina are assimilated Omanis, but of Persian origin, and Shiites. Along with the Khojas, or Hyder-abadis, who are Shiites of Indian origin, they are amongst the leading merchant class. Their families tend to have strong links up the Gulf, and you will often find that brothers or cousins are carrying on business in Kuwait, Bahrain, Qatar, Dubai, and even Basra and Baghdad. The Khojas have similar links, though often more strongly with Karachi or Bombay. Although these people are Omani citizens with Omani passports, there is an element of the second class in them; there are restrictions that they have to bear which more Omani Omanis do not suffer. This goes too for that other main class of imported Omani, without whom the country would not function at all, the Baluch. They too live in specific quarters of the town (for instance, Takiya, on the way to Sidab) and though they are Omanis, have second-class attributes. But, as we shall see, the true Omanis don't live on the coast at all; that is, and always has been, one of the main problems for the country.

There is another group of persons living in Muscat who are of great significance and importance to its working—the Indians. In recognition of this, they are the only other country to have resident diplomatic representation; there is a Consul General of India, who lives in a large and rambling house behind the chief

Hindu merchant. Without the Indian community, both merchant, artisan and secretarial, ordinary life would grind to a halt.

Thus, on a normal day, there are three flags that flutter over the Muscat skyline, the blood-red flag of the Sultanate flying over Fort Merani, the Union Jack (in its consular form) and the Indian national flag. On festive occasions, there are two blood-red flags on Merani, two on Jalali, one over the main gate and one on the school, besides less official ones; but there has been no flag on the pole above the palace for nearly ten years.

If you walk out of the town by either of the two main gates you can on your way check up, if you can read Arabic, on the latest Government announcements. There is no such thing as an official gazette, and if there were it would be most irregularly published judging from the paucity of notices that are stuck up on the gates. Most of them are from the Customs Department and hint at some esoteric transaction that has either taken place, or shouldn't, meaningful only to those versed in commercial dealings with India; but occasionally there is a notice from the Governor of the Capital, bald and direct in its message but hiding a wealth of secondary meaning if you understand the code—announcing, for instance, that dolls may not be carried in public in the streets of Muscat.

These pieces of paper, glued rather inconclusively to the walls of the gates and the Customs House, are the only apparent means of direct communication between the legislature (i.e. the Sultan) and the people. They are a bit like, but not nearly so interesting as, a school notice-board; as if all the teams and society notices were subtracted, and the poor schoolboy was left only with the edicts of the bursar and the headmaster.

If you go out by the smaller gate, the one for pedestrians, you find yourself opposite the only official school in Muscat, the Sayyidiya; there is a brother one in Muttrah, of identical size; the school in Muscat was established in 1940, and that in Muttrah in 1959; the Muscat one has a fine looking boarding house in its grounds, but since its completion in 1964 not one single student has lived in it, and now it stands there in permanent sullenness, its windows cracked and broken and thick with dust. Such is the potential of state education in the Sultanate: a maximum of 640 boys up to a standard that with the best will in the world can be claimed to be little more than primary. And private schools are rigorously controlled, to the extent that they are hardly permitted at all; so the Omani boy must seek his further education elsewhere.

Turn away from the school, and you pass one of the main mosques of Muscat, the Ali Mousa, on whose roof on a summer evening you can see the congregation bowing in silent unison, as if in training for a P.T. display. Religion is still very much a part of life for the average Omani, and you will find thirty-six mosques in Muscat (in Muttrah there are forty-five but three times the population). Religion means also graveyards and these, sited with no apparent reason, and only recognisable by a mass of rather large stones lying around, are almost as common in Oman as date trees. As the town planners discovered to their infuriation there are at least sixteen to be counted in Muttrah and seventeen in Muscat, and every single grave is sacrosanct, unmovable.

Behind the Ali Mousa mosque is the main food suq of the town, full of burasti cafés where there are always plenty of people gossiping and sipping tea or coffee. The children clamour for rather sinister looking cubes of flavoured ice, sold out of a large thermos, the Muscati equivalent of ice-cream. Further up the hill behind the suq proper is the fish and meat suq, a place of grotesque smell, particularly late on a summer afternoon when the remnants of a day's sale are lying on a fly- and cat-infested slab; the fish though, is fresh every day and delicious. Nearby is the only public lavatory I have seen in Oman, a circular concrete erection of traditional French design, a most unexpected piece of municipal munificence; maybe, who knows, inspired by Ottavi* or one of his French consular successors. You can scramble up to one of the old watch-towers just above and get one of the best views of Muscat, looking straight out to sea between the two forts. (On one occasion, in 1782, they bombarded each other across the harbour —the Imam Ahmed bin Said in Merani versus his two sons, Seif and Sultan, in Jalali, who were holding a third son Said as hostage. Said escaped, Ahmed relaxed his shooting, and the forts were saved for the cameras of posterity.)

Outside the main gate of the town you can either take the con-

* See page 51 below.

crete road to Muttrah or walk up past the Bank to the Wadi
Kebir, at the top end of which is the Al bu Said graveyard. Sand-
wiched between these two routes is the Harat al Dalalil (quarter
of the auctioneers, of which I never learned the tradition) in the
midst of which is the solid concrete grey mass of the American
Mission and its Women's Hospital. Past the Bank, the British
Bank of the Middle East, which from 1947 to 1967 was the only
Bank in the Sultanate (as I write they are digging an enormous
hole within the walls which will one day next year—or the year
after—turn into the Eastern Bank, and soon the same will happen
just outside the main gate for the Ottoman) past the B.B.M.E.
flows the Wadi Kebir, and quite literally flows, if ever there is
enough rain. One day the water filled the vaults and turned all the
rupee notes to sodden pulp.

The Wadi Kebir is today the main water supply for Muscat.
Two private pipelines actually bring water into the town for
certain favoured houses, but otherwise donkeys plod to and fro
strapped up with four-gallon tins, or men trudge with goatskins.
It was not many years ago that the house in which we lived was
entirely supplied by a caravan of goatskin carriers, moving to
and fro like an army of ants. Some of the wells have pumps now,
but several are still worked by bullocks, and the peculiar creaking,
more like a screeching, of the rope moving over the wet wooden
pulleys of the zigbara, makes a haunting accompaniment to the
silence of a hot summer afternoon.

Around the wells are some trees and plots of grass, a brilliant
green blotch amongst the lifeless volcanic hills. If you walk up
past the wells and beyond the last burasti huts of the village of
Tawiyan al Alwiyat, you come to first one, and then another,
small concrete dam in the wadi; these help to prevent too much of
a flood pouring down into Muscat after a storm. On one occasion,
at the end of a sudden rain in July, I saw them full of yellow sandy
water and in them was a great splashing and shouting of boys
happily having a swim; a more elderly group had a transistor and
were picnicking by a pool wholly surrounded by oleanders, nearly
invisible.

If you walk far enough up this wadi, and take the right turn-
ings, you can cross a pass and come down into Beit al Falaj,
beyond Muttrah. One day I walked some way up, climbed a hill,

and found myself looking straight back at Fort Merani through
the wadi gap, and hearing again the plaintive call of the wells.
The old track to Muttrah leads off the Wadi Kebir, near the last
burasti huts, and I tried to find it; but it has long ago been
obliterated by falling stones, and you can merely guess the route.
I later discovered that the younger generation of Muscatis not
only don't know where the old track is, but are not even aware
that there used to be one. Like rights of way in England, I
suppose.

So, back through the gate and home again to our great white
house, best known in Muscat as the old French Consulate—Beit
Fransawi, they say with a knowing nod; and up on the rooftop,
surrounded by those hills which, when the death of the great
Sayyid Said bin Sultan in 1856 was publicly announced, were
almost shaken, we are told, by the wailing caused throughout the
town. It is a good place to sit, look out over the other rickety
rooftops of Muscat to the two trusty old sentinel fortresses of
Merani and Jalali, and think of the events that brought Monsieur
Ottavi, the best known of the French consuls, to Muscat to the
very same roof. He may have done the same some evenings
when he had nothing else to do.

Muscat itself has been mainly involved with the more recent
history of the country, from the time, that is, that the Europeans
first impinged upon the coast; with what might be described as
international diplomacy, even if diplomacy has often been a
euphemism for exploitation, or downright invasion.

Muscat means 'the place of falling', referring either to a land-
fall, or to the harbour itself (falling of the anchor chain). There are
assumed references to it by Greek authors, and various writers
from the ninth century onwards have mentioned it, mostly in a
marine context as a port from which voyages to India and further
east were started. It is not at all clear at what period, and under
whose rule, Muscat prospered and was built up into the imposing
place that Albuquerque found when he arrived in its harbour in
1507.

The speed and energy with which the Portuguese moved into
the Indian Ocean area after Vasco da Gama's circuit of the Cape in
1498 is astonishing. When Albuquerque left Portugal in 1506 this

was his second voyage to the Indian Ocean, and his firm intention was to establish Portuguese control over the whole area. This he proceeded to do with the utmost singlemindedness and complete disregard for human life or property. Reaching Oman in 1507, he first burnt a fishing fleet that he found, presumably peacefully fishing, off Ras al Hadd; he then threatened the people of Qalhat, temporarily leaving them unharmed only because they immediately accepted his overlordship; further up the coast the people of Qaryat objected to his demands, and their town was pillaged and burnt. So he arrived in Muscat, and this is what he found: a large and populous town with behind it a plain as large as the square of Lisbon, all covered with salt pans; he found orchards, gardens, and palm groves, and an ancient market for horses and dates; it was, he said, a very elegant town, with very fine houses, and supplied from the Interior with much wheat, maize, barley and dates, which was exported by sea; the city of Muscat was part of the kingdom of Hormuz. Albuquerque immediately demanded that it should pay allegiance, and tribute, to him, but sensing quickly that he was about to be double-crossed, gave orders for the town to be sacked, and all shipping in the harbour to be destroyed. This was done, some prisoners were left behind with their noses and ears lopped off, and Albuquerque departed for Sohar, Khor Fakkan and finally Hormuz which he captured in October.

Muscat's first impression of Portugal (and international diplomacy, if this was it) was not a comfortable one; and it was nearly 150 years before the Omanis got their final revenge on the Portuguese, who were dislodged from this their last toehold in Oman on 23 January 1650. The way in which tradition says it happened is an appealing romance; unfortunately, historians reckon that the tradition is no more than a myth, but nevertheless it is too good a story[6] to suppress altogether.

The Imam of the moment was Sultan bin Seif, who the previous year had replaced his cousin, who had already succeeded in removing the Portuguese from almost the whole coastline of Oman. Sultan quickly decided to finish the job off, by ejecting them from Muscat. He set off with his army from Rustaq, his capital, and made a number of unsuccessful attacks on the town. Then one day he received a letter from an Indian merchant called Narutem, telling him to attack on Sunday. Narutem had a daughter whom the Portuguese commandant wanted to marry, and the only conclusive way Narutem could think of foiling this desire was to have the Portuguese driven out; clearly he was a man to be reckoned with. Narutem persuaded the commander of the Muscat garrison to empty the water from the cisterns of the two forts, and provisions and gunpowder from the stores, on the grounds that, since a long siege was to be expected, everything should be renewed and fresh. Then he wrote his letter to the Imam.

So, on Sunday January 23rd (although the precise date is, of course, just part of this story, nevertheless 1650 is now generally agreed at least to be the right year) Sultan bin Seif duly attacked, and sure enough, all he had to contend with on the walls were a lot of drunken Portuguese soldiers; they were killed and left 'prostrate like the trunks of uprooted date trees'. He then captured the two forts, and the battle was nearly over; except that one of the Portuguese officers, named Cabreta, made a counter-attack with a small group of soldiers. This party were, however, overpowered and retreated to the cotton market, where the final assault on them was made with spears and rotten eggs. This improbable combination of weapons finished Cabreta off.

I am glad to say that Narutem and his family were exempted from taxation for the rest of their lives; and, in spite of the eggs, the memory of Cabreta is retained in the name of the corner tower on the Muscat walls, still known today as Burg Cabreta. And that was the end of the Portuguese in Oman.

Between 1507 and 1650 the Portuguese had established, and maintained more or less continuously, a trading empire in the Indian Ocean area. It was purely a commercial affair, into which colonisation never at all entered their calculations. If, for commercial reasons, a base had to be established, and indeed this was the case, then it was established; the purpose of the base was, however, no more than as a safe anchorage, a taxation and export centre, and the Portuguese had no interest in the local inhabitants except as a source of labour or revenue. If they kept quiet they were left alone, if they became tiresome they were suppressed.

The Oman coast was by no means the centre of this commercial operation, but it was an important part of it, and during the course of time the Portuguese established four main bases on it:

at Qaryat, Muscat, Qalhat and Sohar. Of these, Muscat was the most easily defensible and the safest harbour, and became the pivot of their Omani operation. The real centre of their activity on the western side of the Indian Ocean was, however, the island of Hormuz, which became, as it were, the regional capital.

During the period from 1507 to 1600, the Portuguese built up the defences and the town of Muscat. There is still an area down near the Customs Office called the Gareza, which was originally a group of buildings comprising the factory, the Governor's residence, barracks, warehouse and chapel of the Portuguese administration; Gareza itself being the Arabic version of the Portuguese word for cathedral. This complex of buildings seems to have been completed about 1531 and the remnants still existed as late as 1895. At one stage one of the buildings, presumably the Governor's residence, had served as a palace for the Al bu Said Sultans (certainly Sultan bin Ahmed used it for this purpose from 1793 when he became ruler until 1800 when the new palace on its present site was completed), and later for members of the royal family. It would appear that it was so used when Miles was resident in Muscat (a detached three-storey edifice, he calls it), but by 1895 Bent[7] could only describe its ruins ('three walls, also a window or two with lattice-work carving'), and mention that it was by then used merely as a stable for the Sultan's horses. Now there is no trace at all of the Gareza, the last rubble having been cleared to make way for the house of the Secretary for Petroleum Affairs.

It was in 1527 that the Portuguese began to build the forts of Jalali and Merani, but in their present form they date, respectively, from 1587 and 1588; Jalali, originally called San Joao was built by Melchior Calaca, and Fort Capitan, later named Merani, by Dom Manuel do Souza Coutinho, and there is a clear inscription to this effect still there above the main gateway. To look at they are fairy-tale forts, all that a boy (or a grown-up for that matter) requires of a fort. Jalali has for some time been the main gaol of Oman, but even so its sinister associations seem somehow out of character. Until recently it was administered directly by the Governor of the Capital whose rigid standards and total lack of sympathetic imagination assisted in creating its horrific reputation, but a few years ago the Army became at least partially

responsible for it, and has mitigated some of its harshest and
nastiest characteristics. But it still remains a very shivery spot,
very much a place to keep out of; some of those inside it have
been in for a very long time.

Merani is a very much sunnier proposition. It is the headquarters of the Muscat garrison, who live there, and who have
turned it into the sort of homely military barracks you can see
anywhere in the world—iron bedsteads, socks over the rail, pin-
ups, and gay tin trunks bulging with the worldly possessions of
the yawning privates. You can climb up and through this old
fortress, peer down old cannon muzzles through embrasures over
the town, walk on the ramparts where today they only fire
salutes, and imagine anything that ever happened to any fortress
in the world. There are probably more old cannons in Merani fort
than in any other one place, and there can be little doubt that its
collection of mint-condition cannon balls (still in their original
wrappings in unopened boxes) is unequalled. An official salute
fired by four of these ancient cannons is a semi-social event of
Victorian melodrama; a lighting of fuses, swabbings, explosions,
smoke rings, and a sergeant ever more wildly leaping from one
gun-team to another giving action signals; as if some faded etch-
ing had suddenly been galvanised to life with the jerky raising of
the Sultanate flag on its staff. Mind you, only just over a hundred
years ago shooting could be a more serious affair, and in 1859
Sayyid Thwaini, the Sultan, had a convicted murderer blown
from one of those guns into the bay.

Under Fort Merani, on the seaward side and almost hidden
from view of the town, is the sub-harbour of Mukalla (dis-
paragingly referred to in John Thornton's 1703 map as 'the hole
for shipps'), where you can see the remnants of the old coaling
station, which nearly caused diplomatic rupture with France in
the early 1900s, and, lying at perpetual anchor, most of the
Sultan's Navy. Round the rocks stand herons, hunched and peering for fish.

Since 1650 only one Portuguese ship is known to have visited
Muscat, and that was in 1956 during a local naval visit from Goa.
After all those years there was no Portuguese flag left to fly from
Merani's masthead, nor had the Portuguese any Muscati flags.
By some well-timed sleight of hand, together with the assistance

of the R.A.F., the day was saved, both Portuguese and Muscat
flags flew from their appropriate places at the correct moments,
and their guns could fire their respective salutes. Protocol was
triumphant. (More triumphant than when in 1931 the French
sloop *Diana* on an official visit was unable to fire a single shot
because she had run out of ammunition.)

The last third of the Portuguese occupation of Muscat and the
coast was a period of gradual decline. At the end of the sixteenth
century two developments occurred which turned out to be the
death knell for the Portuguese: the accession to the throne of
Persia of the great Shah Abbas in 1587, and the first contact of
Britain with Persia, the Sherley mission of 1598. The latter was
quickly followed in 1600 by the granting of a charter to the East
India Company, and a British interest in the Indian Ocean area
was firmly established. In Persia their first contact with Shah
Abbas was followed by the granting to Britain of a trading post on
the island of Jask, just up the coast from Hormuz, in 1619.

The interest of Persia was to expel the Portuguese from
Hormuz, that of Britain to extend its trading interests. The two
sides combined in 1622, defeated and turned the Portuguese out
of Hormuz; this was a totally unjustified piece of belligerence by
the East India Company, the sort of thing that the later invention
of the telegraph put an end to. (The first overland cable to India
passed through Jask, and a branch, installed in 1901, led down to
Muscat.) Indeed the East India Company realised it had gone too
far and subsequently declined to join the Persians in further
conquest, specifically against Muscat. Shah Abbas, however, captured both Khor Fakkan and Sohar on his own; he also allowed
Hormuz to waste away, and established a new base at the old
fishing village of Gombroon, and called it Bander Abbas.

In the last few years of their tenure of Muscat, the Portuguese
strengthened their defences, and dug themselves in, but all to no
avail. The town wall and the defensive towers perched high over
the passes to Sidab, Kalbuh and Riyam, were all built in this
period, but, when the time came for Narutem's plot, they proved
to be little more than they are today, grand gestures of more
scenic than military significance. Sultan bin Seif ignored them, and
that was the end of the Portuguese.

Sultan bin Seif was the second Imam of the Yaariba dynasty of

Oman. When he was elected in 1649, he found a country more united than it had been for many years, from which the Portuguese had already been almost evicted, and which for the first time in its history was tentatively looking out to sea, following with a quizzical gaze the backs of the departing Portuguese. Other foreigners were already hovering in the area, to take their place; indeed, there was during the seventeenth and eighteenth centuries in the Gulf area a tidal flow of European commercial activity, with successively the Portuguese, Dutch, British and French being cast up on the shore. Oman itself was least affected by the Dutch, who apparently did no more than lease an office in Muscat in 1670 to make sure that their mail kept moving, although it is probable that they had some sort of loose naval alliance with the Omanis for some years;* it was most affected, in the long term, by the British.

British interest in the area started almost coincidentally with the beginning of the Yaariba dynasty. In the 1650s general contact between Sultan bin Seif and the British and an agreement for a 'factory' type base for the British seemed imminent. In 1650 Colonel Rainsford was sent by the President of the Council of the East India Company in Surat to negotiate a treaty, but because of the untimely death of Rainsford the treaty was never signed, and Britain had then to wait 139 years before she had one. Sultan bin Seif, and even more his successors, decided that they did not want any European settlement established on Muscat soil and, with the memory of the Portuguese, one could hardly blame them.

The Yaariba dynasty led Oman into very considerable prosperity both at home and internationally, under the leadership of Sultan bin Seif (1649–68) and his son Seif bin Sultan (1680–1711)— nothing is more confusing than the very common Arab habit of inversion of names from one generation to another†. Sultan began the process, by building up his Navy after the expulsion of the Portuguese, and mounting a number of expeditions to liberate Omani settlements on the East African coast that had been subjected to Portuguese domination. Seif completed the job, so that by 1698 practically the whole coastline from Mogadishu to Cape

---

* An envoy of the Lord General of Batavia arrived in Muscat in 1672 on a commercial visit.

† See page 66 below.

Delgado was controlled by Oman. He also sacked the town of Salsette on the Indian coast and for a time conquered and ruled Bahrain in the Gulf. At home he was responsible for many public works, in particular for the restoration of falajs and the construction of new ones. 'Oman was strong and prosperous under his sway',[8] but when he died in 1711 this prosperity quickly declined.

It declined into the Hinawi-Ghafiri civil war of 1719 to 1724, to a period of virtual anarchy after, to the Persian invasion of the Batina in 1743, and to the founding of the Al bu Said dynasty by Ahmed bin Said in 1749. They have ruled Oman to this day.

Ahmed appears to have started life as a merchant; he was introduced to the then Imam as a man 'discreet in judgement and very courageous'[9] and became in effect his chief confidant and business assistant. After some years he was promoted to be Wali in Sohar, where 'he was urbane to the rich and poor, to the learned and ignorant, and his condescension to all ranks raised him in general estimation.' He was also, as was undoubtedly necessary in those times, cruel and treacherous—treacherous, I assume, because he was ambitious. At any rate, his final coup to dislodge the Persians was to sign an agreement with them and then invite them to a grand celebratory feast at the fort in Birka. There, when they were duly bloated with food, they were slaughtered by the waiting Omanis. In the critical circumstances of Oman at that moment he had some justification for such behaviour. It also had the great advantage of consolidating his own position.

It needed, however, a lot more consolidation than this. Ahmed may have conceived of himself as the founder of a brave new Omani dynasty, but most of his subjects would have been far less optimistic. The country was in chaos, unrecognisable as the internationally influential power of 1700; Ahmed's first job was to create peaceful conditions at home, and at the same time to reconstruct the Navy for his foreign policy. No doubt it was the merchant in him that persuaded him to look outwards across the seas, and not to peer introspectively into those mountainous and religious fastnesses behind him. However that may be, he looked outwards, and his Al bu Said successors have ever since continued to do so.

What Ahmed saw when he looked outwards was, however, something rather different from that which his predecessors had seen. Into the Indian Ocean had come the French, and their attitude was subtly different from that of the Portuguese, Dutch and British; assuredly their interests were primarily commercial, but commerce built, where possible, on colonies rather than factories, and they viewed the British already in the area just as they looked on them in Europe, as enemies. For them, the Indian Ocean became an extension of the European struggle for power, against the British.

Into such a framework Oman fitted as a most necessary, indeed vital, potential ally on the political plane; commercially too she was the pivot for the Gulf area, having the same importance as the islands of Qishm or Hormuz had once had. This was because she now was potentially (as she had in fact been under the Yaariba) a marine power in her own right instead of just a pawn in the game of geography.

For the last half of the eighteenth century, then, Muscat gradually became a magnet to which both France and Britain were drawn, seeking there alliance and priority of favour. Later, in the nineteenth century, French influence dwindled after the defeats of the Napoleonic wars, and the part that Oman could play in the increasingly tough world of big power politics was reduced; added to which, her own base was increasingly threatened by the Wahhabi invasions. The position of 1800 then quickly reversed, and it was Muscat's turn to seek friendship on the best terms she could. Although she did her best to play France off against Britain, it was an unequal struggle, and both parties knew it. But it constitutes a fascinating sideshow of history, very much part of the Muscat mystique.

France had started busily. As early as 1667 de Lalain, a French envoy to Persia, was advocating the seizure of Muscat and its retention as a naval base. More explicitly in 1699 and again on many occasions between 1707 and 1719 aides-mémoires and draft treaties were drawn up by French representatives in Persia (one of whom, Monsignor Peter Paul, enjoyed the grandiose title of Archbishop of Ancyra and Vicar Apostolic for the Dominions of the Mughal Emperor) for alliances which included provisions for the conquest of Muscat—something that the Persians desired as much as the French. These documents defined exactly what the French presence would be, and what advantages there would be to France from owning Muscat; invariably the forts of Merani and Jalali were to be part of the French share. In the event, however, nothing came of any of this drafting, and the Omanis were probably unaware of the potential danger. In a more practical way, France had obtained Mauritius, which she named Ile de France, in 1715 after the Dutch had departed from it. Under its vigorous Governor, La Bourdonnais, it was built up between 1735 and 1740 into a flourishing base and colonial possession. Trade expanded, chiefly in that most valuable of commodities, slaves. One of the chief French traders, a man called Morice, drew up in 1777 a most elaborate plan for the annexation of Kilwa (one of the Omani possessions on the East African coast) as a forward base of operations, but it was never followed up, primarily because of the need at this time to keep a friendly relationship with Ahmed bin Said.

The first direct contact of the French with Muscat seems to have been as late as 1749 when for the first, but not the last, time French privateers attempted to attack British vessels in Muscat harbour. Action of this sort culminated, in 1781, in the seizure of a Muscati frigate, the *Saleh*, off Sohar, and in these circumstances it is surprising that the French were as well thought of by the Omani rulers as they appear to have been. Admittedly, a replacement *Saleh* was returned, even though it was nine years later, and 'not worth a quarter of the old one', but the secret of their success was probably that the Imam himself, as well as the main merchants, owned ships that were engaged in direct trade with Ile de France, and the French Governor there was careful to treat them beneficently, and to exchange well-chosen gifts with the Imam from time to time; at the same time the French Consul General in Basra had struck up a personal friendship with Ahmed bin Said. In 1785 a mission led by the Comte de Rosily came to Muscat; according to French sources[10] he was given permission, in spite of the virtual ban that had been imposed ever since the time of Rainsford, to build a factory; if this were so it seems unaccountable that the French did not build it. Equally strange is the fact that when in 1790 the new *Saleh* was ceremoniously presented to Ahmed bin Said, by now the ruler, the French also took no quick action to appoint a consul in Muscat—which, together with a free house for him, was offered. There seems some doubt, however, about the offer of a factory, and two years later in 1787, the 'ban', according to Captain Francklin, was still on. As for the consul, it was not until 3 March 1795 that a decree was issued in Paris announcing the establishment of a Muscat consulate, and the appointment of Monsieur Beauchamp as first Consul. For some unrecorded reason (possibly because he is described as a distinguished astronomer and well-known traveller), Beauchamp had still only got as far as Egypt by 1799; while there Napoleon diverted him to Constantinople, where he was arrested and imprisoned; he never saw Muscat. And, in the end, no French consul arrived to live in Muscat until Monsieur Ottavi came to live in my house in 1894.

Napoleon when he landed in Egypt in 1798 was on the first leg of his intended conquest of British India; Muscat would be *en route*, and so Napoleon wrote to Sultan bin Ahmed, who had succeeded Hamad bin Said as ruler in 1792, as follows:

A l'Imam de Muscat;

Je vous écris cette lettre pour vous faire connaître ce que vous avez déjà appris sans doute, l'arrivée de l'armée française en Egypte. Comme vous avez été de tout temps notre ami, vous devez être convaincu du désir que j'ai de protéger tous les bâtiments de votre nation et que vous engagiez à venir à Suez, où ils trouveront protection pour le commerce. Je vous prie aussi de faire parvenir cette lettre à Tippoo-Saib par la première occasion qui se trouvera pour les Indes.

Bonaparte.

It was dated 25 January 1799, but the Imam never read it, for it was intercepted by a British agent. But that hardly mattered as it turned out, for a few months later Napoleon withdrew from Egypt and landed in France.

However, even if Sultan had read the letter, it is doubtful whether it would have had the desired effect, for only three months earlier he had signed a treaty with the Honourable the East India Company, a treaty which on the face of it gave Britain everything, Sultan practically nothing, and the French notice to quit. It is amazing to find such a swift switch of allegiance as this; a matter of years before the French had seemed to be making all the running, but now suddenly here was Sultan signing up (for the first time, for there had been no previous treaty between Muscat and any outside power, apart from the early trading agreements of the type signed by Wylde* in 1646) with the British. Possibly it was as a result of French inaction since the de Rosily mission of 1785; perhaps Sultan had been persuaded that, in spite of what was happening in Egypt, the British would win the day; maybe contacts and trade with Ile de France had slackened off, or soured. However that may be, so favourable to Britain is this treaty that it is almost embarrassing to read.† Even so, Wellesley, the Governor General in India, was suspicious still of the French, and also of the Imam's apparent volte-face towards Britain and away from France, and so sent to Muscat again to consolidate this first treaty with a second confirmatory one. This was signed in early 1800 by Captain John Malcolm, Assistant Resident at Hyderabad (afterwards Sir John Malcolm, Governor of Bombay), on behalf of the East India Company, and Sultan bin Ahmed; its immediate effect was to install Mr. Bogle, a surgeon, in Muscat as Britain's first diplomatic resident representative, doubling this job with that of private physician to the Imam.

Wellesley's suspicions may have been well grounded, for Sultan's correspondence and connection with the French did not snap off as one might have expected from the terms of the two treaties signed with Britain. Nor did Napoleon's vision of his conquest of Britain in India die. And so, two years after the Malcolm treaty, we find Sultan writing to Ile de France, to complain of something the British were doing, and asking again for French representation in Muscat, and Talleyrand writing a memorandum to Napoleon in these words:

> Mascate est une place importante. L'Imam qui y gouverne, et dont la domination s'étend fort avant dans l'interieur des terre et même sur quelques districts de la côte de Mozambique est un prince indépendant sous tous rapports.

Wellesley might well have agreed with the final phrase.

* See page 65 below.
† For the text see Appendix 2.

Late in 1802 Talleyrand and Napoleon appointed Cavaignac to re-establish contact in Muscat, and stay, if accepted, as Consul there, and sent him off with Decaen, the new Captain General of the East, who was leaving to take over in Ile de France. Cavaignac arrived in Muscat on 3 October 1803, and found Sultan out of town; he was told he could not disembark his baggage or occupy the house that he was under the impression had been made available to the French Consul, before the Imam returned and gave express permission (Bogle was behind this, claimed Cavaignac). When he did return, he gave Cavaignac a very negative answer to his requests, and Cavaignac who had arrived with so much hope in his heart, left Muscat a disappointed man. Testily and with poor grace he wrote: 'Ce pays et ses inhabitants sont tout à fait misérables. Le souverain n'est qu'un chef de Bedouins.' All France required in Muscat, he added, was 'un agent commercial de la dernière classe.'

It may be that the judgement of Auzoux on the character of Cavaignac, that he was 'un personnage léger et prétentieux' was correct; on the other hand, Cavaignac had his supporters, who were perhaps less blinded by the imperial associations of an Imam than their superiors—for instance, Decaen's interpreter, who had this strikingly derogatory opinion to make: 'Je sais que l'Imam de Muscate fait un assez grand bruit en Europe . . . pour moi, qui ne me suis jamais servi de lunettes, je ne le vois, et ne le considère que comme un pauvre prince bedouin, qui cherche à faire accroire aux autres qu'il est quelque chose et qui, dans le fond, n'est qu'un zéro.'

At any rate, Wellesley had won the day, and the Bedouin chief (or the zero) had made his choice. This was no doubt the crux of the matter; so long as Sultan could play both sides against each other, he would do so, but when it came to the crunch, he could only, as he saw the facts, choose Britain. There is little doubt that he was encouraged in this by his desperate need for direct help; his absence from Muscat when Cavaignac landed was because he was engaged up the coast in opposing the Wahhabis; that they turned back was through no compulsion from Sultan, but only because of the news of the assassination of the Emir Abdul Aziz back in Saudi Arabia. He was sure the Wahhabis would return,

and he needed help; he reckoned he would get more from Britain
than from France.

He was, no doubt, right; but Britain was by no means as forthcoming as he hoped. Sultan himself, however, was killed in a
fight with pirates in 1804, and there seemed every likelihood that
Muscat would slither quickly back into local anarchy. But two
years later Said bin Sultan, at the age of eighteen, murdered his
cousin who was at the time reigning in Muscat, and so started his
own fifty-year reign, which, in spite of many tribulations, ups and
downs, gave Muscat its greatest prosperity and power since the
heyday of the Yaariba.

In his long reign Said had to contend with and balance the
Wahhabis, whose prime purpose was to convert Oman to their
puritanical form of Islam; the British, whose main concern was
to suppress piracy and the slave trade; France, which was forever
trying to widen its commercial and political influences; the
Americans, who came in on the fringes of the game; the East
African Arabs, who were nominally under his control and were
the source of great commercial wealth (primarily slaves); and his
own family, who were as ready to stab him in the back as he had
his cousin Badr bin Seif in 1806. In this power game Said was, on
the whole, successful; so was Britain; the Wahhabis were intermittently; while France made great commercial profit, but less
political headway.

Said's first preoccupation was at home with the Wahhabis. He
tried hard to obtain British assistance to defend himself against
them, but Britain refused to be drawn into commitments concerning what she considered to be the internal affairs of Oman—a
phrase and a concept that remains well used, and most useful, for
diplomats still. Said retaliated by signing a Treaty of Amity and
Commerce in 1807 with the French; this was a partial revenge for
Decaen after the failure of the Cavaignac mission of 1803, but of
no practical use to Said versus the Wahhabis. Said, realising that
his hope continued to be from the British side, helped them whenever he was asked, so that they should be indebted to him as far as
it was possible to make them. The British needed his help on two
counts; first, a chronic situation, against the French, and secondly
to suppress piracy, which was rampant and vicious throughout
the Pirate Coast.

As Napoleon's European empire declined, so did his eastern one; in 1810 Decaen was evicted from Ile de France, which henceforth became British and Mauritius, but the French retained their hold on Madagascar, and so remained in the Indian Ocean picture.

A little later, in 1814, the Wahhabi dynamo also ran down, and Said was at last free to develop his own state. He did this first at home, and then abroad; in the late 1820s his eyes turned to Africa, and after his first stay in Zanzibar in 1828 he was always happier to be in Africa than Arabia. From 1840 his main centre of rule was Zanzibar, and he visited Muscat increasingly infrequently, leaving his affairs there in the hands of a governor. His preoccupation in conquering the coast of East Africa led him into continual trouble with the moralising, slave-suppressing British, and into some queer alliances.

Mombasa was his greatest problem, with its powerful and almost impregnable Fort Jesus, originally built by the Portuguese in 1593 (a few years only after Jalali and Merani); Said badly needed reinforcements to help him overcome it, but where was he to find them?

In 1833 he sent an embassy to Madagascar, to Queen Ranavolana in Antananarivo, offering himself in marriage to her. He also asked for the loan of two thousand soldiers to help him conquer Mombasa. This was, Said thought, a possible solution to his dilemma. It would be attractive to register a wedding between a Sultan of Oman and a Queen of Madagascar, but such an unlikely liaison was not to be. She answered in a letter written in English, which a Captain Hart was able to retail to Said; she regretted she could not marry him herself, because it was against the law of her country, but she offered a young princess in her place. She also offered any number of soldiers, and asked if Said would purchase on her behalf a coral necklace. Said thought hard, but ended by not taking up the offer of the men, for fear of what the British would think, and how they might react; nor did he marry the princess (she would have been his second political princess wife, for six years earlier he had married the sister of the Prince of Shiraz), and it is not recorded whether Queen Ranavolana got her necklace.

This was not Said's last contact with Madagascar, however, for five years later he offered Queen Seneekoo of Nossi-be his protection; she readily agreed and signed a treaty with Said under which she would pay 30,000 dollars a year and duty on exports and imports if he would take charge of the fort and protect her and her people. Unfortunately, however, Said did nothing about his side of the bargain, so that Queen Seneekoo in 1840 was obliged to switch to the French for protection. Said complained to Britain, and Palmerston became cautiously involved with the Quai d'Orsay over Nossi-be; he discovered, however, in time that interference on behalf of Said in this far corner of the Indian Ocean would be full of diplomatic danger.

Said's link with Whitehall was remote and must have been equally befogged with incomprehension on both sides, for Said was in the schizophrenic situation of dealing with the Foreign Office over one half of his kingdom, and the India Office over the other; and vice versa. Somewhere in regal co-ordination above the two was Queen Victoria. Her only knowledge of Said can have been through exchange of personal gifts, and these were a pretty rum lot. Soon after her coronation the Queen sent to Said her portrait, and later a four-poster bed; this was followed in 1842 by a state carriage and harness (which nine years later Said sought permission to give to the Nizam of Hyderabad, since, even if he had wanted to use it, there were no suitable roads in Zanzibar for this purpose), and in 1844 by a silver-gilt tea service. (I remember seeing in Madagascar a large oaken sideboard which had been presented by Victoria to Queen Ranavolana; one wonders who was the adviser on royal gifts.) The only recorded gift of Said to Queen Victoria was the Kuria Muria Islands,* for which the Foreign Secretary somewhat embarrassedly gave him a snuff-box in return.

1833 was a year of varied hope for Said, for besides his Madagascar foray, in that same year there arrived a Mr. Roberts in Muscat. He had left America the previous year to negotiate commercial agreements on behalf of the American Government with a most improbable trio of countries—Cochin China, Siam and Muscat. Having satisfactorily disposed of the first two, he arrived in Muscat to receive a most friendly welcome and three days later he went away with a signed Treaty of Amity and Commerce

* See page 158 below.

safely in his pocket. The Americans, however, were of no assistance to Said when it came to reinforcements for his Mombasa war. He was left to his own devices; he got Mombasa in the end, but never by force of arms.

There are a few echoes of this American contact with Muscat. A portrait of Said hangs in the Peabody Museum in Salem, Massachusetts, from which town there was a considerable mercantile contact with Oman in the middle part of the nineteenth century. Later, in 1880, the American Government appointed as their consular representative a British merchant named Louis Maguire, who the next year switched his allegiance and became the Consular Agent for France. Archibald McKirdy, a partner in W. J. Towell and Sons (a firm that still exists under that name in Muttrah today—it was sold to its present owners in 1900) then became American vice-consul, and remained in the post until a career diplomat, a Mr. Coffin, was sent out from America to take up the post in 1906. Two other Americans followed him in the post, with a local merchant, also from the firm of W. J. Towell, as vice-consul, until in 1915 the Consulate, housed in the large rambling Zawawi building crouched under Jalali (the same building was used as the Indian Consulate General fifty years or so later) was finally closed. The 1833 Treaty remained operative until in 1958 a new treaty of 'amity, economic relations, and consular rights' was signed.

The last years of Said's life and reign were largely spent in Zanzibar, which is where he liked to be, but he paid occasional visits to Muscat. There his influence over his people weakened both from treachery within his family, and in the later years from the renewed threat from the Wahhabis. While he lived Oman still had a role to play, but the seeds of disintegration were there, and it only needed his death to make them bloom.

His last visit to Muscat was in 1854; what with one thing and another he did not leave until 15 September 1856, and two months later died of dysentery on board ship, cheated of a last view of Zanzibar. In Muscat his son Thwaini took over, in Zanzibar another son, Majid; and the split inherent in this arrangement was formalised by the Canning Award of 1861 under which Zanzibar agreed to pay an annual sum of money to Muscat; it said:[11]

The annual payment of 40,000 crowns is not to be understood
as a recognition of the dependence of Zanzibar upon Muscat;
neither is it to be considered as merely personal between Your
Highness and your brother. It is to extend to your respective
successors, and is to be held to be a final and permanent
arrangement, compensating the ruler of Muscat for the
abandonment of all claims upon Zanzibar, and adjusting the
inequality between the two inheritances derived from your
father, the venerated friend of the British Government, which
two inheritances are to be henceforward distinct and separate.

In 1861, it was clearly reckoned that Majid of Zanzibar had the
best of the bargain—indeed, the annual revenue of Muscat at the
time was estimated at 130,000 crowns to the 206,000 of Zanzibar
—although it has turned out differently in the end. The Zanzibar
subsidy, once Thwaini died in 1866, became a sort of bureaucratic ping-pong ball between the Treasury, Foreign Office, India
Office and Government of India, and caused innumerable files to
be filled with intricate civil service logic and counter-logic. At the
same time, in those penurious days of the Sultanate, it was a vital
part of the Muscat exchequer's income and its payment became a
de facto weapon in British hands with which to influence the
ruler. From 1873 its payment was made by the Indian Government and London combined, from 1883 by India alone, from 1947
by London, and still to this day it is paid. In 1873 the 40,000
crowns were valued at 86,400 rupees, and this was the amount
that was paid until in 1912 an extra 100,000 rupees was added to
induce the Sultan to sign an arms control edict. In 1967 the payment amounted to £6,500, which was the sterling equivalent of
the Rs86,400 of 1873, and I have failed to establish for how long
after 1912 the extra Rs100,000 was paid; perhaps it was a once-
for-all bribe to get that edict signed.

Said's death hastened the decline of both parts of his kingdom.
Majid's successors hobbled along in the face of increasing
European interest and encroachment in East Africa, particularly
from Germany, until finally in 1890 Zanzibar, together with
certain other lands, was parcelled out to Britain in the general
African carve-up, as a protectorate.

In Muscat too the solidifying power of Said quickly dis-

4

integrated under Thwaini, his son Salim, and then Turki, one of the sons of Said. This disintegration occurred for a number of reasons. There was, primarily, the excision of the East African empire and the large loss of trading revenue—Muscat thrown back on itself was a very different proposition from Muscat plus the wealth of Zanzibar. Then there was a fresh wave of Wahhabi invasions from the north and west; there was a resurgence of Imamate power in Oman proper; there was the new era of maritime power based on the steamship, in which Muscat could not compete; there was dissension in the ruling family; and there was Britain forcing the Sultan to suppress his slaving activities, which were about the last mainstay of his weakening economy.

The writing was on the wall: Muscat slid down the scale of influence, and ended up by scarcely maintaining her independence. In 1895 Sultan Feisal bin Turki actually lost Muscat to an invading army from the interior, and had to be reinstated with the help of the British Government. It was hardly surprising, therefore, that we find it being seriously mooted that Britain should take over Muscat, as it had taken over Zanzibar, as a protectorate; it is even less surprising that Curzon should have favoured such a move, particularly after his semi-regal progression round the Gulf area in 1903. A visit to Muscat was part of the itinerary, and a special red carpet had to be laid upon the beach for him to walk from the boat to the Consulate steps; moreover, he had to be moved from boat to carpet without wetting his boots, and this was engineered by the local manufacture of a sort of sedan chair. This remains, allegedly, as one of the Consulate's museum pieces —it is a rather poor quality kitchen chair, with a couple of bare poles attached to its sides. The boat was rowed by a specially trained crew of local sailors, and Curzon must have been more than usually intolerable throughout his visit. 'I have little doubt', he said, 'that the time will come . . . when the Union Jack will be seen flying from the castles of Muscat.'[12] He was wrong; the old principles of non-interference in internal affairs of the Gulf states won through, and the Sultan was shored up in a shaky independence, buttressed by his British treaties—Friendship, Commerce and Navigation (1839, 1846, 1891), Anti-Slavery (1822, 1839, 1845, 1873), Communications (1864, 1865) and Cession of Land (1891).

However, in spite of this fundamental weakening of Muscat, it spluttered back on stage, under the spotlight of European rivalries, during the last years of the nineteenth and first of the twentieth centuries; and there was a faint echo of the struggles of one hundred years previously between France and Britain. In 1891 France and Russia allied themselves to reduce the power of Britain in the Gulf; in Muscat, France led the way, although Russian ships also began to pay visits to the harbour—and indeed, amongst the graffiti of ships' names and gulls' droppings littering the rocks of the harbour, you may pick out the names of many Russian ships, most of them more modern visitors than the *Nijni Novgorod* in 1893, but there they are. (There is also at least one Chinese signature on the rocks, unless it's a naval jape.)

The French, in this last effort to dilute, or remove, British influence, worked on two lines of action: they tried to obtain a coaling station for themselves, and they gave French flag protection to Muscat vessels. The former was a fairly straightforward business: first they tried in Sur, then in Bander Jissa, a few miles down the coast from Muscat, but however much the Sultan may have wished to oblige them he was faced by his 1891 Agreement which constrained 'himself, his heirs and successors, never to cede, to sell, to mortgage, or otherwise give for occupation, save to the British Government, the dominions of Muscat and Oman or any of their dependencies'. Monsieur Ottavi, the French Consul, who had taken up residence in 1894 in Muscat (in this house, as you will recall) could not do much about that, and had to be satisfied with the offer by the British of the use of half of the coaling facilities they had in Mukalla cove, part of the Muscat harbour.

To prevent Ottavi from offering French flag protection to Omani vessels was less simple. It would not have been enormously important anyway if the vessels were not slave traders; this was in clear contradiction to the principles of the 1890 Brussels Slave Trade Conference which had been signed by France. Finally, in 1903, it blew up into a full-scale diplomatic deadlock when simultaneously a French flag dhow was detained by the Sheikh of the Beni bu Ali in Sur, and three people of Sur arrived in a mailship at Muscat claiming the protection of the French Consul. It took an arbitration of the Hague Tribunal to settle this oddment of an international dispute, and with it died any further serious French activity. French consuls, however, continued to live in our house until the end of 1920 (one of them died in it, having been there only one month), but not until 1945 did the French Government return the lease to the Sultan.

So we are back where we started, on the roof, looking out over Muscat town lying in the sun like an old scabious pie-dog asleep in the dust. If Ottavi were miraculously returned to Muscat to-morrow he would immediately feel himself at home: a few new-fangled gimmicks around the place, some of the old buildings a generation more crumbled and cracked, but the people would be just the same, doing the same things: tribesmen squatting out the day on a doorstep, rifles at hand, negroid fishermen carrying poles of fish to the market, multicoloured Baluch women at the wells, children playing happily in the alleys, Indian merchants, dark with sweat, making for a godown, old men lurching under the weight of their loads to clear the jetty, men talking out the hours wherever they meet together. And then, descending from the roof at sunset, he would involuntarily turn to the large iron ring set into one of the wall embrasures, to loosen the rope and lower the French tricolor from its masthead. *Mon dieu*, no flagpole, no rope. But the ring is still there.

❧ Muttrah ❧

Muttrah is a joint between Muscat and the Batina coast. It is a moot point whether it is more closely related to Muscat or its hinterland, but I, for one, feel closer in Muttrah to the Batina farmers and the date growers of the Interior than to the administrators, such as they are, of Muscat. Even the traders who have offices in both towns seem more sophisticated in Muscat; as if when they leave for their Muttrah business they involuntarily change from dark grey suits to something more reckless, checked, and earthy.

Therefore I think of Muttrah as a part of the coast, and, looking back into history, this seems to be right, for seldom does Muttrah figure in the same paragraph as Muscat, nor does its capture or recapture ever seem to have any great political significance. It is Muscat, or nothing. Muttrah remains the southern port of the Batina, and the commercial centre for the Sumayl Gap.

It just happens to look, superficially, a bit like Muscat. It has a similar bowl of a harbour, and a sea front crescent of faded Indian Ocean type houses, and a grey fort looking down on it in a spirit of slightly responsible recklessness. Only one fort, though; where the second might have been, facing it across the harbour, is only a solitary watch-tower. And the fort, when you come to look at it closely, is like a wafer compared to the Muscat cakes, hardly more than an operatic silhouette upon a pointed spur.

Muttrah is considerably larger than Muscat, has a much bigger suq, and has three times the population. Its suq is filled, not with refrigerators and cameras, but with bales of gaudy cloth, piles of kashmir head scarves, strings of skull caps; the harbour is littered with dhows, but never a B.I. boat.* The narrow alleys of the suq are crowded with bedu, with Batina Baluch, with sweating porters; there is a constant clack of coffee cups, a babble of

* British India Line; always referred to as B.I.

bargaining, and the rich metallic jangle of Maria Theresa dollars; the merchants squat cross-legged, squeezed in beside their wares, as if in a rented tomb space in a catacomb. Some of these recesses have been brightened with neon lighting strips and may contain such profitable lines as cosmetics and medicines; others may be blank padlocked wooden doors, their owners either asleep, ill, or away for the date harvest. The corners of the suq that I like best are the group of spice sellers, surrounded by concentric circles of baskets full of subtly different dried grasses, seeds and dusts, and backed by bundles of shrivelled tobacco leaves; and the pot sellers, standing amongst staggering stacks of every size and shape of simple pottery jar, some from Bahla or Rustaq, many brought down from Iraq by dhow. You can buy a lot in that suq, from a Chinese (Peking) tricycle to a Penguin book, from an old bedstead to a gramophone record, from a Mexican gold sovereign to a ton of dates; but the oddest thing that I ever saw was a silver model of a very Victorian warship, complete with six cannons detachable in pairs, two ship's ladders artistically hanging over the sides, and one splendid anchor caught up in the prow; all wonderfully out of scale, made in Bombay, and costing £54.

Muttrah is the commercial centre of Oman. There the simple necessities of life are bought and sold; cloth, rice, coffee versus dates and limes. That has always been the basis of the economy, and it still is in 1967. The addition of oil as an export will one day transform the way of life, commercial and social, as it has done nearly everywhere else in the Arab world, but this has not yet happened.

In Muttrah, then, are the manipulators of money, whose skills must overcome the fiscal peculiarities of the country, which are as variable and inconsistent as most other things. If you are a Muttrah merchant you must be equally versatile at least in rupees, annas, naya peis, dollars, pounds, baizas, dinars; annas do not exist officially, but are referred to as often as naya peis, which no longer exist officially either; there are now 64 baizas in a rupee, which used to contain 16 annas and later 100 naya peis, and which is still valued at the old pre-1966 Indian devaluation rate, but only 3 baiza and 5 baiza coins exist for small change; the Maria Theresa dollar (M.T.D.) (officially pegged at 5 rupees, but unobtainable at that price) is divided into 120 Omani baizas, which are quite different from Muscati baizas (needless to add, Dhofari baizas are different again); exchange rates tend to be described in terms of rupees to a Kuweiti dinar, but may equally be in terms of the Bahraini dinar which used to equal 10 Muscat rupees before the 1967 sterling devaluation, or in terms of M.T.Ds. (referred to indiscriminately as dollars or riyals, which may alternatively be U.S. dollars or Saudi riyals in a different context) to 100 rupees; and you must also be on your guard for rupees to the M.T.D. or rupees to the gold tola bar. And once you have mastered that lot, you must start on the difference between a Muscat maund, which equals 24 kiyas, each kiyas representing the weight of 6 M.T.D., and an Omani maund, which equals 24 kiyas, each kiyas representing the weight of 6 Omani baizas, remembering that 5 Omani baizas are the same weight as 1 M.T.D. and that in Arabic a maund is a mun; 200 Muscat maunds equal 1 bahhar, which is the same weight both on the coast and in the Interior but varies when applied to different produce, a bahhar of salt or firewood being equivalent to 400 Muscati maunds.

Oh, I forgot to tell you that a Muscati rupee is worth 1s. 6d., and a kiyas weighs 5.9375 oz.

Curiously enough a maund (or mund or mun) is a weight of far greater pedigree than might be imagined, and, though this is less surprising, of great complexity; in the heyday of the East India Company (and, for all I know, still) it represented something different in almost every area of the Indian Ocean region, from 90 lb. 4 oz. in Bussorah for grain to 2 lb. 8 drams in Bettlesakee for coffee (3 lb. for other goods). Mind you, if the Muttrah merchant must be proficient in currency manipulation today, it is nothing to what the East India Company official needed at his fingertips. The maund was not the only weight or coin to fluctuate its value; the Spanish dollar was worth 5s. 4½d. at Surat, 5s. 3¾d. at Bombay, but 6s. 8d. ('about') at Bussorah; the bahhar varied between 222 lb. 6 oz. (equivalent to 10 frazils) at Judda and 814 lb. (40 frazils) at Bettlesakee. In the handbook[13] on this general subject published in 1789, and issued, no doubt, to all young recruits to the Company, it may be easy enough to check up the number of budgerooks in a Muscat Mamoody, but one is really up against it when one has committed to memory a list of coinage values only to read 'The above is the calculation on real silver rupees (Surat or others), which often rise or fall in value. There are also imaginary rupees current in Tattah, in which denomination the Merchants keep their Accounts.' Sometimes you feel fairly certain that the Muttrah merchants too have read that last sentence and have taken it to heart.

The whole Muttrah suq is bisected by a concrete road which leads down what used to be the old wadi to the sea; indeed, after a heavy storm this road reverts to nature, and becomes a torrent of water. This is rare, however; usually it is awash with people and carts, and Land-Rovers nudging their way through the crowd with a multifarious hooting of horns. Land-Rovers are the modern equivalent of a camel train, and except where the road is concreted, between Muscat and Muttrah, with an extension to Beit al Falaj, are the only rational type of car to use. They carry people or goods, or both, in profusion and disarray, springs strained beyond endurance, tyres without a vestige of tread, and wheels in crazy disalignment; there is no such thing as writing off a vehicle in Oman, and its economic life stretches to the scrap heap.

The older form of transport, camels and donkeys, have a park just outside the main gate (the one that is solemnly shut at night and guarded by the Beni Umr, even though it has become detached from the city wall on both sides), and camels are permitted no further; donkeys may continue on to Muscat under certain controlled conditions—chiefly for the cartage of lucerne, which may not be carried in bulk by any other means.

Muttrah is a place that throbs with life; it is never comatose like Muscat, even on a hot summer afternoon when most of the shops are blankly boarded up. Particularly is this so down on the beach where the children play all day in spite of its being, amongst everything else, the public lavatory. Seen from the corners of the coast road from Muscat, the Muttrah sea front appears charming and attractive, but the smell and the dirt and the rubbish down there are pungent and pervasive; though one particular smell connected with drying fish, which some residents of Muscat can still clearly recall, and which was probably the same 'peculiar and disagreeable odour'[14] which saluted the senses of J. B. Fraser in 1821, has now been swept away. It is a dirty town, with pools or rivulets of filth all about it; unhealthy from too many people, no sanitation, too little water, too much poverty. If you drive through the empty town on a summer night, the stale stench of the day hangs over the streets like a noxious mist; and then you see that the street is not empty, but lined with the corpses of sleeping persons, seeking in the open a dilution of the town's semi-solid supply of air. In the winter it is not so bad, but still the foxes slink out of the hills to scavenge round the town.

The dirt is in strong contrast to Muscat, which people always find surprisingly clean. This is at least partly due to Muscat's regiment of women who, bent over the frond brushes they always like to use, sweep the streets in the dim indefinable dawn, and who have vanished, like wraiths, by the time most people are up and about. But why the same shouldn't be done in Muttrah, particularly as the Municipality is a joint one, is an unsolved mystery.

On the way out of Muttrah towards the wells, and on the left of the road, is the Muttrah Mission Hospital, known throughout Oman, an oasis of medical service for the people. In more recent times Government clinics have helped to spread the burden of medical care, but the Mission Hospital remains the only centre in the country for surgery and treatment of serious disease (except that now the Oil Company has a spanking new hospital which is available to its own employees). The Mission is the Arabian Mission of the Dutch Reformed Church in America, and of the same organisation as those in Bahrain, Basra and, formerly, Kuweit.

The Basra Mission was opened in August 1891, by Cantine and Zwemer, and the Bahrain Mission two years later. In November 1893 Peter Zwemer arrived in Muscat to open a mission there also, and 'he hired a native house, one of the best in Muscat, only to be compelled to move out to make room for a French consul,[15] —the house, therefore, the one in which I lived, and Ottavi was the Consul; bad luck for Zwemer. However, he was able to purchase some land and have it registered with the Sultan and that is the nucleus of the present Muscat premises; by 1909 they had two acres including a graveyard (which, curiously, seems to be used only for non-Europeans; Europeans have been buried in the Christian cemetery by the sea), and in 1908 the Peter Zwemer Memorial School was opened, having cost $1,200. The Women's

Dispensary, now expanded into the Women's Hospital, cost a further $1,300 and was opened in 1913. In 1909 the Muttrah medical work was inaugurated with the arrival of Dr. Sharon Thoms, father of Dr. Wells Thoms who runs the hospital today. On 15 January 1913 Dr. Sharon Thoms fell from a telegraph pole, which was to link the Muscat and Muttrah Missions, and died.

This setback, together with the start of World War I, compelled the Mission to close down, and it was not restarted in Muttrah until 1928 with the arrival of Dr. Paul Harrison. He purchased the present hospital site, and started building in 1935. Dr. Wells Thoms came in 1939 and has been in charge ever since, a remarkable family history of service to Oman. The hospital today has a T.B. wing and a leprosy ward besides the usual medical facilities, and it has general control over its sister establishment, the Women's Hospital in Muscat.

More and more medicine is badly needed in all the country of Oman, where the diseases of poverty are endemic; but this is evident enough even from Muscat and Muttrah where limbs are wizened and sometimes stunted beyond repair, and the eyes of children are already gummed with trachoma, and there are plenty of older men being led through the dangerous streets, quite blind. Nor can one repress a shudder when one sees clanking heavily along in chains outside the hospital itself a mindless, but presumably dangerous also, idiot man.

Muttrah pulsates with life, with commerce, with activity of one sort or another, but, in spite of its fort and the innumerable towers scattered over the hills around it, it does not figure much in the history books. The fort is almost certainly Portuguese, although probably built on a previous Arab site (indeed the site is so obviously reserved for a fort that no doubt they were built and rebuilt through the ages) but it can never have been intended to withstand a long siege, for its capacity is too cramped; it feels almost brittle, serving more as a gesture than the real thing. Like Jalali, it is today a prison; you can visit it for photography as long as you take with you one of the Wali's men who will persuade the guards to open the great wooden gate for you, both on the way in, and, more importantly, out.

From up there you can get a fine view of the town, and even forget the smells; the dhows, with their square sterns floating at anchor like a fleet of Elizabethan galleys; a long boat creaking in to the customs jetty loaded to the rowlocks with sacks of rice; a few broken foundations in Arbak cove across the harbour, where a jetty used to stand, as disconsolate as Mukalla in Muscat (and where it is planned to put the new jetty when it is finally built); the Wali's house beneath, and the grey bulk of the Mission Hospital beyond groves of burasti huts; the walls of the Khoja quarter just traceable, whose gates are still locked at night like a Warsaw ghetto; the grey spiky volcanic rock all round the cove and the town, like a protective armadillic armour. But best of all, on a stormy winter evening from a corner of the coast road, you can look back at Muttrah, its sea-front houses bright white from some last quirk of light, and behind them the black hills etched out of Wagnerian clouds, with, dead centre in a pool of clear sky, a crescent new moon.

❊ Batina ❊

The Batina is a long sweep of coastal plain stretching from Muttrah/Muscat, where the mountains meet the coast, in a crescent to Khor Fakkan/Dibba in the north, just short of the Musandam peninsula where the mountains meet the sea again; the very top of this coastal plain was cut away from the Sultanate in the early nineteenth century (it was Said bin Sultan who, rather insultingly, had to agree to this after buying off one of the Wahhabi attacks on the country) when the present boundary was established at Khatma Malaha, a few miles north of Shinas, but the hills of the peninsula itself are again, technically, Sultanate territory. Batina is derived from an Arabic root meaning 'to be hidden', usually used in relation to the belly, and you may think of the Batina coast, therefore, as the soft underbelly of the country, protected above by tough mountains, and lying comfortably in the warm waves of the sea.

The Batina coast is quite flat; its sea-line is a long two-hundred-mile beach, lapped or pounded by the sea, and broken only by the estuaries of wadis which create semi-saltwater khors of varying size. Apart from some areas of mangrove swamp growing around a khor, the coastline is almost continuously edged by a belt of agriculture, and behind that is a flat expanse of gravel plain, littered with dry, unproductive trees and shrubs, which extends back to the foothills of the mountains. At various points along the coast are a succession of small towns, which sound like the roll-call of an L.M.S. branch line long since grassed over in disuse; change at Sib for Birka, Musanna, Suweiq, Khaboura, Sahm, Sohar and Shinas. Percy Cox, when he was British consul in Muscat, evoked the grand imperial manner of a Curzon when he went visiting these places; always, he wrote[16] 'it was my habit to wear a bathing suit under my clothes when landing along the coast if there were not a flat calm.'

The Batina has two assets—sea-water, and therefore fishing;

fresh water, and therefore agriculture. The fresh water is from well sources, and depends upon the subterranean flow from the mountain range; the occasional flooding of the wadis is mostly wasted, ending up in the sea, for there is no system of water conservancy as yet. It has not been needed, for the wells (and they have developed enormously since diesel pumps have been widely used) have always sufficed for the limited requirements of the garden owners along the coast. The two main products are dates and sweet limes (of a shrivelling bitterness in spite of adjectival euphemism), although there is now an ever-widening variety of vegetables and fruits being grown—tomatoes, beetroots, carrots, cauliflowers, peppers, cabbages, radishes, broccoli, melons, papaya, mangoes, bananas, guavas.

The other traditional pastime of the coast is fishing: for sardines, sharks and a wide variety of most excellent edible fish. Some years ago there was a thriving export of dried fish to, for some obscure reason, Ceylon, but now most of the consumption is local, either on the coast, or taken up by camel load to the interior. Much of it is dried (and some varieties smoked), either for animal fodder, in the case of sardines, or for human beings, in the case of sharks (a particular delicacy, it seems, for the Arabs of the interior, but very definitely an acquired taste).

There is no doubt that the Batina is, potentially, a garden area of great wealth; it has a market that could stretch from Muscat to Kuweit, water enough, and proved capacity to produce. But, of course, this is a dream needing a tremendous capital investment in terms of water conservancy, agricultural education, and marketing development; with the arrival of oil revenues, there is now the possibility of realising the dream. The Batina is an existing asset which many others of the Arabian Gulf oil states would dearly have liked to possess; let's hope that one day it will have the agricultural riches that it is capable of producing.

Already something has happened; there is, for instance, an experimental farm, belonging to the Development Department, at Sohar, where research into improved strains of fruits and vegetables most suited to the coast is carried out, and the devoted staff of the farm help the local farmers in every way they can to put a little science into their work. It is a pretty dispiriting job though, both from lack of funds, a most limited co-operation from the authorities, a fundamental conservatism amongst the people and restrictions of one sort and another. However, it is a beginning, and some of the results in the farm are most encouraging for the more munificent future that is hoped for.

The new Batina road is another improvement of almost revolutionary quality, although as you rattle down it in a cloud of dust you may think this a ridiculous exaggeration. I have just been reading some notes of a journey I made from Muscat to Sohar only seven years ago, before the graded road had been started, and I can relive only too painfully the appalling twelve hours of bumping through villages and wadis and round date groves and through ever thickening envelopes of dust, and compare with that, most favourably, the three hours it takes today. (And you only have to go back to 1930 to do the journey by camel with Bertram Thomas in seven days.)

So there is progress; but it is still very slow, rather like electoral reform in the nineteenth century, not at all what one expects from the jet age of 1967. And, looking at those notes again, I am afraid the gardens themselves along the Batina are very little changed, nor is the administrative system controlling the lives of the inhabitants.

The Batina road has been graded in a more-or-less straight line behind the garden strip, so that as you drone down it you pass only the dry grey waste area which fills the space between the wells and the hills. On a summer's day there is nothing inland to be seen behind the heat haze, but in winter the drive becomes transformed by the magnetising presence of the mountains, sometimes remote and tantalising, sometimes so close that they seem to block out the sky. On the other side is a continuous line of palm trees, and sometimes, as the road edges closer to them, you pass a newly dug garden with some fresh lucerne and a couple of papaya trees looking like Japanese sunshades. Occasionally an empty barrel and worn tracks mark the turn to one of the towns.

These towns are all very similar, and it is an active feat of memory for the occasional visitor to remember which is which. There will be a beach with dirty discoloured sand and some dunes behind it; fishing boats drawn up, and nets laid out to dry; a rim of burasti huts, and a huddle of houses, with the Wali's fort growing out of them in a square tumbledown gesture of greatness, topped by the red flag of the Sultanate, sometimes so faded as to look, for one revolutionary moment, like the white Imamate one. There will be a small suq, with some camels and donkeys tethered outside it to crooked poles, and a few Land-Rovers, the taxis of the coast; maybe a 3 ton lorry, piled with at least six tons of people and goods (I was assured that on one occasion an Army patrol stopped an overladen 3 tonner and ninety-six people were ordered off it). Perhaps one or two more prosperous white-washed houses will be there amongst the burastis and the mud huts, and then behind them the date groves, interspersed with limes and other fruits.

Limes are a profitable fruit. The market is primarily Iraq, where the particular tang of the Muscati lime is a *sine qua non* of local rice spicing, and is equally a compulsory addition to a cup of tea. The limes are dried before being exported, and turn a rather un-pleasant black colour; once dried, however, they can be kept for at least a year or two for the merchant to pick the right moment for selling. The Batina grower will sell for about Rs15 to Rs18 per maund depending on the season (a maund consists of about five hundred limes). A garden of four or five acres can easily produce half a million limes a season, which works out at over £1,200 gross income to the farmer; this in a country where labour costs no more than about Rs4 per day is a considerable sum. The whole-saler will sell for well over £400 per ton, around Rs20 per maund. The biggest wholesaler—alleged by many to be a virtual monopo-list—lives in Sahm, next door to Sohar, and behind his houses you can see the limes piled into bunkers like coal, awaiting ship-ment either direct to Basra, or to Bahrain as an intermediate call. Limes are normally valued in rupees as being primarily a Batina business; they are grown widely in the Interior as well, but, in typical contrary fashion, are of a different quality there, and turn yellow, not black, when dried; their value is about one-third less than the Batina variety.

Dates are the other way round; being primarily an Omani produce they are valued in M.T.D.s, and the Batina varieties are generally less valuable than the Omani ones. They are split, generically, into dry or wet dates; dry are of inferior quality, and are usually boiled before being used as animal fodder. Large quantities are exported to India. The value of dates varies tremendously according to their quality, and also the season, but as a rough average dried dates will fetch 40 to 60 rials per bahhar, and wet dates up to 100 rials and more per bahhar. The average yield of a tree may be 12 maunds, which gives an income of, say, Rs15 per tree of dry dates, and double for wet dates. The number of varieties of date is enormous, and like everything else are distinct for the coast and the interior; the official number of varieties of coastal Batina date is twenty, and of interior Omani date sixty-two.

The export of fish has died away in recent years, but one merchant told me that about ten years ago he used to export 4,000 to 5,000 cwt. of fish per month for ten months of the year; at that time it was worth about Rs30 to Rs35 per cwt. f.o.b. Muttrah, so he handled about £100,000-worth per year.

Practically all this wholesale trade, whether for internal consumption or export, is handled by the Muttrah merchants—except that Sahm happens to be the centre for the lime industry. Statistical information is extremely limited in the Sultanate, but the Government handbook gives the value of total exports of dates in 1962/3 as over £100,000, and limes as just under £100,000.

The towns, the whole coast, are basically similar: bright and lively in winter with a marvellous background of blue sea, and the white sails of fishing boats curling up into blue sky; hot and heavily humid in summer, when you long for the afternoon breeze to riffle the air. A summer's night in the open is no drier, but a lot hotter, than lying in a moorland mist for twelve hours. But however much they are the same they are different, and have different associations, these Batina towns.

Sohar is the Batina capital; and difficult though it is to imagine today, it has at various times been the capital of the country. Ibn Hawqal[17] writing in the tenth century, says: 'Sohar is the capital and is on the sea. Its traders and commerce cannot be enumerated. It is the most developed and wealthy town in Oman. The rest of Islam hardly knows that a town such as Sohar with its wealth and development exists on the Persian sea.' This is heady stuff for a place that looks like Sohar does today, and one wonders why and how it became such an influential place. Admittedly it is situated at the coastal end of one of the three or four main passes through the Omani mountain range, the Wadi Jizzi, and one can only assume that the Khor beside the fort, now silted up and almost sealed from the sea, was once navigable and provided the harbour which is alleged to have been a parasang in length and a parasang in breadth.

However this may be, and in spite of ups and downs, Sohar was undoubtedly a thriving and important town; when Albuquerque arrived in 1507, having sacked Muscat, the great fort of Sohar was said to require one thousand persons to defend it. Discreetly, however, it surrendered to Albuquerque, and Sohar soon became one of the chief Portuguese 'factories' in Oman.

At the end of the Portuguese era, and under the Yaariba dynasty, Sohar maintained its influential position, to the extent that in 1645 the Omani leader, the Imam Nasir, wrote to the British to offer them trading facilities there. The next year Philip Wylde arrived to negotiate an agreement on behalf of the British and duly signed one. It was the first, though quite private and unofficial, treaty between the British and Oman and this gives it an immediate notoriety; but it is also worth noticing for two of its clauses*—one, that licence was given for the British to exercise their own religion, and secondly, that the British were permitted reserved powers of justice for their own subjects. Of these, the former was liberal enough, but not particularly surprising since the Arabs were used to Christians from the presence of the Portuguese (during their occupation, an Augustinian church was built in Sohar, with a friar as permanent curate; this must have presented something of a shock to a town that was one of the three† where the Imam could lead the Friday prayers) and a colony of Jews had long been established in Sohar (this tradition of religious tolerance has lasted down to the present day and is common to all the Gulf states). The clause giving extra territorial jurisdiction is more remarkable, being a forerunner to the whole Gulf system of British law which, in the case of Oman, was only finally retroceded with effect from 1 January 1967. What is odd is that the first official British Treaty of 1798 did not include such a clause, although the American 1833 Treaty did; the British added theirs only in 1839, almost two hundred years after Wylde.

* Others are worthy of note too; see Appendix 1 for the full text of this treaty.
† The other two are Nizwa and Rustaq.

During the Yaariba era, for nearly eighty years, Sohar prospered and, in the Hinawi-Ghafiri civil war of 1724–8 which
effectively ended it, appears to have been outside the mainstream
of battle and to have remained remarkably untouched. From the
end of the civil war until the beginning of the Al bu Said dynasty,
that is from 1728 until 1749, there was a confused period of
internal rivalry in Oman, to some extent representing a continuation of the Hinawi-Ghafiri war (this was a basically tribal
affair about which more will be heard later), and only significant
because the Persians were invited by Seif bin Sultan* on the
Hinawi side to assist him. This gave the Persians an opportunity
to return to the Oman coast, which at various times they had held
and lost; in 1743 they took Muscat, and a few months later they
forced the Wali of Sohar, Ahmed bin Said, the future founder of
the Al bu Said dynasty, to surrender Sohar to them.

Ahmed bin Said, since by this time there was no one else,
assumed the leadership of the Hinawi element, and retired to
Birka, where he managed to concentrate most of the trade that
had previously belonged to Sohar. The Persians, for their part,
did not stay in Sohar long and, in circumstances that are somewhat obscure, gave up first Sohar and then Muscat, to Ahmed.
Ahmed then staged the celebrated feast at Birka† where he had
the remaining Persians murdered, and never again have they
returned to occupy any part of Oman. At this point the Imam, a
Ghafiri named Bilurub, was deposed, and Ahmed bin Said, the
proved strong man and saviour of his country, was elected Imam
in 1749.

Sohar from this time lost the influence and prestige that it had
continually possessed for at least the previous 1,500 years, since
Muscat now became the single capital and focus of the coast; in
spite of this, however, Sohar managed to maintain an outward
impression of importance, to the extent that, after Ahmed bin
Said's death, it became nominally independent; an independence
that was ratified in the terms of the Pact of Birka in 1793 under
which Said, Qais and Sultan, the three sons of Ahmed, obtained

---

* A grandson of the one mentioned on page 38; this Seif was elected Imam on four
separate occasions, the first (subsequently disallowed) being when he was aged only
twelve.

† See page 39 above.

respectively Rustaq, Sohar and Muscat. Later, in 1849, its independent status reached its formal height when Hennell, the Resident in the Gulf, actually signed an anti-slavery treaty with Sohar (whose signatory was Seif bin Humoud and who, having just ousted his father from his rule, was murdered by him next year) as if it were one of the Trucial States. Two years later, however, Said bin Sultan reabsorbed Sohar into his dominions in spite of existing treaties and from then on, although there were claims of independence by certain Walis, Sohar has never been more than a wilayat. Sometimes in the turmoil of family strife a strong Wali would denounce the authority of the Sultan in Muscat, but retribution would inevitably follow, and, particularly in the chaos of the second half of the nineteenth century in Oman, this retribution often ended in slaughter.

Indeed, one of the more unpleasant examples of the pursuit of power in Oman comes from Sohar in 1866 when Sayyid Thwaini, who had succeeded in 1856 to the Muscat portion of Said bin Sultan's inheritance, was murdered by his son Salim—shot while asleep in the Sohar fort. Today the fort is far more peaceable, and is likely to cause death only through its own collapse; the Wali took me up to its roof one day, and I was apprehensive throughout the rickety trip. The view from between its embrasures is a typical Batina one, a carpet of palms one side, and the sea the other; but you do get also an outline impression of the old walls, now reduced to rubble except where a disconsolate arch is shakily reared over the road into the town.

So much for Sohar, capital of the Batina—except for one last flicker of drama. In 1952 the present Sultan, incensed at last into action by the Saudi occupation of Bureimi, called for his Army to gather there. The tribesmen rallied to his call, and one can picture the scene as being similar in most respects to the preliminaries of any Sohar battle for the preceding hundreds of years. Eight thousand of them are said to have been there, ready to march (well, to pick their way) up the Wadi Jizzi to Bureimi. The Sultan arrived to lead, or at least to enthuse, his loyal subjects. Excitement sizzled. But then came the deflation of anticlimax. Britain had second thoughts, and ordered their Consul General in Muscat to express them to the Sultan. He dutifully rattled his way from Muscat to Sohar, emerged from his car with cramp, and expressed them. With a strong belief that this was all wrong, the Sultan told his people to go home. Looked at in retrospect, Oman has never been the same since; or, perhaps, the Sultan hasn't; either way, that decision at Sohar was a great deal more influential than must have seemed at the time to the Foreign Office official who signed the telegram in London.

Down the other end of the Batina, almost hidden from sight, is the only solid material evidence that the Sultanate is living in 1967: the oil terminal of Mina al Fahal. Strictly, I suppose, the Batina ends at Qurm, where, after two hundred miles of sandy beach, some rocky outcrops meet the sea, forming a series of small coves. On top of these hills has been built Ras al Hamra, the housing area of P.D.(O.), easily the finest site for an oil camp in the whole Gulf region. Scattered over the hills lie precisely angled air-conditioned boxes that are as far removed from the ram-shackle burasti villages of the coast as A.D. 1967 seems to be from A.H. 1387. And beneath the houses, in a wide bay, are the instal-lations themselves, dominated by a group of six gleaming crude tanks tucked into a crook of the hills, and out at sea an oil tanker contentedly subsiding into the water as it fills with oil. Looking in at this unlikely scene is Fahal Island, arching out of the water like some petrified whale, once again after 414 years deserving its title of Victory Island.*

The main road bypasses all this, and except for the square out-lines of the houses which you can see as you drive along, you could be wholly insensible that Muscat was now an oil state. Per-haps, if you were using your eyes you would recognise the flattened right of way of the pipeline which serves as a sinuous underground umbilical connection between the coast and the oil fields 175 miles over the hills and far away. If not, you might arrive at the Rui Gate without a thought of oil.

Rui is a small village a mile or so from Muttrah, which serves as a market garden for Muttrah and Muscat. It has a watch-tower on a hill above it which at a particular moment of dusk looks like a great owl brooding over the village. Beside the road is a sort of Omani fish-and-chip shop, a large open roofed kitchen where

---

* In 1553 the Portuguese destroyed the Turkish fleet here and called Fahal the Island of Victory.

they bake fish whole; you see the donkeys pattering along from Muttrah fish suq, a pannier bag slung each side with the forked fish-tails sticking out of the top, on their way to replenish the grill, and the smell of cooked fish pervades that stretch of road.

The Rui gate is a customs check point, explicable only when one has grasped that there is a fundamental difference between Muscat and Oman; this difference is illustrated at Rui by the customs duty which is levied on all produce 'imported' into Muscat and Muttrah from the Interior. The rate is $7\frac{1}{2}$ per cent for most, but not all (e.g. dates 5 per cent, tobacco 15 per cent) of the main products of the country. There is also a Muscat/Muttrah Municipality tax (at 10 per cent of value) payable on goods consumed in, or imported through, the Municipality. These taxes are not collected at the Rui gate, but if you arrive from the direction of the Interior and have goods for resale, you must obtain a chit from the officials there and then sell your goods through the official broker in a public auction in Muttrah. You pay the broker the tax rate plus 5 per cent (i.e. normally $12\frac{1}{2}$ per cent) of the proceeds, and he is then responsible for passing on the appropriate percentage to the Customs and Municipality. All sales of produce must be made through the broker, and not privately, a custom noted, incidentally, by Fraser when he visited Muscat in 1821. This, as you may guess from previous observations on weights and measures, is but the bare bones of a system that is infinitely more complex in reality. Indeed, the system is totally incomprehensible to the ordinary man; there is a Customs manual, which you may purchase for Rs5, but it leaves you with as many, if not more, questions than you began with; there are customs officials, whose expositions seem clear enough until you sit down to think about them, and who, when re-questioned, either do not answer, or produce an answer that is in contradiction to other statements that you thought were facts. It is very muddling. However, one may safely sum it all up by saying that everything is taxable to some degree or other, which is one good twentieth-century characteristic of Oman.

All, or some, of this is known by the Rui gate officials, whose red flag flying over a mud hut signifies their official status, and whose two gates force everyone to halt before going out or coming in. Exit check is a further mystification, incidentally, and I am still not clear whether its purpose is to assess an export tax (which exists) or to check that those going through have the relevant permission to do so.

Between Rui and Muttrah there is not a lot of space, but squeezed into it is Beit al Falaj, round whose fort is clustered the Headquarters of the Sultan's Armed Forces (SAF), and in whose very limited plain, called the Saih al Harmel, is the official civil, and military, airport of the country. Most visitors to Muscat arrive there nervously watching hills approaching ever closer to the wing tips of their aeroplane as it slews in through some not very obvious gap. Nothing larger than the planes which land there now will be able to in the future, and one day there will be a Muscat International Airport out, perhaps, at Azaiba which already is used by P.D.(O.) and by any other plane that may have strayed by inadvertence or force of circumstance to the area.

If you happen to be out there early you will most probably see groups of camels and donkeys strung along beside the airstrip from Rui to Muttrah suq loaded with firewood which they bring in bundles down the Wadi Adai from the Saih Hatat; if you are even earlier, you may find them encamped behind the Rui gate waiting for it to open. These silent strings, creaking a bit when you get up close to them, kicking up a light mist of dust in a breathless morning, are a slowly dissolving symbol of the past; a few minutes later, the Land-Rovers have woken up, the Provosts (themselves a veteran, if not antique, aeroplane) splutter to life, and the mechanised dust of another day takes over.

Beit al Falaj fort is said to have been built as a Sultan's week-end country house about 150 years ago; indeed, I have been told that the engineer of this fort was the same man who built my house in Muscat. Perhaps. If it were, he would more readily recognise his handiwork in Muscat than the pleasure palace in Beit al Falaj, where the disciplines of army life have drained away any last traces of dissipation; although, to tell the truth, any visiting soldier must get quite a military shock to see how dishevelled it is.

But it is really Qurm that is the southern end of the Batina, a little fishing village on a khor that is in fact the estuary of the Wadi Adai whenever it is in spate. You can often find two or three camels down there by the water's edge, their owners having plodded down in that curious lunging camel movement from

Sumayl, or further up the Gap, to buy fish, probably a sack or two of sardines to sell as fodder back home. Across the shallow stream the beach sets off in a wide curve north, with herons standing sentinel along the sand. You can see a cluster of burasti huts, the first of the coastal fishing villages, and drawn up on the beach a couple of badans, which are the most common of the larger fishing boats, with their pointed sterns jutting up like enormous beaks against the sky. If you are lucky, you may see a flock of flamingoes down there, a carmine admixture to the sea or the sky, and on the khor itself you will be unlucky not to enjoy the flash of a kingfisher; indeed, bird life is prolific on the Batina, and someone has claimed to have seen almost every variety of ordinary European bird there; in fact, you are advised to bring with you to Muscat the bird guide-book you would use in England, not some exotic encyclopaedia of Arabian or Indian varieties. Apart from birds, the beach is pitted with crab holes; if you sit there silently the crabs emerge from their holes or from the sea like some midget army on manœuvre, and if you move there is a flicker and a flurry and they have vanished. They have magpie characteristics and will triumphantly carry off down into their holes anything you leave on the beach.

That's where the Batina begins; on to Sib, where the Treaty was signed, to Birka, where Ahmed bin Said slaughtered the Persians over dinner (there is an inscription over one of the doorways in the fort referring to the great man—but not to this particular exploit of his), Musanna, Suweiq, Khaboura, where the Wali will take you to his special reception burasti on the beach, to Sahm, Sohar and its invitation to historical rumination, and then to Shinas and the area they call the Shumaylia (the Little North) where the tobacco comes from. And that is where it ends.

Muscat to Ras al Hadd

The coast south of Muscat is a continuation of the rocky inlets of
Muscat itself, with an occasional fishing hamlet clustered round
the stony exit of a wadi, or a larger village in some clearing which
the mountains have not obliterated. First comes Sidab, which
seen from the pass above it provides a foreground to a long and
magnificent view down the coast, where the crags jut out into the
sea in a Norwegian fjordscape: black rock, blue sea, a crescent
sliver of sand, and blue sky filling every cut in the mountainous
horizon. Sidab is one of the main fishing villages of the Muscat
area, and the beach is often crowded with houris, drawn up in neat
rows as if in a south-coast car park.

Perhaps it is even better to go to Sidab by sea, out through the
tidal race beside Muscat Island, past a few coves unapproachable
by land, and so, with a careful backward glance at the sinister
silhouette of Jalali, into the gay semicircle of Sidab. You would
probably not notice if you did not know that in two of those
hidden coves is the Christian cemetery of Muscat, administered
and serviced by the British Consul General. The temptation to
land and look at the tombstones is too great to withstand; most
of them are sad, almost pathetic, reminders of what it was like to
be in the Navy in the nineteenth century—young, invariably
young, members of ships' crews who ended their lives in the un-
bearable heat of the Gulf. Amongst them, however, is one
surprise, a firm and legible inscription: 'In loving memory of
Thomas (Va)lpy French D.D. entered into rest May 14 1891
First Bishop of Lahore and First Missionary to Muscat'.

Bishop French was a typically Victorian missionary who, having retired at the age of sixty-five from Lahore, could not bring
himself to settle in England, and chose Arabia as a fresh field for
his work. He arrived in Muscat on 8 February 1891, and immediately declined an invitation to stay from the British Political
Agent, Colonel Mockler, in case he should compromise him. He

found a dirty room to live in, but then, with the help of the American Consul,* transferred to Muttrah. His activities must have seemed suspect and incomprehensible to the locals; he would go to the coffee houses or the street corners, and read the Gospel to anybody who would listen—'I cannot', he admitted,[18] 'say that I have met with many thoughtful and encouraging hearers or people who want Bibles and Testaments.' He determined to go inland, and on May 5th sailed for Sib in a small boat, but by this time his health had collapsed and a few days later he had to be brought back; on May 14th he died in the Consulate in Muscat.

He was not the only missionary to die in Muscat. In the very same boat as French travelled from England came also the first of the American Mission members, Cantine and Zwemer, to see where they might inaugurate their missionary activities.† They ended up in Basra, but it was only three years later that Peter Zwemer, in November 1893, arrived to open a branch in Muscat. This, a properly organised, professional (when compared to the amateur efforts of French) undertaking has blossomed into the Mission Hospital set-up of Muscat and Muttrah today. However, *en route* to today, their second missionary, George Stone, died in Birka in 1899 in similar circumstances to French, and is buried near him in the cemetery; Dr. Thoms (the father of the present incumbent of the Muttrah hospital) died in 1913 from a fall while erecting a telegraph pole; and last year Dr. Huisingveld was shot in the hospital grounds. They too are buried in those coves.

The earliest legible date on the tombstones is 1866. I have not been able to establish when the cemetery was officially consecrated, and wonder where earlier European travellers were buried. For instance, William Francklin baldly records in the journal of his visit to Muscat: 'On the 25th January (1787) Captain James Mitchell, our fellow passenger, died . . . we interred him the same day, on the shore, at Muscat.'[19]

Beyond Sidab is a shiny white-sanded beach, much favoured for swimming, and further on Bustan, from where there is a prolific traffic of donkeys carrying vegetables and fruit to Muscat market. Beyond Bustan is Bander Jissa, where Monsieur Ottavi angled for

* Archibald McKirdy, see page 48 above.
† See page 57 above.

a coaling station, then a piratical collection of creeks and deep-water inlets before you get to Qaryat.

At Qaryat you are back in history again. It was one of the main coastal towns which Albuquerque, you may recall, threatened during his first foray upon Oman, whose inhabitants were slaughtered by him because they failed to take the precautionary tactics of the people of Qalhat, and submit to him.

Qaryat is sited on a wide flat saucer of plain where the mountains have, temporarily it seems, receded from the water. The town itself is today a dune or two inland, and a salty khor to one side of it, once presumably the port, is now silted up. It is very much like any other Batina town: ringed with date groves, dominated by a fort inhabited by the Wali, and with a busy suq. It is a great fishing centre, and a corner of the suq is given over to fish which lie in that glazed hardening state which is peculiar to them when newly caught. You may find there rows of sharks, some of them those sinister hammer-head brutes (which do not look really dead, but just to be lying in wait for anyone unwary enough to tread close enough to either of their hideous stalks of eyes) and also sting-rays, almost as nasty as hammer-heads; there are also more peaceable and edible-looking fish. Sharks are laid out in the sun to dry, then carved into strips of what looks more like leather than fish flesh, piscine biltong; and then taken into the Interior by donkeys or camel, where it is considered a delicate addition to rice. As for the ray, once you have inspected its vicious sting which looks like an auger shell, you are likely to give it a wide berth when you happen to see one through your mask while swimming off Ras al Hamra. Near the suq sits a man roasting fish over coals, the Qaryat *restaurateur*.

Qaryat was important, and to a lesser extent still is, because it is situated at the end of two routes into the Interior. The main one is through the Wadi Miglas to the Saih Hatat and the town of Hajir, an area where much of the tobacco sold in Muttrah suq is grown. From this route you can branch off on tracks down to Bander Jissa on the coast, or across to the Sharquiya inland, and if you continue along the main route far enough it comes down the Wadi Adai, and so to the Rui customs post and Muscat.

The Wadi Miglas, which starts (coming from Muscat) just after the village of Suwaqim in a twist of the river bed, and looks like blank cliff until you drive right into it, is an impressive boulder-strewn gorge in which it would be most unpleasant to be caught during a flood. It is, I suppose, about ten miles long, and emerges into the plain of Qaryat. This plain used to be one of the breeding grounds of horses, which years ago were the most immediately striking of Omani exports. Albuquerque mentioned them, and so did Ibn Batuta when he arrived in Qalhat; so did many other travellers including Marco Polo.

Today, however, there is hardly a horse to be seen in Oman, either because they are no longer of commercial interest, or perhaps because the skill to rear them has been lost. However this may be, horses used to typify the wealth of Oman, and now are so infrequently seen as to demand comment; and where once the plain of Qaryat might have been full of them grazing, now the only product of the plain is salt, which is dug out from salt-pans and sent to the Interior or to Muttrah. As you may recall, salt is measured by a bahhar that is, together with firewood, twice the weight of a bahhar applied to anything else; firewood, curiously enough, is the other main product of the Saih Hatat, and all those donkeys and camels that you see streaming in to Muttrah at first light with their loads of wood started out the previous morning or afternoon from the area of Hajir.

The other route from Qaryat to the interior is the Wadi Thaika, through what is generally known as the Devil's Gap, so narrow is it; impassable for Land-Rovers. If you follow it through, six miles of this 'grand and curious gallery' as Miles[20] describes it, you come, over the watershed, to the Wadi Tayin that leads round and down to Ibra and Qabil, the centre of the Sharquiya. This route starts at the southern end of the Qaryat plain, between Hail Ghaf and Dagmar; Hail Ghaf was founded in the early nineteenth century, is the seat of the senior sheikh of the Beni Battash, and is famous for its mangoes, its main street being an avenue of enormous mango trees whose shade makes it seem more European than Arabian; Dagmar is, so I was told, derived from the Arabic 'A tyrant has died', and is now almost dead itself.

I like Qaryat: the drive from Muscat up the Wadi Adai, through the Saih Hatat, with a roller bird at each small falaj garden, to Suwaqim and down the Wadi Miglas, is a cameo of almost any trip in the Interior. The fish, and the boats drawn up in ranks along the beach, and the mango trees of Hail Ghaf, typify the Batina. So, in one day's drive, you can feel the whole country, and contact a slice of its history. And behind the plain stand the mountains, dominated by Jebal Aswad, steely blue and shimmering in the heat.

The next place of importance down the coast is, or rather was, for it hardly exists today, the elusive Qalhat; elusive in the sense that it is nearly impossible to come to grips with the magnificence that once must have existed there. Marco Polo wrote: 'This city has a very good port, much frequented by merchant ships from India and they find a ready market here for their wares, since it is a centre from which spices and other goods are carried to various inland cities and towns. Many fine war horses are exported from here to India, to the great gain of the merchants. The total number of horses shipped to India from this port and the others I have mentioned is past all reckoning.'[21] Ibn Batuta visited Qalhat about fifty years later, and in spite of a most painful walk there from Sur with bleeding feet he was also able to remark upon the beauty of the city, in particular a fine Persian mosque which remained until Albuquerque rased it to the ground in 1508. When Albuquerque first arrived it was still a 'beautiful strong town, but not so populous as heretofore, whose buildings are after the style of those in Spain.'[22] On his first voyage up the coast, Albuquerque spared Qalhat, whose Governor prevaricated and promised to serve Portugal, but in 1508, on his way back, he landed there again and burnt the city. This seems to have been the end of Qalhat which had already been struck by an earthquake at the end of the fifteenth century, and had never wholly recovered.

Certainly Qalhat today looks as if it had been struck by a long series of earthquakes. My arrival there one Monday morning in February was, like Ibn Batuta's, on foot, but I had been able to pick my way for a large part of the distance from Sur by Land-Rover, so was not even limping. Once you can drive no further, you join a cliff path beyond a stony beach, and, all agog, set off for Qalhat. The only immediate evidence that anything might have once been there is a square tower with a domed top which stands forlornly across a broken stony piece of ground, and a wall that crosses from coast to mountain in front of your path. On further inspection you may find what look like two enormous cisterns, one of which is situated at the end of a small wadi channel, and the other without any apparent source of water at all. There is a path along a wall above a khor, behind which a wadi vanishes into the hills; there are a mass of foundations of rooms of houses, or shops, in squares; and there are millions of potsherds. There are also the remains of two towers, which do not look very old, on the other side of the khor, above which the modern village of Qalhat is squeezed into the side of the wadi around a pale tree or two.

None of this is very inspiring; nor is the coastline itself more hopeful of ancient anchorages, nor the small rubbled plain between coast and hills a particularly spacious site for a city. But there it was. Why there, when only a few miles away is the ancient town of Sur, complete with a much larger and deeper creek, and a route leading straight up behind it into the Interior? Well, the reason appears to be that what is true today was almost wholly the reverse some hundreds of years ago: whereas now there is practically no fresh water at Qalhat there used to be a falaj system leading down the wadi from the hills, and, according to Miles,[23] 101 wells to supplement this supply, dug presumably around the mouth of the wadi (101 sounds a mystic and suspect figure, and I do not know whether this information came from oral tradition or documentary evidence). Whereas today the khor is a poor rather stagnant tongue of water, it used to be a deep-water harbour leading right up to the debouchment of the wadi from the hills; if this were so, it would indeed have been a very fine anchorage, and it therefore must have been so. These two assets, vanished today, would have immediately made its potential superior to that of Sur, where there is no fresh water at the coastal village, and the khor, though impressive enough, is liable to silting from the bar off shore. At Qalhat the water is deeper more quickly, and the shore is a cliff rather than a sandy bay.

There remains the problem of access inland. It is true that the Wadi Hilm does, with some difficulty, provide a donkey path which emerges finally into the Wadi Beni Khalid, and so down to the Jaalan and Sharquiya, and I can only assume that this was a sufficiently simple alternative in those days to the very much easier and more obvious route down the Wadi Falaij to Sur. Possibly tribal affiliations *en route* had something to do with it. At any rate, it is clear that the Wadi Hilm route was used, even if the longer but easier journey via the Wadi Falaij was the more common one.

When Qalhat was founded is not known, but it is recorded that Malik bin Fahm,* when he first migrated from Yemen to Oman, descended to the coast at Qalhat (from the Nizwa area) to re-group his forces and leave his womenfolk before challenging the Persians, who were based on Sohar at the time, about A.D. 200. Possibly the Persians had previously founded Qalhat, and perhaps been ejected, for certainly it later became, under the Kingdom of Hormuz, the main port along the coast; alternatively it may simply have developed into a centre, outstripping its more ancient neighbour Sur, as a result of its favourable site. Assuredly it declined because the earthquake destroyed its advantageous position, and no one bothered, or was able, to re-establish it. In fact, there was no need for Qalhat, once Muscat, whose pre-decessor in influence and facilities it was, developed; already when Albuquerque arrived, you may remember, 'Qalhat was not so populous as heretofore' and Muscat was 'the principal entrepôt of the Kingdom of Hormuz'[24] and was exporting as many horses as Qalhat did when Marco Polo visited it.

But all this, in the midday sun, is, even in February, a hot imaginative effort as you trip over the splintered rocks above the sea, picking up pocketfuls of pottery, hopefully seeing them as relics of ancient trading. The most delicate is the misty olive green of Chinese celadon, and I would have liked to have looked back at the graveyard of Qalhat clutching a whole bowl under my arm. But I fear there is nothing whole left there, just fragments of history heating in the sun.

There is a theory that Sur, twenty miles on down the coast (an hour on foot followed by an hour in a Land-Rover), was the original home of the Phoenicians, and that when they moved to Lebanon, and settled in Tyre, they used the same name. Tyre, in Arabic, is written with precisely the same Arabic letters as Sur. According to this theory, which derives from the report in Herodotus that the Phoenicians came from the Gulf area, the

* See page 100 below.

Phoenicians learnt their seamanship in the Arabian seas, and exported the knowledge to the Mediterranean. It is a pleasant concept, particularly if you happen to be standing on the rocky spit by the Sur creek which is similar to that at Tyre, but more modern scholarship has thrown so much doubt upon it that we must, for the time being at least, forget it. However, the origins of the Phoenicians are by no means clear or agreed upon, and maybe one day some new archaeological evidence will revitalise this moribund theory.

If not Phoenician, Sur is undoubtedly an ancient settlement and port. Its bay is reasonably sheltered, and its long creek a haven; and situated as it is in a wide plain at the base of the Wadi Falaij with an easy route up into the Interior, it is a natural site for a town. Its one disadvantage is, as I have mentioned, its lack of fresh water. In fact, Sur is split into two parts, Sur al Sahil, the town on the coast round the creek, and Balad Sur, a large village among date palms a few miles inland. It is in the former area that there is no water; in Balad Sur, well water is readily available and is today piped into Sur al Sahil where there are about six or seven water points to which the people go to fill their tins at three baizas (Omani ones) for four gallons.

Sur is even today renowned for being different; its people are supposed to be difficult, and independent minded to the extent of being suspect. This is their nature; for centuries they have lived in and off the sea, and they looked outwards to India and the East long before the Yaariba or the Al bu Said began to do the same from their Muscat base. They administered the trading entrepôt between southern and eastern interior Oman and India before Qalhat developed, and they continued, I imagine, in a less sophisticated way than Qalhat, to do what they had always done, even during the heyday of Qalhat. Albuquerque referred to Sur as a fishing village and ignored it—rightly, because the Kings of Hormuz had ignored it and built up Qalhat instead; but Sur has had the last laugh, and even if it's a bit down at heel and forgotten today, it is a great deal better off than Qalhat; and is, even if this is no great virtue, easily the next most important port in Oman after Muscat and Muttrah.

In fact, Sur has certain parallels with Muttrah. If you drive into the suq it is a throbbing mass of selling and buying in a wide square, rather like a piazza; stalls full of cloth, stalls full of vegetables; bananas from Tiwi, tobacco from Hajir, garlic from the hills; and a great corner of it given over to fish: large fish, small fish, dusty fish, gutted fish, slices of fish, entrails of fish; ordinary sharks, hammer-head sharks, sword-fish and sting-rays; a smell of fish and blood and guts that in the morning is almost an aroma, but in the late afternoon a vicious stench. In Sur there is no Government tax on fish or fishing nets, as there is elsewhere in the country.

Round Sur suq is a square of shops, amongst them a 'workshop for all kinds of radio', a watch repair shop, and two carpenters' workrooms where they make the heavy carved doors and lintels used in many Omani houses—for instance, in my Muscat house. The wood comes from the Malabar coast, and you could buy a set of two doors and a lintel for Rs500. From the square narrow streets lead towards the beach, with important shops hidden dimly behind unimportant doors; outside are donkeys quietly waiting to be loaded, or camels, couched and chewing, patiently permitting their girth straps to be tightened round sacks of rice, belching out their commentary on town life. On close inspection you will find that many of these shops are run by Indian merchants, who have been established there for generations; this in itself is evidence of the wide trading activity of Sur, and its potential wealth in terms of trade. Even so I was surprised to see crates of ginger ale and tonic water for sale, and to be offered by one of the sheikhs, straight from its tin, a piece of a Huntley and Palmer's Dundee cake with my coffee.

Framed at the end of one street I saw the silhouette of the stern of a dhow. This was the only one being built at the time I visited, and there it was cradled on the upper beach, well shaped and perhaps half complete; round it were carpenters sawing, workmen hammering in enormous nails with uncanny precision, and others drilling holes with a drill mounted on a bowstring. Sur was, and still is, the centre of dhow building in Oman (Muttrah is the only other place you might conceivably find one being built), but its activity is much reduced from what it was. Miles reports that in 1874 eight dhows were built and launched; today only one or two will be ordered in a year. A dhow of largish size, say 200 tons, will take about five to six months to build, and will cost about Rs80,000 without the engine; that will be imported from Bahrain or Dubai and befitted after launching. To see one of these great skeletons being enlivened with decks and mast as it rests on the sands is an encouraging salute to the traditions of local industry, and a poignant reminder of how Sur in its day must have resounded to the bangings of the boat builders.

The beach itself is a wide shallow curve of dirty sand, the bay full in the evening of returning fishing boats; dogs are scattered like crabs over the sands, and children in as great profusion; flies come in hordes. At the far eastern end is a rocky outcrop under which the creek scours inland, and under it is the village of Aygah where the Beni bu Ali live. You can only cross to it by ferry, which leaves from near a collection of buildings; one is the customs house (in 1928 the Beni bu Ali sheikhs decided to establish in Aygah their own independent customs post over which they hoisted their own flag, and it took the Sultan two years and the assistance of the British Resident in the Gulf to get the flag down and the customs post back to the Sur side of the creek), another the Sultan's house, and a third a water point, from which the inhabitants of Aygah must take their fresh water. Beside the creek are beached dhows, being scraped or repaired, and in some cases derelict. There is a wide grey dismal expanse of wet mud at low tide, and beyond and behind the town you can see camels being led through shallow water, fording their way to the sands beyond, and the route inland.

In Sur I recall visiting one sheikh who gave audience in a cramped room made more cramped by an enormous four-poster bed on which his visitors sat in rows: he himself was of massive arthritic bulk and looked, when sitting cross-legged on the floor, like the Big God Nqong just about to give, for a change, the camel his hump. The talk tended to be of the outside world, at least as far as India, and the Arabian Gulf and East Africa, and they told me that three thousand people of Sur are at present working abroad. After the introspective conversations of the Interior and the parochial chatter of the Batina, it was stimulating to find a town that was not thinking always of itself, and could take foreign ideas in its stride.

One thing that Sur has always taken in its stride, in its independent way, is the seamy side of trade—arms traffic, slavery,

6

smuggling; not that, at least in the earlier days, this was seamy trade, for slavery was a natural part of life, arms traffic equally so, and smuggling a far less pejorative term when customs posts had not been invented. But later, and particularly in the fullness of the Victorian era, Sur became anathema to the British, one of whose primary aims in the area, as has been described, was the elimination both of slavery and illegal arms traffic.

Sur was an ideal centre for this sort of thing; firstly, it came naturally to its citizens, as it had for centuries; secondly, the harbour had always been primarily a dhow harbour for local craft, and had never developed into a more sophisticated colonial port; then again the independent spirit of Sur had always been a most practical thing, so that the Sultan in Muscat could never guarantee any control over the town; and there was an organisation to deal with the fruits of this trade, both in Sur, and up-country on the routes into both Oman and Saudi Arabia. One might add that the traffic in rifles continues today, and I was assured that I could buy any number of new American rifles for 300 riyals apiece (about £150, very expensive; no doubt there is a proper and bargainable price attainable for those with time on their hands).

It was in 1822 that the British first managed to induce the Sultan (Said bin Sultan) to sign a treaty limiting traffic in slaves, but still in 1841, for instance, about four thousand slaves were estimated to be imported through Sur; subsequently, as things became more strictly controlled by the British, and each successive treaty limited the official possibilities for slavery more closely, the people of Sur started to use the French flag, a practice that was actively encouraged by the French (led by Monsieur Ottavi from his base in our Muscat house) in the late 1890s. In the first few years of the twentieth century it continued to flourish, even if not at the high level of the 1840s, and it was not fundamentally broken until the 1905 Hague Court arbitration went against the French and virtually forced them to stop facilitating the practice in Omani waters, and, even more importantly perhaps, the Portuguese in Mozambique helped to suppress the source of slaves. There, in 1902, the Portuguese Governor discovered a slave market established in a creek called Samuco (about two hundred miles north of Cape Delgado), arrested those involved and deported them to Angola for twenty-five years;

many of them were Omanis, and a lot from Sur. This psychological and practical blow to their fortunes was, I suspect, of rather greater significance than the threats of the Great Powers, or the judgement of the Hague Court.

The British, so involved with Oman during the nineteenth century, and for ever being dragged further into its affairs by that peculiar British aptitude for greater involvement the more such involvement is asserted to be unwanted, did not often become entangled in Sur itself; but on the occasions they did, there was usually drama. France, the French flag and the sailors of Sur demanding protection from the French Consul in Muscat all caused drama and, as we have seen, ended in an appeal at the Hague Court. Wahhabi devastation of Sur in 1865 led to the bombardment by British gunboats of Qatif and Dammam, a fine piece of imperialist drama; this, incidentally, occurred because during the sacking of Sur a large number of Indian merchants (technically under British protection) were maltreated and lost their possessions, but whether such a fine distinction as this was recognised by the Saudi merchants shelled in their turn in Dammam must be a matter for grave doubt. The greatest drama connected with Sur was, however, the Beni bu Ali expedition of 1820, and its 1821 successor, an episode traumatic enough, one would have thought, to have warned the British off Sur for all time.

The Beni bu Ali were the only tribe in Oman to have accepted the new creed of Wahhabism (and indeed they remain nominal Wahhabis today). Their tribal area is in the district of Jaalan in the eastern corner of the country; their main centre was, and remains, Bilad Beni bu Ali, and their chief port Al Ashkhara—port being a euphemism for a group of burasti huts collected at a point on the beach where it is possible to get boats ashore through the surf.

In 1820, the Beni bu Ali had recently renounced the rule of the Sultan of Muscat, Said bin Sultan, who was preparing to launch a punitive expedition against them. In the same year, they attacked and ransacked a ship belonging to an Indian merchant, who immediately complained to the Government in Bombay. Informed of this, the Political Agent for the lower Gulf, Captain Thompson, sent letters of complaint to the Beni bu Ali, who promptly murdered the pilot of the cruiser *Mercury* when he landed at Al Ashkhara to deliver them. Thompson reacted by offering to join Said's planned expedition against the tribe. Said was delighted, and must have been extremely surprised suddenly to find the British most uncharacteristically prepared to march with him against what can have been to him no more than an unruly tribe; they were acting just as he had always wanted them to, but in a way that he had given up any hope of seeing practised.

Said and Thompson agreed to land their force at Sur rather than on the open beaches of Al Ashkhara, and march up the Wadi Falaij behind Sur to Bilad Beni bu Hasan, a town whose tribe was friendly to Said, only a few miles from Bilad Beni bu Ali. On November 9th they attacked the Beni bu Ali. Out of a total of 402 men under Thompson's command, 317 were killed in the battle; and Said reckoned he had lost a further 400. It was a disaster.

Thompson reported to Bombay, and sought reinforcements for a second reprisal expedition. The reaction in Bombay can be imagined, both against Thompson personally and in terms of the distortions and magnifications of the task of revenge that was required; for whatever else might happen, no one now doubted that the British had got to humble the Beni bu Ali; such were the imperatives of imperial diplomacy.

On January 10th Major-General Lionel Smith was appointed commander of the Beni bu Ali expeditionary force. Fifteen ships sailed from Bombay, with another eleven for the horses. At the end of the month they landed at Sur, and encamped spaciously; on February 10th the Beni bu Ali made a surprise night attack on the European camp, and killed twelve persons including one British officer. For two more nervous weeks Smith waited at Sur for the animal transport promised by Said; and on February 24th the force at last began to advance. It consisted of 2,695 men, and included infantry, twelve-pounders, and heavy siege guns. If ever there was a case of escalation, this was it.

On March 2nd Smith finally revenged His Majesty upon the Beni bu Ali, but not without a tough battle in which he lost 28 killed, and had 165 men wounded. Smith was left with a large number of Beni bu Ali prisoners; the wounded, old men and young boys, were entrusted to Said who is alleged to have treated them so brutally that most died in imprisonment; the remainder

Smith took to Bombay, but after about two years they became so much of a burden to the administration there that they were sent back to Bilad Beni bu Ali with large grants of money to enable them to rebuild their homes and falajs, all of which had been destroyed during or after the battle.

So, the net result of this extraordinary episode in British-Omani history was that Bilad Beni bu Ali was destroyed and re-built with British money; a lot of people were killed; Thompson was court-martialled, but effectively acquitted; Said was given a sword of honour for his part in the first battle by the Indian Government; the booty from the Indian merchant ship was never recovered, nor the murderers of the pilot of the *Mercury* dis-covered; but, in a curious imperial way, honour was, I suppose, satisfied all round.

The Beni bu Ali are still at Bilad Beni bu Ali and Al Ashkhara today, and are as perverse as ever. No European can safely land in their territory without invitation, and P.D.(O.) have still not managed to do any work, geological or survey, in the area; the last time they tried they were told (only fairly politely) to get packing. Government control over the Beni bu Ali appears to be about as effective as it was in 1820; their sheikhs, however, waywardly consider themselves particularly loyal to the Sultan, but in a personal capacity which takes no account of the Sultan's Government; in the mid-twentieth century this tends to lead to misapprehensions. The Beni bu Ali keep, too, their quarter of Sur, Aygah across the creek, and together with the Jenaba of Sur carry on their immemorial trading activities as best they can.

Just out of sight from Sur, at the last corner as you descend from Bilad Beni bu Ali, or the Sharquiya, is an arched gateway standing solitarily over the road; the place is called Rafsah, and beneath it at the edge of the wadi is a bright green snatch of garden, where someone has tapped the water. This gate limits the territory of the Masharifa, a tribe that straddles the Wadi Falaij; it used to be a customs, or more correctly, an extortion post. As the traveller passed through, a chain was let down like a sort of portcullis, and a challenge was sounded: 'Hinawi or Ghafiri?' If he was Ghafiri, as most of the inhabitants of Sur were (but the Masharifa were not), he had to pay a tax, or transit fee, of five bezas. There is no sign of the chain there today and the camels march through with an extra sniff and a belch to show their opinion of progress.

Beyond Sur are two large lagoons, Khor Jerameh and Khor Hejareh. These were once the favourite haunts of pirate ships and, more peaceably over the centuries, collecting places for dhows waiting for the monsoon to relax sufficiently for them to set out for India, and the further East: even to China, with which the Arabs of the Gulf have traditionally traded, notably in the eighth and ninth centuries, when the Abbasids ruled in Baghdad, and the T'ang Dynasty in China.

Then, at the end of the coast, you at last reach Ras al Hadd, the most easterly piece of Arabia. I had always imagined it to be a sort of cousin of the Cape of Good Hope, where the full force of the Indian Ocean swirled past the calmer tributary sea of the Gulf of Oman. But not a bit of it. The hills decline into a flat sandy spit before they ever reach the point, and Ras al Hadd turns out to be an insignificant piece of plain with an apologetic corner to show where Arabia can stretch east no further. On this plain are the incongruous remnants of an R.A.F. landing ground, used as a staging post during the Second World War—chipped concrete runways and a dilapidated shed or two. A mile away, facing the southern coast is a small village of burasti huts, with a fort standing above them and a Sultanate red flag flying; and, if you go to call on its inmates they will proudly and repeatedly assure you that they are Hinawis (i.e. nothing to do with the Beni bu Ali) and loyal servants of the Sultan, as if you had been sent down as a spy to test their sincerity.

There they live, quietly carrying on with their business of fishing, or doing nothing, oblivious that they are within sight of one of the world's busiest shipping highways. When you first see a tanker passing round the corner, you merely comment on it; but after being there an hour or two you suddenly realise that there has not been a moment of time when you have not seen one tanker, or two, or even three. There they go, in a ceaseless follow-my-leader, a mobile chain stretching from Europe to Kuweit. That would be a sight for those ninth-century dhow captains, waiting for the monsoon to unleash them for their journey to India.

The other extremity of this eastern side of Arabia tapers into the Musandam peninsula, an inhospitable area which, although separated from the rest of Muscat and Oman by fifty miles of Trucial State north of Khatma Malaha, is also nominally Sultanate territory.

In practice, the Sultan has a Wali in a town called Khasab, whose influence extends about as far as the limits of the town. Most of the remainder of this mountainous promontory is inhabited, where there is any inhabitant at all, by a peculiar tribe called the Shihuh. They speak an Arabic dialect that is unknown elsewhere, are troglodytes (according to the evidence of Bertram Thomas[25] who also produced a hypothesis that they should be equated with the Shuhites of Job—Bilduz the Shuhite), and are alleged to make a barking noise, like dogs, after a meal. It is hardly surprising that they object to outside influences, even those rather inconclusively wielded by the Sultan.

The top of the peninsula is nearly cut across by two deep fjords that do not quite meet; they bear the imposing imperialistic names of Elphinstone and Malcolm Inlets, and deep down in Elphinstone Inlet is a small island on which the Persian Gulf telegraph cable once terminated, prosaically called Telegraph Island. The terminus was only there from 1864 to 1869, since it was quickly found that no one could live in such an inhospitable spot. Inhospitable it might be, but Curzon imagined it to be of potential strategic importance. By 1904 its importance had become actual rather than potential; it seemed to Curzon a vital, pivotal, link in the defence of British influence against the Russian threat. It further seemed to him necessary to erect flagstaffs there, a proposal that he had first put forward in 1901.[26]

One can image the bureaucratic flurry that must have begun in London when the mail brought in Curzon's proposals. Such was the Civil Service organisation at that time that even the smallest matter was likely to pass over the desks of the India Office, Treasury, Foreign Office, Cabinet Office, Admiralty, Committee of Imperial Defence and often end up with the Prime Minister. On this occasion Curzon managed to persuade both the India and Foreign Offices to agree to three flagstaffs on Musandam peninsula, and up they went; but without flags, for there was no decision as to what flag should fly on them. Not the Union Jack, surely, for it was not British territory (though nobody was very

sure whose it was); perhaps, said the Foreign Office, the Blue
Ensign of the Royal Indian Marine. Good heavens, no, said the
Admiralty, who had not even realised the flagpoles had been put
up. If there is a flag there, we may have to defend it. Defend it, said
the Committee for Imperial Defence, not a bit of it, you must take
the flagstaffs down again. And down they came, except for one on
Telegraph Island which was permitted to remain, without a flag,
since that island had long had British connections, and no further
precedent could be said to have been set.

It is improbable that any of their Lordships in London appreciated that all three flagstaffs were anyway quite invisible from the
open sea.

OMAN

※ Oman ※

The way into the Interior is via the Treaty of Sib.

It illustrates the basic differentiation between Muscat and Oman, and has achieved a certain notoriety primarily because it was kept secret and was, therefore, assumed to have within the text something worth secreting. Since nobody knew for sure what was in it, anybody could claim that it contained whatever he happened to want it to contain; claims of this type were normally made, as is customary in such situations, by those opposed to the Government in power i.e. the Sultan in Muscat. In retrospect, it is ludicrous, and tragic for Muscat and Oman, that the text remained unpublished for so long.

The Treaty of Sib was essentially a document of and for the moment. In it the Sultan said that he would respect the traditions of interior Oman, and the sheikhs of interior Oman said that they would accept the status of the Sultan. There was no more to it really than that, but of course the terminology of the document suited the time, the place and the actors involved, and is anything but precise when it comes to arguments on interpretation between international lawyers.

Muscat and Oman are not considered distinct for nothing, and it is not by chance that the local people, when they leave the coast to go into the interior, say they are going to Oman. Interior Oman has always been, in a real sense, separate from coastal Muscat. That is not to say, however, that Muscat and Oman have been, and therefore still should be, two independent states.

To define the extent of Oman is in itself not at all simple. Its limits, in so far as it has had any, have ebbed and flowed throughout history in sympathy with the power and influence of individual leaders, tribes and tribal groupings. The most meaningful definition would, I think, be the area which has accepted the Imam as its leader, primarily spiritual, but also partially temporal; the Imam being the elected head of the Ibadhi sect of

Islam. This is one important clue to Oman—that, as a concept, it is largely founded on a religious base.

The Ibadhis are a very old schismatic sect of Islam. In 657, during the reign of Ali, the Fourth Caliph, there emerged a group called the Kharijites who believed that the original principles of Islam were being forsaken; a year later at Nahrawan Ali defeated them, but legend has it that two persons escaped the disaster and settled in Oman. Whether these two, or others, established what became known as Ibadhism, named after one of its main protagonists, Abdalla ibn Ibadh, is not important, but Ibadhism managed to root itself impregnably in the mountains of Oman, and there it remained, and still remains, long after it was expunged from the rest of Arabia; other pockets remain, however, in parts of North Africa.

Ibadhi philosophy contains elements of democracy, although in practice it has turned out conservatively traditional to the point of being reactionary. Ibadhis believe, for instance, in the election of the Imam by the whole community, that he should rule with the advice and consent of his people and that, if he loses popular support, he may be deposed. Ibadhis differ from most other Islamic communities, who have Imams or Caliphs within their system, in their belief that it is not necessary to have an uninterrupted succession of rulers; if there is no suitable candidate, then the office of Imam can remain vacant. On the other hand, Ibadhi beliefs tend to be very conservative, being based on early Islamic sources—the Quran and Hadith. However, because they interpret them in their own way, they diverge acutely from the Sunni ultra-conservatives, for instance the Wahhabis.

In general, the central and southern parts of the Interior of the Sultanate contain Ibadhi adherents, the rest being Sunni (apart from the Beni bu Ali who were converted to Wahhabism). Throughout their history the Ibadhis have, with gaps, elected Imams, and the Treaty of Sib was, in 1920, signed on the one side by the representatives of the Imam. This, however, begs the question of why it was necessary for a treaty to be signed, and what stresses had caused a situation which was, after all, if you consider the Sultanate as one country, virtually a state of civil war.

This situation had been reached because of the attitude of the Al bu Said dynasty to the Imamate. Before the Al bu Said, the country had only intermittently been involved with the outside world, and certainly the activities of the people on the coast had not interfered with the traditional ways of the Omanis of the Interior. Admittedly, the Yaariba dynasty had begun the process of looking outward, from an interior base, but this was a relatively unsophisticated activity which took into account the traditions of the Omanis, and all the Yaariba leaders were, by definition and election, Imams. It is arguable that the very fact that all Yaariba leaders were Imams was an indication that the Imamate as a non-temporal office was already subjugated to the pull of temporal power politics, that it had lost, or at least was losing, its primarily religious identity; this may well have been so, for, as if by divine right, the first Sultans of the Al bu Said dynasty were also duly elected as Imams. Their subsequent error, or, perhaps more correctly, their realism, led them to ignore the Ibadhi basis of their religious power; they began to forget their Omani roots in their flirtation with international interests. In this the real catalyst was Said bin Sultan, whose whole life, much of it outside Oman, was devoted to the development of commerce and international influence, and for whom the traditions of the interior Omanis were blinkered bigotry. He never resented the fact that he was not elected Imam, he never gave a thought to it; but the Omani leaders began to resent the fact that he ignored them and the Imamate concept. They resented it still more when the policies of the Sultan in Muscat began to impinge upon their own way of life. This happened in what might seem to us a most irreligious context, the gradual suppression of slavery and arms traffic, both imposed, as we have seen, on the Sultans by the British as a *quid pro quo* for their real or imagined support to the Sultanate.

Ibadhism does not require a continuous Imamate, and when Said bin Ahmed, the second of the Al bu Said dynasty, died in 1810 there was a gap for sixty years; it is worth remembering, too, that for the last seventeen years of his life Said had not been ruler (he was deposed in 1793), although he nominally remained in his retirement, and until his death, Imam. For a large proportion of these sixty years Said bin Sultan was ruler, and his personal power and prestige was such that the Imamate question remained more or less dormant. But when he died in 1856 things altered fast.

The personality of Said bin Sultan had barely managed to glue together the pieces of his Muscat coastal empire during his later years; when he died and Thwaini, his son, succeeded to the Sultanate of Muscat, the parts became quite unstuck. Turki in Sohar, and Azzan bin Qais in Rustaq, who were already, in effect, independent princes, became even more detached from the theoretical central authority of Muscat.

Rustaq is a typical Omani town, strategically placed at the exit of a wadi from the mountains, walled and with a massive castle, watered by falajs, and with extensive date groves round it. Its main peculiarity is that, as an Omani stronghold, it is on the coastal side of the mountain range; it has served, therefore, as the centre of Omani activity in the east, and has often acted as capital, or at least sub-capital, for the Omanis. It was, you may recall, the base from which the Yaariba dynasty ruled. During the years following Said's death it was to figure prominently in the turbulent course of Sultanate history.

Indeed in 1846, well before Said's death, there had been a gathering of many of the Ibadhi leaders there for the express purpose of electing a new Imam, but this effort fizzled out when three chosen men in succession declined to stand for the office. During the Sultanate of Thwaini, Rustaq remained effectively independent under Azzan, who was himself part of the Al bu Said family, in fact a great-great-grandson of Ahmed bin Said; it was Azzan who, threatened by Thwaini, called on the Wahhabis for assistance, which they gave with such enthusiasm that they ended up, in 1865, by sacking Sur.

The next few years in the Sultanate are distorted with religious and tribal rivalries, and personal ambitions, the whole thing being intermittently thrown even further off balance by the activities of the British authorities in the Gulf, led by Colonel Pelly, the Resident in Bushire.

Following the Sur episode both the British and Salih bin Ali al Hirthi urged Thwaini to take measures against the Wahhabis. Salih bin Ali was senior sheikh of the Hirth and of the Hinawis of the Sharquiya,* one of the most powerful personalities of the interior; Salih and his successors were from this time, and up to the present day, of enormous influence in Omani history. On this

* See page 115 below for Hinawis and Ghafiris; pages 128 et seq. for Sharquiya.

occasion, however, nothing positive resulted from Salih's initiative, for Thwaini was murdered in Sohar by his son, Salim, and Salim called off the planned retributive action against the Wahhabis.

Next year, 1867, Turki, the Wali of Sohar and uncle of Salim, took the field against Salim, and advanced on Muscat. He was already threatening the town when Colonel Pelly entered the arena, forced Turki to accept paid exile in India, and thus officially underwrote Salim as Sultan. Salim then tried to have Salih murdered, even though, in Turki's campaign against him, Salih had personally refused to join the other Sharquiya tribes in alliance with Turki; this proved to be one of Salim's more stupid actions, for Salih promptly joined the other interior tribes to plan for Salim's downfall.

Indeed, he effectively took charge of the proceedings, and quickly linked up with Said bin Khalfan al Khalili; Said bin Khalfan was a member of another venerated and important Omani family which has figured prominently in the history of the country, and it was Said's grandson, Mohammed bin Abdulla, who was Imam from 1920 until 1954. The Hirthi/Khalili combine contacted Azzan bin Qais in Rustaq and organised a pincer movement upon Muttrah, the former from Sumayl and the latter from Rustaq via Birka. They duly met up at Muttrah, took the town, and then marched into Muscat. Salim fled to Fort Merani, but 'being almost paralysed with fear'[1] had to be carried up the steps; locked into the fort he recovered himself, began to bombard Muscat and kept this up for forty-eight hours. Into this operatic battle sailed Colonel Pelly, who, in an unsuitably direct fashion, set about helping Salim until reminded by telegram that he should not use any force on Salim's behalf. Whereupon Salim quickly came to terms with Salih and Azzan, agreed that they had deposed him, and sailed off to Bander Abbas under Pelly's protection.

Azzan was elected Imam in October 1868, the first since the death of Said bin Ahmed, the third, and so far the last, of the Al bu Said to have thus been honoured. He did not last long. He started, however, with a burst of success, and by the middle of 1869 had control of Bureimi, Dhank, Bahla, Nizwa, Manah and Izki; he even defeated the Beni bu Ali down in the Jaalan. He was

quickly in trouble, though, on two counts: on the one hand he
alienated the Ghafiris,* who found the Imamate under the
influence of Salih and Said bin Khalfan far too Hinawi-orientated,*
and on the other the British never acknowledged him as Sultan.
The mark of official British acceptance was of importance not
only because of the general British influence in the area, which
under Pelly was more direct than under previous Residents, but
also because it would, or at least was assumed it would, bring
payment of the Zanzibar subsidy with it. It so happened that at
that moment an academic and political wrangle of the first order
was raging between the Foreign Office and India Office as to
which should make this payment, and the argument was not even
partially resolved until 1873; if Azzan had not been Sultan it is
possible, but in fact not very likely, that some temporary arrangement would have been reached earlier, but the British anti-Azzan
group was far too strong to encourage such a solution. Pelly,
having twice supported Salim, was resolutely opposed to Azzan
who was considered, probably correctly, by the authorities as
being the representative of a reactionary, potentially anti-British
movement. This was bad luck on Azzan, who in many respects
had, at least temporarily, wider control over the country than any
ruler since Ahmed bin Said. However, without official imperial
British support behind him he was doomed; and his end was
hastened by other imperial British actions.

In 1870 Turki was released, or at least permitted to escape,
from his Bombay restriction, and sailed for the Trucial Coast.
Although he failed dismally in his first efforts to drum up support
for his cause, he was later backed by his brother Majid from
Zanzibar with financial aid, and this enabled him to get going.
Late in the same year he successfully ambushed the forces of
Azzan near Dhank, and the tide began to turn. Turki picked up
allies like a snowball, and ended up by marching on Muttrah with
a combined column of Beni bu Ali and Beni bu Hassan, a remarkable feat of very temporary alliance. Azzan was killed in battle in
Muttrah in January 1871; Turki became Sultan; he was duly
given official British acknowledgement in August, and that was
the end of the Imamate for another forty-two years.

* See page 115 below for Hinawi and Ghafiris.

During these years the Sultanate became weaker, and by 1910 was virtually confined to Muscat and Muttrah, where the British, for their own reasons, kept the Sultan in theoretical power over the country. The interior became a foreign hinterland, where two men in particular added to their tribal power and prestige, Salih bin Ali in the Sharquiya together with his sons, Abdulla and Isa, and Himyar bin Nasir of the Beni Riyam, the leading Ghafiri tribe. So strong, for instance, was Salih that in 1874 he captured Muttrah and had to be bought off by Turki, and in 1895 he captured both Muttrah and Muscat and besieged Feisal bin Turki (who had succeeded his father as Sultan in 1888) for three weeks in Merani fort; again he had to be bought off—but not before a Bombay newspaper was able to quote a report from its special Muscat correspondent that 'for three days we were the witnesses of the extraordinary spectacle of a Sultan bombarding his own palace'.[2] After this occasion the British announced that they would not tolerate any further attacks on Muscat and Muttrah, and thus effectively guaranteed whichever Sultan they recognised; a far cry from their earlier protestations about non-interference, and a forerunner to the support given for the Sultan in the civil war of 1957-9.

In 1912 the Sultan, encouraged by the British, who added to their advice a promise to increase his subsidy by a lakh of rupees (for how many years is slightly obscure, but probably just for the one year*), issued an edict whereby all arms imported into the country had to pass through a Government warehouse in Muscat. Such a control was the last straw for the Omanis of the Interior, who in 1913 made their opposition to the Sultan explicit by electing Salim bin Rashid al Kharousi as Imam, with the backing of Isa bin Salih for the Hinawis (he had succeeded his father who died in 1896) and Himyar bin Nasir for the Ghafiris. They occupied Nizwa, Izki and Sumayl. In the same year Taimur bin Feisal followed his father as Sultan in Muscat, and the British put in a force of Indian troops at Beit al Falaj. In 1915 the Imamate forces attacked them, but were heavily repulsed; there has been no attack on Muscat since.

After their defeat, a first meeting was held at Sib with the

* See page 49 above.

British Political Agent as chief negotiator; on the Imamate side were Isa bin Salih, Himyar bin Nasir and the Imam's chief Qadi. No agreement was reached. In 1920 the traditional 5 per cent duty on goods brought from the interior to the coast was raised to the penalising level of 25 per cent; in the same year the Imam was murdered by a Wahiba tribesman, although this seems to have been quite coincidental and an assassination that was in no way politically oriented. A new Imam was elected, Mohammed bin Abdulla al Khalili, grandson of Said bin Khalfan who had been so much involved in the election of Azzan bin Qais in 1868. In September there was a second meeting at Sib, and the Treaty was signed.

What it said—as was finally and conclusively discovered the other day when the fifty-year rule on official documents was reduced to the thirty-year rule, and it became available to readers on request—was this:

In the name of God, the Compassionate, the Merciful.

This is the peace agreed upon between the Government of the Sultan, Taimur bin Feisal, and Sheikh Isa ibn Salih ibn Ali on behalf of the people of Oman whose names are signed hereto, through the mediation of Mr. Wingate, I.C.S., political agent and consul for Great Britain in Muscat, who is empowered by his Government in this respect and to be an intermediary between them. Of the conditions set forth below, four pertain to the Government of the Sultan and four pertain to the people of Oman.

Those pertaining to the people of Oman are:

1. Not more than 5 per cent shall be taken from anyone, no matter what his race, coming from Oman to Muscat or Muttrah or Sur or the rest of the towns of the coast.
2. All the people of Oman shall enjoy security and freedom in all the towns of the coast.
3. All restrictions upon everyone entering and leaving Muscat and Muttrah and all the towns shall be removed.
4. The Government of the Sultan shall not grant asylum to any criminal fleeing from the justice of the people of Oman. It shall not interfere in their internal affairs.

The four conditions pertaining to the Government of the Sultan are:

1. All the tribes and sheikhs shall be at peace with the Sultan. They shall not attack the towns of the coast and shall not interfere in his Government.
2. All those going to Oman on lawful business and for commercial affairs shall be free. There shall be no restrictions on commerce, and they shall enjoy security.
3. They shall expel and grant no asylum to any wrongdoer or criminal fleeing to them.
4. The claims of merchants and others against the people of Oman shall be heard and decided on the basis of justice according to the law of Islam.

Written on 11 Muharram, corresponding to 25 September 1920.

The Treaty said this because these were the points which needed settlement so that the country could revert from near civil war to a rational atmosphere of peace which in turn could provide the possibility for normal development. To turn the document into a text for juristic claims by academic international lawyers could only be fruitful for the lawyers themselves and it is inconceivable to imagine that any claim could be conclusive; when you realise that Wingate himself commented of the document that its phraseology was deliberately ambiguous and that his intention was to lead the tribes into believing they had their independence whilst at the same time the British Government could deny to the Sultan that the arrangements they had made derogated from his overall sovereignty, you begin to comprehend that the Treaty of Sib is today no more than a legal quagmire.

What the Treaty really confirmed was that the people in interior Oman had a practical and historical right to a way of life that in certain respects followed different guidelines from those regulating the people who lived in Muscat and on the coast. It also confirmed that at that moment of time the Imam, as leader of the interior tribes, had sufficient power and influence to insist on exercising that right. It did not say, and neither the Imam nor Isa bin Salih would, I believe, have claimed this, anything about interior Oman being an independent state; an element of independence, yes, but not an independent state as we today would interpret that concept—if only because our current concepts of independence and state are different from those that pertained in 1920, and even more divorced from any concept in vogue in Oman at that time.

From all this it must at least be apparent that the interior Omanis are different from the coastal Muscatis, independent minded if not nationally independent. The difference is partly religious, but Omanis have not been always, or even exclusively, Ibadhis; the other side to their difference is their tribal nature and to understand this it is necessary to dig back into history and see how little their character and traditions have been diluted by the passing centuries.

Omani mythology has it that the founder of Oman was Malik bin Fahm. Like so much mythology there is little doubt that this is based on the facts of history (which will be unfolded proof by proof as the textual critics, the professors and the archaeologists extend their work), and certainly the story[3] it gives for the origin of the Omanis is epic and colourful.

Malik bin Fahm lived in Yemen, and one day one of his tribesmen complained that a nephew of Malik had killed his dog. Malik angrily announced that he would not stay in a country in which such insults could be perpetrated, and prepared to leave; he was joined by a numerous party and set off.

A fanciful reason for leaving, though not an impossible one in a society where honour could be slighted in ways that seem peculiar to us. Malik is undoubtedly a historical person, but the reason for his departure was more meaningfully linked to the bursting of the Mareb dam, an event that finally terminated the influence and culture of the Yemen civilisation. This happened in the second century A.D.; it resulted in a complete decline of Yemen, and to a great dispersal of tribes. One group, under Malik bin Fahm, dog or no dog, migrated east to Oman.

Malik arrived in due course near Nizwa, and found that the country was under nominal control of a Persian Marzaban, or Governor, who was ruling from his capital at Sohar. Having deposited and settled all the families and heavy baggage in

Qalhat, he sent a message to the Persian Marzaban and said: 'I must positively settle in a district of Oman', but he added that he would be quite prepared to do this without evicting the Persians if they so wished, but that if they attacked him, he would assuredly defeat them and banish them from the country. The Persians, not very surprisingly, refused to accept this sudden ultimatum from a wild collection of Arab tribesmen appearing from out of the desert. They prepared for war, and set off from Sohar, up the Wadi Jizzi, with a large force that included some elephants; and on his side, Malik also prepared for battle.

The Persians advanced with thirty or forty thousand men, and encamped at Selut, near Nizwa, where Malik opposed them with six thousand men, of whom two thousand cavalry were commanded by his son Hunat. Malik himself led his army on a piebald charger wearing a red robe and a yellow turban twisted round his helmet. 'Advance with me', he shouted, 'against all these elephants, and attack them', and they attacked them with their spears and swords, and shot arrows at them; and the elephants turned round in terror and began to trample the Persian soldiers; 'and you could hear nothing but the clashing of iron upon iron, and the crashing of swords', and the battle continued until night fell.

It continued in this epic fashion all next day, and on the third day too; until Malik met the Marzaban in single combat (having disposed already of three other Persian leaders in single combat one after the other) and 'smote him on the crown of his head, and his sword split his helmet, and his brains became visible, and he gloried in his death'. And that was the end of the battle. The Persians asked for a truce, and returned to Sohar, and Malik returned with his men to Qalhat where their wives awaited them.

The story continues that during this period of truce the King of the Persians, infuriated at the insult imposed upon his Governor in Sohar, sent out reinforcements under the command of another of his most experienced Marzabans. When Malik heard of this he wrote again to the Persians, and told them he would turn them out of the country if they did not leave; and when they refused, he advanced on them and defeated them in another battle, in very much the same way as on the first occasion, except that there was no single combat and it did not last quite so long. And that was the end of the Persians, and, as in all good epics, the Omanis prospered and settled down to develop their new country, and Malik ruled for seventy years and died at the age of one hundred and twenty.

Malik bin Fahm has a certain Homeric quality, but his spirit remains alive today. Tribesmen of Yemeni (or Azdite) origin will assure you that Malik was their great[n]-grandfather,[n] being equivalent to however many years their imagination can encompass; the time-span is unimportant, it is Malik who counts. And, to bring fantasy literally to ground level, the falaj that is specifically mentioned in the text of the Omani epic, the *Kashf al Ghummah*,[4] as having been dug by Malik before his first battle with the Persians, can still be seen in Manah, overgrown and unused now, but certainly the remains of a falaj. Malik, then, is very much part of the mythology of Oman; there is no reason to suppose that he did not rule, that under him the Persians were not driven out, that in his time there was not an influx of Yemeni/Azdite tribes to Oman.

Malik, incidentally, is genealogically descended from Azd as part of the Qahtan line of Arab ancestry; these tribes are usually referred to as Yemeni, in that they settled in Yemen. The other line from Adnan (which includes the family of the Prophet Mohammed) originally settled in the northern part of Arabia, and its tribes are generally referred to as Nizari. Both lines settled in Oman, Malik bin Fahm's Yemeni Azdites being one of the settlements of that particular line.

It is interesting to find in Izki, one of the oldest Omani towns, that one of the quarters is called Yemen, and another Nizar, even to this day. There can be little doubt that this is a direct reference to the ancient tribal division that existed; and indeed Yemen today is primarily a stronghold of the Beni Ruwaha, a tribe of impeccable Qahtani descent, and Nizar belongs to a branch of the Beni Riyam, who are of direct Nizari descent. The old divisions are still very much alive.

After Malik there is a long period of historical lacuna, covered by hardly more than a paragraph in the *Kashf al Ghummah*. Historians seem agreed, however, that from A.D. 200 until about A.D. 600 the Azdite tribes were in continuous control of interior Oman, and that the Persians regained control of the coastal areas, not only of Oman but also Bahrain and right round the coast to Yemen. Almost certainly the local Persian capital was Sohar again, for that is where Amr bin al As found them when he arrived in Oman in 630 as emissary from Mohammed to order the conversion of the country to Islam.

Some years later, probably about 680, there were fresh invasions of Oman from Iraq and Persia under the general direction of the Moslem Governor of Iraq, Al Hejjaj, and for the next seventy years or so Oman was governed, at least theoretically, by an appointed Governor from Iraq. Towards the end of this period, however, an Omani, who had been made Governor and then deposed, allied himself with the Ibadhis, and gradually gained control of the country. In about 750 Al Julanda bin Mesud was elected first Imam in Oman. And from that day to this Oman has remained largely Ibadhi, and, although with long gaps, Imams have continued to be elected when and if there has been a suitable or acceptable candidate.

Just to complicate the definition and description of Oman, there are in fact two different Omans. The first, and most important, is the Oman I have been trying to disentangle from Muscat. The second is the traditional provincial division of the interior, which is in reality the kernel of the wider Omani nut—it is the central geographical core, the area in which Malik bin Fahm settled, known as Al Jauf; roughly from Bahla to Izki, but including the Jebal Akhdar down the Sumayl Gap and round to Rustaq. North-west of this lies the Dhahira, Ibadhi still, but gradually more diluted as the country extends north, and certainly more open to ideas or force that might infiltrate south from the Trucial Coast. South-east of Al Jauf lies the area known as the Sharquiya, the eastern province, also strongly Ibadhi, but leading its own existence, and rearing its own group of influential leaders. Nizwa, centre of Al Jauf, has often been the capital of the Imamate, and the wild mountainous country of the Jebal Akhdar and its foothills has provided a refuge for Ibadhism and the Imamate during periods of territorial subjection to outsiders; there have been plenty of invaders throughout history, and the refuge has been needed, and well used.

Nizwa is dominated by the great circular tower that overshadows, literally, the suq, and, metaphorically, the rest of the town and the surrounding countryside. It was built by the Imam Sultan bin Seif, the one who was responsible for the final ejection of the Portuguese from Muscat. He died in 1680, and it took him twelve years to build the Nizwa fort; it is supposed to have cost 80,000 crowns, and to have been financed by the spoils taken from the sacking of Ras al Khaima. It is a splendid piece of fortification, 120 feet in diameter according to my approximately paced measurement. In it lives the Wali, a slim man of powerful presence, who dispenses the rule and justice of the Sultan. To reach him you pass a number of guards at various gates at ground level, a horse rather miserably tethered beneath two palm trees next to a well, and a group of prisoners, who will good naturedly wish you good-day, in spite of the chains around their ankles; then up some stairs, round a corner or two, up more stairs to reach a rickety roof whose beams are only too visible where the mud has chipped away. There the Wali greets you, and takes you off to conversation and coffee. One day, sure enough, after a particularly heavy series of rainstorms, the roof gave way, and until it was patched up you had to go to another house in town to find him.

You can climb to the top of the tower and walk round a raised rim, peering through one embrasure after another; and look down on the flat geometry of the suq roofs, the houses scattered through the palm trees, the main street leading out towards the Government farm, and across and up to the ridge of the Jebal Akhdar range, the mountains lying in a sort of tilted slab of grey rock angled to the hot blue sky. There are some holes in the roof of the tower, and somewhere many feet below them the more sinister of the dungeons. Encamped on the roof in cheerful disarray of iron bedsteads and littered clothes are a section of the Army on guard in the tower; and fluttering high above all this the red flag of the Sultanate, where not so long ago flew the white flag of the Imamate.

Up there you can barely hear the noises of the town, which are in fact at their most concentrated down in the suq, hidden beneath roofed paths just outside the fort compound. This is one of the largest and busiest suqs in the interior, a focus of trade for miles around; indeed, only Ibri can compare with it. There I always liked to search the silver suq for an antique piece of jewellery (always difficult to find), to marvel at the Breughel-like interior of the meat suq, and to poke around the dark caverns behind the working copper-smiths for an old coffee-pot or piece of traditional Nizwa ware.

Nizwa is also famed for the halwa made there. Halwa is—no, it is describable only in terms of two expressive quotations; the first is from Samuel Zwemer, a missionary, who says[5] 'hilwa, which to the acquired taste is delicious, but to the stranger smells of rancid butter and tastes like sweet wagon grease'; and Theodore Bent warns[6] you that if you are fond of it, do not watch it being made 'for niggers' feet are usually employed to stir it, and the knowledge of this is apt to spoil the flavour'. Bent's theory is, I believe, quite apocryphal, but I am sure he is right about the principle; eat, but ask no questions.

Beyond the suqs of Nizwa is the town, of square mud walls and wooden doorways, and beyond and around them the palm groves, which in Oman are to be found wherever there is water. The oasis of Nizwa is large, watered by a large wadi which is usually flowing, however weakly, but after heavy rains will be in spate and quite impassable; whatever inconvenience this may cause, no one will complain, for its means the falajs will be full for another year.

If you drive down what might be described as the main street, on the road to Bahla and Ibri and towards the mountains, the wadi slowly opens out; on one side it is fringed by date groves, with mud or burasti houses hidden amongst them, on the other by a series of sturdy mud buildings which look like mosques. In fact they are the special 'tabsils', where in season the 'mabsila' dates are cooked; this is a generic term for dry dates, whose quality is such that they are not normally eaten but are boiled and then exported as cattle fodder. A very thriving trade in these dates exists in Oman, and at the right time, in July, curling columns of smoke rise into the Nizwa sky from these buildings and the piles of dates are brought to the tabsil, as to a coal bunker, and shovelled into cauldrons. Then they are laid out on the stones to dry, so that, at this season, the wadi is patterned with slabs of colour: the deep porphyry of dates, the fresh green of limes, that slowly turns to a bright dry yellow, the deep hot red of peppers, the startling orange of discarded date fronds, with the multi-coloured cottons of the women moving up and down or squatting stationary on the stones.

At the corner of this wadi, where the road turns left to Bahla through the bare hills that encircle Nizwa, is the Government Experimental Farm, a delightful and well-ordered spot. The best occasion at the farm is Farmers' Day, when all the local dignitaries turn up and as many of their retainers as can find a way in. A huge marquee is set up, suitable speeches are made, followed by a cere-monial circuit of the gardens. In the marquee hundreds of Omanis patiently and soundlessly wait, in long well-drawn lines, squatting on one knee with their rifles and camel sticks pointing to the roof like a plantation of young spruces laid out by the Forestry Commission; they wait for a cup of coffee, and then lunch, and are impervious to the speeches and the great men on the dais. Round the marquee are various European visitors look-ing rather overdressed and self-conscious, but no one is as impres-sive or authoritative as the Wali, resplendent in his flowing gold-fringed light brown abba. Behind all this, lunch is being boiled in five large cauldrons, and then laid out in huge round dishes ready for the signal to eat; sixty-six dishes of rice I counted, and several police to guard them.

Six hundred and fifty, or so, years ago Ibn Batuta visited Nizwa, and what he said about it was this:[7] 'the city is at the foot of a mountain and is surrounded by gardens and rivers; it has beautiful bazaars, and the mosques are large and scrupulously clean. It is a custom of these people to dine in the courtyards of the mosques; each of them brings his own food, and they assemble together and eat in the court of the mosque. They are a bold and brave race and the tribes are perpetually at war with each other. They belong to the Ibadhi sect and pray on Fridays at noon four times.' Except for eating in the mosques things have not changed too much. Today the tribes are no longer at war with each other—not with rifles and bullets at least—but even in this Ibn Batuta is not much out of date, for up to as late as 1920 and the Treaty of Sib they were. And never more so than in this area of Nizwa, the traditional capital of the Imamate, a centre to be captured, there-fore, by anyone presuming to power, even though he did not choose to use it as the capital himself.

Alternative Imamate capitals were normally Bahla, not far from Nizwa, and Rustaq on the Batina side of the mountains, although individual rulers might reside temporarily in other centres. Bahla is an hour or so of rattling in a Land-Rover from Nizwa, and must once have been a magnificent place, for even today you can sense this from the remnants of the wall that surrounds the town for a distance of about eight miles, the longest and largest in Oman, formerly guarded by a special detachment of slaves. It encloses not only the castle and the present town, but also a wide expanse of date gardens and fields of corn and general agriculture. Bahla was for a long time the capital of the Nabahina dynasty, who were in general control of Oman for four or five centuries before the Yaariba, from about the mid twelfth until the early years of the seventeenth century. The great fort must have been built and rebuilt many times, and what is left today is still as impressive as any castle in Oman.

As you drive round a corner and first see the line of the wall snaking over the hills you see also, at the right season, small yellow rectangles of ripe corn, or, a few weeks later, stooks among the stubble, or the winnowing of the ears. The road curls, almost as if it were a country lane, in a gouged wadi overhung with trees and occasional cotton plants skirting the edge of the wall, and then, round another corner, you see the castle itself perched on a rocky height, bedraggled with broken battlements, but still fiercely clasping its ancient history round its towers, a red Sultanate flag sharply defined above the elephant-grey of its walls. In a part of the castle that is best preserved lives the Wali, one of the few in Oman who functions with a positively executive regard for the clock. The fort is built in the waist of the town, and the wall vanishes from sight from it, ballooning out to encompass and preserve the city in both directions. It did not always succeed in this, and one razing of the fort is reported in 1610; this being so, the present fort is no doubt a Yaariba rebuilding, in the same tradition as Nizwa, Jibrin, Rustaq and Al Hazm.

A few miles from Bahla, away from the mountains in the beginnings of the gravel plain is another castle at the oasis of Jibrin, where, says Miles,[8] 'under a grand old tamarind tree we camped for the night very comfortably.' I expect it was the same tamarind tree that I saw, and under it some fine horses tethered, one with a foal. Jibrin is a peaceful fort, built as a home, and used by the Imams, or ex-Imams, as a sort of retreat. Bilurub bin Sultan bin Seif built it in about 1670 and founded a school beside it. It has latticed and stone-mullioned windows looking out over the flat plain and towards the sharp line of the Jebal Akhdar, whose highest peak is roughly opposite, and many of the rooms and ceilings have their old painted beams; one only hopes that the Sultan will preserve this castle which is unique in Oman for its peaceful, almost idyllic character. Mind you, it has its dungeons—four of them in ascending degree of unpleasantness—but what you remember is the deep red of the painted beams, the 'winter' room, the Imam's private Majlis (complete with hidden corners for guards and a false floor), the schoolroom at the very top where the breezes and the view would surely beguile students, even though, we are told, they were provided with bananas from the Imam's private garden to keep them alert, and a special chamber for the women in which a well hole descended through to the ground beneath, provided with a golden chain and bucket, for making saffron. The Wali of Bahla, who holds the key of the castle, is a good guide, and when you leave the guards will give you, if you are lucky, special dates soaked in some sort of fermented juice, a succulent dish of latent potency.

In the wadi a few miles from Nizwa is the ancient town of Manah, where Malik bin Fahm is supposed to have dug the falaj that bears his name. When I visited Manah there were more flies concentrated in it than any other place I ever went to in Oman, so that I was quite unable to appreciate how Wellsted[9] (admittedly 130 years ago) could wax so lyrical about his approach to the town: 'as we crossed the open fields, with lofty almond, citron and orange trees yielding a delicious fragrance on either hand, exclamations of astonishment and admiration burst from us "Is this Arabia" we said "this the country we have looked on heretofore as a desert".' I asked the Wali about the ancient falaj, of course, but he was uninterested; anyway, I went off and found it, broken and dusty in a field and half covered over with dead grass. To tell the truth, it didn't look very ancient.

Nearer the mountain range, indeed tucked almost into it, is another group of towns, Ghafat of the Beni Hina, Hamra of the Abriyeen, Tanuf and Birkat al Mauz of the Beni Riyam. All these places, together with the castles of Jibrin, Nizwa and Manah are the real Oman; Ibadhi, Hinawi and Ghafiri, Yemeni and Nizari; tribal, bellicose, more city-states than a nation.

Ghafat is in a crook of the mountains where Jebal Kaur sticks out almost at right angles from the main range, a monstrous landmark which in winter can be seen equally from the road south of Izki or the road south of Ibri. It is said to be the largest 'exotic' in the world, and the geologists love to wrangle over whether it appeared one primeval day from the guts of the earth, or was tossed over from the sea. Ghafat is the capital of the Beni Hina, the tribe which gave its name to the Hinawi grouping of tribes in the great Oman civil war in the early 1600s; it is an extensive series of date gardens with full falajs flowing through them, and in the centre a collection of neat two- and three-storey mud houses, solid and emanating an air of strength and wealth. The ruling sheikhs are the Awlad Zahir, the sons of Zahir, a powerful family. Abdulla is the senior, two more are Walis in Mudhaibi and Sumayl, and four more hang around in the corridors of power, with the eighth in prison in Jalali—a hostage, maybe, for the family. The Awlad Zahir played a dubious role in the Imamate troubles of 1955-9, and there are many stories of their anti-British outlook, but Abdulla is a wonderful Omani host and a tremendous talker about the world and its problems. Before a visit to Ghafat you need to read the newspapers and listen to the radio, for you may be questioned, as bowl after bowl of fruit is put before you, about anything from the shooting of Kennedy to the British constitution to the quality of space rockets. After several hours of this you will be rewarded with a succulent lunch.

Across a wide wadi from the Ghafat gardens rises Jebal Kaur, aridly frowning down on to the plentiful water of the town; the wadi leads to a plain, and in this area could exist a huge development of wheat production. Half-way down, beside a falaj, is an archetypal lone tree (and marked as such on army maps) beside which is a peculiar model of wheat-grinding machine (and the only one so far permitted in the Sultanate) tended by a couple of Sheikh Abdulla's men. Often a family will encamp there, perhaps for days, hoping to get a lift to Ibri or Nizwa. If Sheikh Abdulla and his brothers were given their head, there would be a lot more in Ghafat and its surrounding plains than that one grinder, and the lone tree would turn into a real bus stop with a motel behind it.

Further along, north-east towards Nizwa is Hamra of the Abriyeen, to my mind the most attractive of all towns in Oman. It is a large place, said to be watered by only one falaj but if this is so it must be the most prolific one in the country; there is a road encircling the gardens and beside it the falaj, and all the gardens at a slightly lower level—you walk down a couple of steps, and then along well-ordered paths with neatly arranged gardens on either side, all very geometrical and systematised; walls, and lime trees spilling over them; sprays of dates like a skyful of fireworks; the bright green of the ubiquitous lucerne, the universal Omani animal fodder. It is almost European in its feel and this sensation is magnified by the town centre with its tall elegant mud houses with wooden windows casting strong Italianate shadows, and a wide flight of steps leading from a sort of piazza to an upper level of the town. In the main majlis of the sheikh, which is a long narrow room, the many windows open straight out on to a grove of lime trees, and what with the burble of water from a falaj beneath and the chirping of birds in the trees, you begin to lose grasp of desert realities; until you re-focus on a room full of bearded Omanis clutching their rifles and their camel sticks, and your Umbrian dreams are dissipated. At the far end of this rural room is another small and rather cramped box of a place, into which I was once put and seated, with honour, on a dais while they all went out and prayed.

Behind Hamra the mountains slope almost from the roofs of the houses up at the peculiar tilted angle of the range towards its highest peak at about 10,000 feet. The mountains are as usual denuded of any vegetation, and burn with a dry glare of flat stone; against the sky they make a razor-sharp grey line on which a goat will stand out as distinct as a ship on an evening horizon.

Hamra is by Omani standards a new place—it was founded during the Yaariba dynasty—and is entirely without warlike pretensions; no castle there, nor walls, just the activities of a peaceful economy; and stuck away under the mountain it was, I suppose, allowed to go its own way. Not so Tanuf, which is equally close, pushed up against the mountains, at the mouth of a massive gorge, whose stream carves its way in twisting corners down to Nizwa. Tanuf must have been a town to reckon with, the capital of Suleiman bin Himyar and before him Himyar bin Nasir, the Sheikhs of the Beni Riyam, Lords, as they liked, and the romantics still like, to think, of the Green Mountain. Tanuf no longer exists. It looks, with due deference to Daniel, like the abomination of desolation. Coming over the brow of a pass from Bahla, you first see a group of a dozen topless palm trees, standing like a cluster of naked telegraph poles; then in the haze beyond you make out the remnants of a whole grove of palms, and then the battered remains of Tanuf town. The town was destroyed, and the falajs cut, as a reprisal against the Beni Riyam for the part that Suleiman bin Himyar played in the Imamate revolution of the 1950s; a revenge, carried out by the rockets of the R.A.F. at the request of the Sultan, in the grand Omani tradition, brought up to date. Not even the ghosts are there today, just rubble; but behind it still the great grey slabs of the mountain, so smoothly tilted that it seems one could roll a ball up the slope, and, stretching to the north-west, the line of the mountain range mistily cut out against the setting sun, and the folding peaks above Hamra and Ghafat on the far skyline. And at its back the tumbling chaos of stones in the wadi, dark in the shadows of the hills, a bolthole up the mountain if things were ever to get too dangerous in the town. Tanuf is, in a sense, a memorial to the ancient way of Omani life; modern developments will change—will sap, if you are an incurable romantic—the other towns of the interior, maybe slowly, but in the end the change will come. Not to Tanuf, however, which destroyed though it may be, will remind future generations of what Oman used to be like.

The Sultan's revenge on Suleiman bin Himyar was implacable; the visible manifestations of his independent and powerful life had to be seen to be destroyed, so that he, and what he stood for, would be destroyed. And so, in Birkat al Mauz too, where he had another fine palace, the R.A.F. were invited to indulge in rocket practice, and the palace is a pitted and broken mess, although it is not so levelled that you cannot admire what it used to be only ten years ago.

Birkat al Mauz, like Tanuf, is built at the end of a large wadi, the Maaydin, that snakes right into the heart of the mountains, and Suleiman's castle lies across its mouth like a massive watchdog

at its master's feet. From here too, if there was danger on the
plain, the Beni Riyam could be up in the unapproachable
mountains in a jiffy, impregnably lodged among the goat paths
and villages, with Suleiman laughing away in the third of his
private castles in the village of Sayq (that too was blasted by the
R.A.F. at the Sultan's request).

Birkat al Mauz has a superb falaj leading out from the castle,
built up on a dry-stone foundation that would do justice to the
Cotswolds. Sometimes it overflows and pours down the main
road. The 'aquaduct' there, perhaps this falaj, or more likely one
the other end of the village that is carried across the road on a
bridge, was built by Sultan bin Seif, who also built Nizwa fort.

Suleiman bin Himyar was senior sheikh, or tamima as it is
called in Oman, of the Beni Riyam, who, after the decline of the
Beni Ghafir, became the leading Ghafiri tribe. As I have inferred,
their tribal territory extended along the base of the mountains,
and also right up on top of them. Hence Suleiman's title of Lord
of the Green Mountain; how he must dream of them from his
exile in Dammam, a place as devoid of romanticism as you could
find, and as flat as the Jebal Akhdar is precipitous.

Until the S.A.S. bullocked their way up the mountain in 1959,
and put a final end to the Imamate war, the Jebal had only once
before been taken in battle, and that was in 972/3 when Oman
suffered one of its periodic conquests. With good reason, then,
Suleiman must have considered himself impregnably safe up
there at Sayq, and reckoned that the arrival of British troops on
top was not at all part of the game. As a permanent reminder that
the mountain is now under Sultanate control Suleiman's house in
Sayq was demolished, and a trim white fort set up overlooking the
village, and inhabited by a detachment of SAF. Particularly in
summer, it is a delectably cool place to live; in winter you may
even wake to see snow covering the parade ground.

It is quite a climb to Sayq. I did it once, by courtesy of SAF,
and have only once been as exhausted from walking, and that was
when I climbed up Mount Hermon one night, watched the dawn
spread over Jordan, Syria and Lebanon, and then came down
again. On each occasion I was equally unfit and unpractised for
such an ordeal. In certain respects, however, this journey was
done in style and comfort; for instance, our party consisted of

eight donkeys, six donkey men, four soldiers, a colleague and myself, and the donkeys took our belongings; but, far more important, we knew we had a warm welcome ahead of us on top, with a bath, bed, food and drink. Even so, there were moments when I was by no means certain that I would reach bath, bed, food, or drink; the path is cruelly steep, and goes on for a long, long time.

I can vividly remember those two October days, starting from Izki by Land-Rover before dawn, loading donkeys in the Wadi Maaydin, and then setting off on foot up and up the mountain. Once you are out of the Wadi, away from the gardens of Sowjra full of limes, bananas and the twittering of bulbuls, the path climbs nearly vertically out of the shadows into the sun, with the hieroglyphs of donkey's hooves on the stone steps up the mountain. You then cross a pass and down to Salut, where we breakfasted off oranges beside a clear stream. Then up another steep ascent for an hour, with views of Shuraija across intervening gorges, its terraces hanging on the cliffs like an Italian Appennine village. It was a six-hour journey, including the stop for those breakfast oranges.

Sayq seemed delightful. There were gardens of lucerne, orchards of pomegranates, peaches, figs and grapes. We strolled along a falaj wall in the shade of trees and there were vines and walnut trees on the far hillside; there was barley, smelling like England, flowers, limes, clouds and some rain. We passed an arbour of trees with their leaves turning into autumnal colouring, and followed a falaj round to its source, the cliffs above scarred by shrapnel.

The trouble with the Jebal Akhdar is that it is a place of great imaginative appeal; you think of fields and trees and animals, and read that once leopards lived up there, and expect a sort of Eldorado. I suppose that I have not helped. The fact is that indeed I saw these vines, peaches, walnuts, barley, pomegranates, and figs, but they exist only in about four or five small villages. The rest is nothing but bare, very stony outcrop, with hardly a vestige of vegetation upon it. The name, Green Mountain, is itself highly misleading, until you realise that the significance of Akhdar is not that it is green, but that it is living i.e. formed out of 'living' limestone as opposed to the 'dead' volcanic outcrops on the other side of the Sumayl gap, and in the foothills round Nizwa. That, at least, is the most satisfactory explanation I have had of the name; it makes more sense than to imagine it received the title 'green' in some bygone age when it really was all green. And, indeed, its old name was not Akhdar at all, but Radhwan, the name given to it by the Beni Riyam when they first settled in the area.

There are a number of routes up the mountain, all steep tracks good only for donkeys, goats, or men. There is a special type of Jebal donkey, as active and tough as goats, for normal donkeys would never reach the top, least of all with a load. The main tracks are the Wadi Maaydin one that I followed, the Qamr track from Nizwa (said to be longer but less steep), another from Mutti near Izki, another from the Wadi Halfayn headwater up to Manaikhir, and one or two from the Rustaq side of the mountains, the best and most used from Awabi. Most, if not all, of these tracks are made easier—perhaps more correctly made passable— by the stone steps cut in them. These steps are quite obvious and without any doubt cut by man; it is thought that this was done by the Persians, who are also supposed to have imported the concept of the falaj into the country. Miles suggests[10] that the work was done by the Persians who were responsible for the tenth-century conquests; this may be so, or it seems to me at least possible that they were very much earlier. What is most surprising, however, is that so much work should have been done for such an apparently unproductive purpose. One begins to wonder whether perhaps the Jebal once was really green after all. I do not profess to know, but I certainly find those cut steps as fascinating to the imagination as almost anything in Oman.

The Persians are also said to have imported into Oman many of the fruits that now are grown in the country, particularly the vine; and Shuraija, that village on the top of the Jebal with its terraces cut out of the descending cliff, is, according to some people, the diminutive form of Shiraz. Up there on the mountain they use the grapes for the time-honoured purpose, as they do in Persia, and never mind Ibadhi precepts in the cold of the winter; and I am told, on the best authority, that Suleiman bin Himyar's cellars in Sayq contained, not rifles and ammunition, but casks of Akhdar '57.

So much for the Jebal Akhdar, except to repeat that its cultivation is limited to a few wadis in the Sayq area (at about 6,000 feet) and that for the rest it is as bare and unproductive as any broken rocky hill. The main peak is 10,000 feet, and that is north, opposite Ghafat and Hamra. There are no longer any leopards on it, but I was assured a special snake lived up there, embossed like a shield.

I have mentioned the Beni Riyam as having been one of the leading Ghafiri tribes, and have also referred to the Hinawi/Ghafiri tribal split in Oman, and this should be explained. This division came about in the civil war which lasted roughly from 1723 to 1728; it ended the Yaariba rule, although confusion continued until Ahmed bin Said inaugurated Al bu Said rule in 1749. The civil war began as the result of a quarrel over succession to the Imamate, and the original protagonists were Khalaf bin Mubarak al Hinai (i.e. of the Beni Hina) and Mohammed bin Nasir al Ghafiri (of the Beni Ghafir). The quarrel sucked in practically every tribe in Oman; those supporting Mubarak were described as Hinawi, and those supporting Mohammed, Ghafiri.

In general, but by no means precisely, the split followed the existing division in the country, between those tribes of Yemeni origin and those of Nizari (or, looking back further and genealogically, to those descended from Qahtan, and those from Adnan). This division was reflected, but again imprecisely, in the division within Oman of Ibadhis and Sunnis, the Ibadhis being more often of Yemeni descent. But it cannot be stressed enough that to make a hard and fast line through, on the one side Yemenis/Ibadhis/Hinawis, and on the other Nizaris/Sunnis/Ghafiris, is both facile and incorrect. And just to make matters more difficult, there have been subsequent switches in the Hinawi/Ghafiri allegiance; most notably and misleadingly the Beni Ghafir themselves, who are now a Hinawi tribe, and it is from them that the Beni Riyam, a strongly Ibadhi and Yemeni tribe, took over the Ghafiri leadership.

All this would be of little more than academic interest if the appellations were not still used today; this they are, although they are meaningful to a differing degree in different parts of the country. The division means most in the east where the Hinawi tribes of the Sharquiya are a close-knit entity under the leadership of Sheikh Ahmed bin Mohammed al Hirthi, a great-grandson of the Salih bin Ali who was partly instrumental in bringing Azzan bin Qais to power as Imam in 1869; grandson of Isa bin Salih, who helped to elect Salim bin Rashid al Kharousi as Imam in 1912, and who was one of the signatories on the Imamate side of the Treaty of Sib in 1920; and nephew of Salih bin Isa who backed the Imamate in 1957 and is now eking out his exile in Dammam.

The Al Hirth

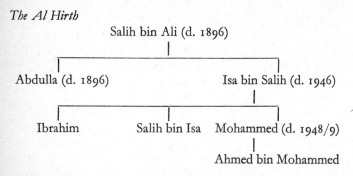

So, the titles and the division lives on; today, it is perhaps more like belonging to a club, or wearing an old school tie, than a very serious business. Even so, the rivalry existed and the memory of it may bubble up, as if, at the end of the day at Lords, the Etonians and Harrovians were to erupt into armed conflict. In Oman, though, the emotions are potentially stronger; somewhere a few generations back there is almost certainly the memory of a blood feud, and that is more potent than the knowledge that your father was bowled for a duck.

The road from Oman to the coast is through the Sumayl Gap. This is the shallowest, widest and most apparent of the comparatively few routes from coast to interior; the other main ones being the Wadi Jizzi (Sohar to Bureimi), Wadi Hawasina (Khaboura to Ibri), and the Wadi Falaij (Sur to Kamil). The most startling thing about the Sumayl Gap is the fact that it is indeed a Gap; a slightly tilted one, of course, for it climbs from sea level to about 2,000 feet at the watershed, but the road has only two or three short stretches of steep gradient throughout its length.

Geologically, it is the Gap between the limestone massif of the
Jebal Akhdar and the dead volcanic hills that lead off to the
Sharquiya, much lower and more ragged, which do not grow into
strong respectable mountains again for a hundred miles or so.
The Jebal Akhdar side of the Gap, however, is a massive wall
that rises solidly up without any warning at all, bare and leaning
slightly inwards at a most surprising angle, like a gigantic slice of
cake. At intervals this great wall is cracked with narrow ravines,
darkly disappearing into the entrails of the mountain. It is a
remarkable formation, of a startling beauty of sharp horizons,
vivid shadows and infinite rock variations. It is sinister only when
it disappears completely from sight, which happens on the
hottest and haziest summer days, and you know it is there only a
few hundred yards away, but it is wholly hidden by a miasma of
heat.

At the interior end of the Sumayl Gap is Izki, a place which has
seldom been tranquil. Today there is a SAF detachment in Izki to
keep official peace, although it cannot cope with the subterranean
intriguings that are the spice of life for all Omanis, and for the
inhabitants of Izki its whole purpose. Izki, or Zikki in its more
affectionate form, is a group of villages whose nucleus is split into
Nizar and Yemen. It lies along and across the rough course of the
Wadi Halfayn, one of the great wadis of Oman, which flows from
the Sumayl Gap watershed deep down into the desert interior,
ending up around the Barr al Hikman. 'Flows' is hardly the apt
word, for it seldom does flow; but it would if there were continual rains and does after particularly torrential storms. Izki's
main water supply, however, is a falaj of great antiquity, the
Falaj al Mulki. This is alleged to be older than the Falaj Malik bin
Fahm at Manah, and must, therefore, be pure Persian; it was said
to have 370 different channels in its original form, where now
there are only two; it is finely maintained, and one of the best
examples of a falaj that I know; near its exit into the open air you
can climb down steps to inspect it, perhaps ten feet below ground,
running in an immaculate stone-roofed tunnel about six feet high,
the water moving swiftly to a depth of about one foot.

Falajs are part of the lore of Oman. Their principle is the same
as that of the Persian qanat, which is one reason why it is
generally assumed they were introduced into the country by the

Persians. The idea is simple, to lead water from its source under or over ground to where it can be used. The construction is described by a nineteenth-century writer[11] as follows: 'A well is sunk upon a descending plain till water is found and a canal cut from the bottom, under ground, descending just enough to convey its water along. A few yards from the first a second well is dug, that the earth, in cutting the subterranean passage, may be drawn out; and the same process is repeated till the spring is conveyed to the surface and made to irrigate the adjacent fields.' So, it is simplest to sight a falaj from the air, for you can then see its course clearly from the slender line of craters, like bomb-holes, that lead from the water source often many miles to a cluster of green palm trees in the desert. Some start at a great depth—the Falaj al Mulki is said to be over forty feet deep at its source—some never go underground at all but, like the Falaj Sahama a few miles from Izki, are led in an open channel from an above-ground water supply; some are many miles long, others comparatively short, some have an enormous flow of water, others are a mere trickle.

A falaj needs continual and skilful maintenance; like the Forth Bridge, when you have got to one end you must start again at the other. It also requires capital and skill to dig. As a result, the falajs of Oman have to some extent reflected the economic state of the country; certainly the second great age of falaj construction was in Yaariba times, when many were renovated, and others built. Since then they have, with certain exceptions, been allowed to fall into disrepair and disintegration. Old dried-up falaj courses can be seen in many parts of Oman, and at the end of them still faintly discernible the dusty squares of what used to be cultivated land.

There is one particular engineering technique used in falaj construction which is both simple and subtle, the syphon. A wadi bed, even if it only flows once in two or three years, is a dangerous hazard for any man-made channel, which would be liable to total destruction from a storm. The falaj makers, therefore, lead the

falaj under the wadi, thus:————————————————: the down-

stream level of the falaj is, of course, marginally lower than the upstream one. Visually, the water vanishes down a sort of well one side, and flows up a similar well the other side. The height of these 'syphons' may be as much as 25 to 30 feet above the wadi level if the wadi has, for instance, cut itself into a ravine, so that, looking at the falaj, one first imagines it has lost its 'bridge' across the wadi; but no, the bridge is inverted and hidden beneath the wadi bed.

The economics of a falaj are also interesting. Occasionally it will have been built by a rich individual for a village, but more often it will belong (unless it is a private falaj serving a private garden) to the village collectively, or at least to a group of landowners. Water from the falaj is, of course, let out from the main channel into individual gardens along its route; what you buy, or own, as a landowner is the right to so many minutes or hours of water per day or week. Normally, the water in a falaj will be divided up over a period of time, maybe a week, or fourteen days, or any other number, known as a 'daur' or 'dauran'—the daur of the Falaj al Mulki is seventeen days. The daur is then divided, normally, into a 'badih', and the badih into 'athrs'. In Yanqul the Falaj al Ain has a daur of seven days, a badih of twelve hours, and an athr of half an hour; thus, there are twenty-four athrs in a badih, and fourteen badihs (or possibly only seven if, for instance, the hours of darkness were to be excluded) in the daur. A landowner will normally own a certain number of athrs—which will not neces-sarily be successive—or, in other words, the right to a certain specified number of half hours of water every day, or every so many days. Water which is not owned as, as it were, a freehold, will be sold annually at a water auction.

The owners of the water, either freehold, leasehold, or occasional, will be responsible for the upkeep of the falaj, and also for ensuring that each gets his right share. Usually they appoint a person, or committee to do this; the man in charge is called an Arif. The economics of maintenance no doubt vary, but in Yanqul, for instance, in the case that repairs must be done, the Arif puts the work out to auction, with bids descending, of course, rather than ascending, and then allocates the cost to the owners on the basis of the number of Athrs they possess. This, I believe, is the most normal process.

Earlier I used the word lore in connection with falajs, advisedly; in many places there exist falaj books, with the history, title, sales, accounts etc. of the falaj. These could be of considerable historical interest if procurable, but are jealously guarded by the Arif, or whoever may be responsible. In Oman they refer to the old Persian falajs as Daoudi (of David), so that it is theoretically possible to trace which are the oldest. In some places they have a semi-pagan ceremony of praying for rain if the falaj level falls dangerously; this has to be performed by some person specifically chosen for his purity. In some towns there is a falaj clock to help settle disputes—a slab of stone marked like a sundial, on which a person may recognise his rights to his water. Falajs may be a potential source for academic study, but are also part of the way of Omani life; and indeed, one of your invariable, almost com-pulsory, conversational gambits will be: 'And how are the falajs? Inshallah, they are full.'

Back to Izki, with the edge of the Jebal a smoky-blue skyline in a breathless evening; some smoked-salmon cloud wisps left over from the sunset; later, a fat moon chasing away the multitudinous stars which recapture the night just before the grey drizzling pre-dawn light removes them for another day. No wonder there is a cave nearby in which an ancient idol called Jurnan lives; to see him you have to crawl through a low opening, and that is guarded by snakes. That is what they say, and I am prepared to take it as read.

Near Izki is the village of Mutti, clamped onto the edge of the Jebal. It is built in the typical and attractive Jebal fashion, of dry-stone walls, and appears immensely solid and purposeful after the mud constructions of the wadis, or the burasti of the coast and desert. Even the camel and goat pens are enclosed stone-wall circles, where in Izki, only a few miles away, they are no more than a circle of camel thorn. One is reminded of the Cotswolds, and can imagine a trellis of roses spilling over the house fronts (roses do grow in Oman, as a matter of fact, especially on the Jebal, but the Omanis themselves have no time for or interest in such decorative luxuries; foreigners, and particularly English-men, will naturally tend them with time-consuming care). Mutti is at the mouth of a wadi so twisted that it is hardly visible, but which is in fact one of the routes up the mountain; when you reach it, the ascent is up well-cut stone steps, as in the Maaydin route, ancient Persian work. Mutti, secretive behind its stone façades, is a place of great suspicion to SAF, and has been ever since it housed rebels in the 1957 revolt. The sheikh there, until he died in 1968, was reputed to be one of the richest men in Oman, but when they came to open up a wall containing his treasure chests it was found to hold nothing more exciting than ancient rifles and antique ammunition.

Further on towards the watershed, known as Nejd Mughbariya, is another of the ravines that slice their way towards the centre of the Jebal. This is the headwater, or more aptly dry-water source, of the Wadi Halfayn. I walked to the end of it one day, a gorge of gigantic proportions, worth the maximum of Michelin asterisks by any standard. It was a November day, still hot in the sun, but cooled by the call of bulbuls and crag martins, by the bright green of the sadr trees, and by the pools of water which became more continuous as I walked further into the mountain. At the end the way was blocked by a great dolomitic crescent of hills, and up on top behind the horizon was Manaikhir; to the left a cliff-face covered with maidenhair ferns and dripping with water, and underneath it oleanders. It was impossible to follow, even with binoculars, the route of the path up the hills, but it went up somewhere there, nearly vertically no doubt—two hours said a man who materialised from the rocks; two hours?; well, two Arab hours. Two hours, maybe, for a tough mountain goatherd. A woman appeared with a flock of goats, and somewhere else in the gorge lived a man in a cave; they set up a weird cacophony of gurgling, whistling, screaming, singing and blowing. The goats seemed to understand. Maybe one of them was Pan. In the sun the sadr trees smelt of Friar's Balsam.

From the dripping cliff-face at the track head to the end of the gorge, and then beyond, runs the Falaj Sahama, now disused like an old branch railway, but built originally by the Yaariba to irrigate lands in the main wadi. Indeed the falaj is like a miniature Alpine railway as it picks its way down the gorge, built up here, roofed over there, with tunnels and drainage arches, and finally a tremendous 'syphon' under the main wadi course. It then chugs gently along open country to a vast cistern beside the road, and then on again to the village that is now only broken mud and the shadowy shapes of fields. The diameter of the cistern is fifty feet, and its depth twelve feet; one day I searched the village site for old remains, but could find nothing more than broken pottery; the village withered away like a dry plant after the falaj was destroyed in a local war, and no one ever had the energy to renew it.

From Sahama it is only a mile or two to the Nejd, signalled nowadays by a cage in which the oil pipeline makes one of its infrequent appearances above ground, in this case to change diameter for the long descent to the coast. As one tips over the watershed, one moves into the Wadi Beni Ruwaha, named after the tribe who inhabit a string of villages starting with Al Mahal, continuing to Al Jenah, Biyyaq, Wobbal and ending with half of Sumayl.

Like many Omani tribes, the Beni Ruwaha are divided into factions, some of whom are so much at loggerheads that it is almost indecent to describe them as of the same tribe. This is the case with the Beni Hisham and the Beni Rashid, both sections of the Beni Ruwaha, and it is no mere idle talk to mention blood feuds in this context. About thirty years ago Seif bin Ahmed al Rashidi killed Mohammed bin Harith al Hishami near Al Mahal. In 1954 the feud flared up during a meeting of the two parties in a mosque in Al Jenah. Twelve people were killed, including Said bin Seif al Rashidi and Abdulla, his brother, and Nasir bin Mohammed al Hishami; a week later Seif bin Ahmed al Rashidi died from wounds incurred during the fight. 1954 is not so long ago, and blood feuds are not easily forgotten or laid to rest.

Sumayl is, if you like, the capital of the Gap. It is a large place, very long, and famous for its dates. Like many Omani towns, it is split into two, Sifala (Lower) and Aliya (Upper). In Sumayl Aliya live the Khalili family, now senior sheikhs of the Beni Ruwaha, an aristocratic Omani family, whose grandfather was Imam from 1920 to 1954; Sumayl Sifala is Ghafiri and Beni Jabir, and in this half is the great husn in which the Wali lives. The Wali at this time was Mohammed bin Zahir*, brother of Abdulla at Ghafat, a member of another aristocratic family, closely related to Ghalib bin Ali who was elected Imam in 1954 at the death of Mohammed bin Ali al Khalili. This is a measure of the importance of Sumayl.

* See page 109 above.

It is an attractive and typically Omani town. The wadi is wide there, and in it there is always flowing water, with pools fringed with oleanders; watch-towers peer up and down the wadi from suitable hillocks. On each side are massed date gardens, with bananas and lucerne and limes crowded in wherever there is space. The town, split as it is, is practically invisible from the wadi bed, although some large houses may be seen lurking amongst the palm trees. The Wali's fort is far away downstream, but perched up on a hill, dominating the lower town and appearing very invincible. The dates for which Sumayl is most famous are the variety called Fard, and in the old days (of the later nineteenth century) they were exported in quantity to America; but then the Americans began their own date culture and inevitably did it far more efficiently than the Omanis.

In Sumayl I learnt that, when people say that a wadi in spate can come upon you so swiftly that you may be drowned in it, that is precisely what can happen, and there is no exaggeration. I was there one evening visiting the Wali, *en route* for Izki. Driving towards Sumayl we could see a storm in the mountains but in spite of a few large warm raindrops we thought we would be ahead of any local trouble. We were wrong. I remember remarking on the sudden change of colour of the water, and in the twinkling of an eye that water was washing the soles of our feet in the Land-Rover; outside it was thigh high, and the pebbles from the wadi were thrown against our ankles like peas in a pod. We retired to the bank, and surveyed the half submerged Land-Rover. The water did not rise further, so we called the villagers to our aid, and between them they lifted the car on to some higher ground; it started without a cough and, led by a man wading in front of it like a Victorian with a red flag in front of a train, it was driven to safety up the bank.

One of the Khalilis appeared like magic, and we were wafted to his house, given mattresses, blankets and dinner, and there we lay listening to the roar of the water until it put us to sleep. In the morning we were woken by the peculiar call of the Sumayl conch-horn, and the sky was fresh blue again, the wadi stones once again uncovered, and we continued our journey.

We were lucky that it was Sumayl with its immediate Arab hospitality. It is not so much fun if you are trapped in mid desert

by one wadi in front of you and another behind. There is, however, only one possible course of action, to wait until the water
has abated; fortunately, a flood is usually over as quickly as it
begins.

The next place on the way to the coast is Al Legeila, the home
of the Beni Jabir sheikhs. This too is an appealing Omani village.
As you crunch through the wadi you can see a trio of well-spaced
watch-towers brooding over the date groves, and behind them the
Italianate rim of the main mountain range. A dry disused falaj runs
to one side, but on the other there are the telltale craters of
another which is in use. At the end of the village there is a long
block of lucerne cultivation that shows up as a palpitating green
in front of the lifeless volcanic hills.

Down a far from obvious path, well hidden from the road,
Sheikh Hamad bin Hamdan al Jabiri has his majlis. It is one of the
most charmingly rustic spots in all Oman, a gravel rectangle set
beside a strongly flowing falaj, overshadowed by a massive mango
tree, and surrounded by date palms, lime bushes, bananas and
lucerne; an occasional gurgling of a pigeon, the thud and tinkle
of a pestle beating out coffee beans, and a barely perceptible
murmur of the women cooking somewhere behind the trees.
Carpets are spread over the gravel, and you can lean back on the
parapet of the falaj and let your fingers dabble the water; large
plates of fruit are served, coffee is passed round according to
immemorial tradition; people appear from amongst the leaves, as
if magnetised by the presence of visitors, and squat impassively,
their rifles straight towards the sky and their camel sticks tickling
the ground around them. Solemnly you exchange the well-worn
Omani phrases, and the servants hover with more fruit, and more
coffee. You begin to wonder if there is a magic in this delectable
place. No; or, if there is, it is swiftly dispelled by a mound of
goat and rice at 9.45 a.m.

After Al Legeila comes Bid Bid, where the Wadi Sumayl is
broad, and at the edge there is always water. Falajs lead off down
the banks, and are edged with oleanders; the background
mountains are purple and invariably you can see a roller bird
colourfully slashing across the sky, or, if you look more carefully,
a red-billed plover at the edge of a pool, camouflaged black and
white among the black and white pebbles. The wadi swings

round ninety degrees, taking its fringe of palm trees with it, passes beneath a SAF camp sited to enjoy the view, and crosses the road again at Fanjah.

One day there will be afternoon coach trips from Muscat to Fanjah for it is only about fifty miles distant, and is a distilled version of all Omani villages: a ford over the wadi, a falaj, date groves, watch-towers hanging like eagles over a steep village, mountains behind. There will be a restaurant there, and very pleasant too. I used to enjoy watching a string of camels plod very purposefully through the shallow water, their big flat feet suddenly appearing as fastidious as their proud noses.

From Fanjah the wadi swings round again, splays out into the Batina, and crosses it to Sib; from there Muscat and Muttrah will obtain their new piped-water supply. Fanjah is, effectively, the end of the Gap even though the road has still to pick its way through the foothills before emerging on to the Batina plain; immediately it gets there you can see the line of the coast and the sea, and, curled into a crook of the hills, glinting silver in the setting sun, the crude oil tanks at Saih al Malah. It is those, of course, that are the omen for the Fanjah coach tours.

Running more or less parallel with the Wadi Sumayl and to the west is the Wadi Maawil, a well-ordered and prosperous area, whose chief claim to fame seems to be that the Julanda kings were of the Maawil tribe. Since the disintegration of that dynasty well over one thousand years ago, the Maawil appears to have lived in peace and to have remained detached from the wars and invasions; certainly it looks like that today.

Then, along the base of the mountain via Nakhl and Awabi is the Yaariba capital of Rustaq, later to play a pivotal part in the Imamate movements of the nineteenth century.

Rustaq is said to mean 'market town', and that, in spite of its political history of intrigue, is what its nature seems to be. It has gardens spread widely over wadis and along falajs, and a country-lane approach to its fort in a scooped out wadi bed shaded with trees; the scent of limes in season, and ripe barley ears peering over walls. There is a large and busy walled suq with three massive gates, with an atmosphere half-interior, half-coastal; salt, fish, dried shark, limes, bananas, walnuts, garlic, all in profusion; auctioning of goats; a scribe squatting in the shade; a camel park, and cafés; copper-smiths and general merchants; and looming above this animated scene the elephant-grey fort and the Jebal. On the gate of the fort one day was stuck a notice, warning the people that a bogus doctor was hawking his wares round town. All it needed was a fairground, and it might have been an international market town.

The fort is called Qalat al Kesra, taking its name from its most ancient tower, said to have been built about A.D. 600 by the Persians from Sohar. There is a story that an iron chain was hung from the gate, and that anyone complaining of injustice should rattle it; the offender would be punished. There is no chain now, but in summer the qadi will sit under a tree by the gate and dispense much the same sort of justice.

Rustaq was the Yaariba capital until they moved down the road to Al Hazm, but its most exciting role was perhaps its nineteenth-century one. When Ahmed bin Said, the first Al bu Said ruler, died in 1783 his sons squabbled continuously about the succession, and in 1793 the Pact of Birka was signed under which Said received Rustaq, Qais Sohar, and Sultan Muscat.* Said had in fact been elected Imam after the death of his father, but then, after a few years, retired to Rustaq and ceased to play the part of ruler. He remained Imam, however, until his death in about 1810, living quietly there. In the late 1850s Azzan bin Qais became de facto ruler of Rustaq, and from this base subsequently, in 1868, was elected Imam, the first one to be elected after the death of Said bin Ahmed. Azzan was defeated by Turki (with the help, be it said, of the British) who became Sultan. Azzan's brother, Ibrahim, however, continued to hold Rustaq on behalf of that side of the family. In 1898 Ibrahim died, and Saud bin Azzan took over Rustaq. There is a story that Saud wished to be elected Imam, and held a congress for this purpose, but failed—owing, some say, to his private predilection for alcohol.

Next year Saud was murdered by his elder brother, Humoud, but in 1903 Said bin Ibrahim was installed (with the assistance of Isa bin Salih al Hirthi) as ruler in Rustaq. In 1912 Said was murdered and Ahmed, his brother, took over. Ahmed bin Ibrahim remained in charge of Rustaq until 1916, when he was expelled, rather

* For clarification of the lineal complexities of these two paragraphs, see the family tree in Appendix 3.

surprisingly, since he was the last of the Qais line, by the
Imamate forces of Isa bin Salih and Himyar bin Nasir. The
results of this were in some ways unexpected. Ahmed bin
Ibrahim was reconciled with the main Al bu Said line, and has
played a large part in subsequent Sultanate affairs. To this day he
is Minister of the Interior in Muscat. His contacts with Rustaq are
still close, and he owns Al Hazm fort, a great angular castle built,
as is inscribed on its massive door, by Sultan bin Seif in 1126 A.H.
(A.D. 1708), who is buried inside it, amongst its crumbling forti-
fications and dusty bronze Portuguese cannons.

This complicated thread of history may perhaps illuminate
slightly the complicated nature of Oman, as well as link it
directly to the present. There is a famous passage in the *Kashf al
Ghummah* about the Omani character; it says: 'Now the people of
Oman are endowed with certain qualities, which it is my hope
they may never lose. They are a people of soaring ambition, and of
haughty spirit; they brook not the control of any Sultan, and are
quick to resent affront; they yield only to irresistible force, and
without ever abandoning their purpose. A man of comparatively
poor spirit, judged by their standard, is on a par as regards
magnanimity with an Emir of any other people. Each individual
aims at having the power in his own hands or in the hands of
those whom he loves. He desires everyone to be submissive to
him, and his neighbour has the same ambition.' That is Ross's[12]
translation, and his comment is deadpan: 'Anyone who has had
much to do with Oman politics', he says, 'must allow that there
are several true points in this description of the native character.'
Amen.

❧ Sharquiya ❧

To the east and slightly south, or if you are no great geographer, to the right of the Sumayl Gap, as you look at the map, is the Sharquiya. This is one of the traditional divisions of Oman and although some argue that Oman province itself extends further east, today it is more or less correct to think of the Gap as the dividing line. The Sharquiya has for many years now constituted the preserve of the Hirthi sheikhs, and the present incumbent, Ahmed bin Mohammed, has a pervasive and expansionary influence.

Unless you take the long road round the mountains via Izki, the way to the Sharquiya is through the Wadi Aqq; you go up to Fanjah and Bid Bid, and then branch left, cutting into the hills just beyond the village of Sarur. The Wadi Aqq is by tradition a strategic route, possession of which has been of importance; it is the way down which the remnants of Captain Thompson's Beni bu Ali expedition stumbled on their return to Muscat. Along it the road forks left for Qabil, and right for Mudhaibi; a little further on it crosses a ridge in the hills, with a watch-tower menacingly poised above it, and looking back you suddenly see a green splash of palm trees—presumably the watch-tower once had some visual connection with the village. Then on, and down a wadi into the wide plain of the Wadi Nam that leads down to the main Sharquiya villages and thence into the Wadi Batha, curling round beside the Wahiba Sands and ending up down by Bilads Beni bu Hassan and Beni bu Ali.

The landscape in this spacious plain has a quite different character from elsewhere in Oman, just as the Bidiya, further on, has a character wholly its own. I think it is primarily the extent of the horizons coupled with the absence of a single indelibly pronounced mountain skyline; down here, instead of the long straight presence of the Jebal Akhdar on one side, and on the other a flat infinite spread of desert, you are in the midst of a more friendly and less rigid mixture of mountain and plain, almost African in its bright contrasts of light and shade; and away in the distance the Jaalan mountains gently dappled.

There are some large villages along this plain, but today they are all secondary to Qabil, the Hirth capital.

Qabil is an intriguing place. Over in one direction are the hills, with pink salmon splashes of colour reaching up their flanks; this turns out to be piled up sand, blown over from the Wahiba dunes, a signal, maybe, that one day the intervening area too will all be sand. Looking south you can see the sharp line of the sands themselves. And inside, like the proverbial spider, is Sheikh Ahmed bin Mohammed al Hirthi, waiting to receive us.

A visit to Sheikh Ahmed in Qabil was always something of a marathon, partly because his hospitality would not permit you to go without lunch and that would not be served before the afternoon, partly because his great range of interests might involve you in discussion about anything and partly because it often meant a night out camping in the open. The visit could always be guaranteed to be of interest in one way or another. The one I shall remember most vividly took place on 5 June 1967; news of the war (or the 'aggression' as the Arabs subsequently insisted on calling it) had by the time we arrived there not yet reached Qabil, but of course the radio had been full of the building tension for days. We discussed the possibilities, and particularly the role of airpower in anything that might occur. At about midday one of his servants came into the majlis and handed him a piece of paper. Sheikh Ahmed looked at it impassively, and then, with a commanding glance round the room, began to read what was written on it. It was the first news that war had broken out, picked up by his wireless operator, and immediately transmitted downstairs. Bedouin ticker-tape. I can think of nowhere else in Oman where it could conceivably have happened this way, with the possible exception of Ghafat, but even there it would never have been carried out with the Hirthi panache. In the conversation that followed Sheikh Ahmed made a revealing remark about the Omanis, when he referred slightingly to the Arabs who involved themselves in these international political upheavals; it was almost as if, in that breath, he considered the Omanis to be a separate and superior race altogether. Probably he does, and a lot of other Omanis would agree with him.

There is a tradition that the 'seven brothers of el Hasa' founded the cities of Mogadishu and Barawa on the East African coast. This was in the tenth century A.D. It is also a tradition that these gentlemen were of Hirth origin. Whether that be so or not, there certainly was a strong Hirth connection with East Africa, a connection that still exists, although it was largely severed by the Zanzibar revolution of 1963. After 1963 a large number of Omanis fled, and many sought asylum in what they considered to be their homeland. The Sultan was not very welcoming towards them, and many were re-ejected, but a large number of those who did manage to stay may be found in the Sharquiya under the wing of Sheikh Ahmed. The Sultan may have had a good point when he made the decision to keep them out; at least he would have had a strong supporter in Captain Rigby, who was Political Agent in Zanzibar in 1857, and said of the Hirth there, who were at that moment trying to oust Majid from the Sultanate, 'their character is vile in the extreme, from long residence here and constant cohabitation with African slaves . . . slave merchants and slave brokers, [they] are cruel sensual wretches, dead to every feeling of humanity'.[13] (One might add that there are quite a few people in Oman today who would readily apply these words to Sheikh Ahmed; he is by no means a universally popular man.) It is certainly true that, in the thriving days of the slave trade, Qabil was bang on the slave route, either from Sur or from Al Ashkhara, two of the main landing points, particularly in the later years when the British were doing everything they could to suppress it.

The Hirth are a strongly Ibadhi tribe, and you may recall* that they played a leading role in the Imamate movement from 1867 until 1957; first Salih bin Ali, then his son Isa, and then Salih bin Isa who supported the Imam in 1957 and escaped to exile in Dammam where he is living today. It was in this most recent revolt that Ahmed bin Mohammed threw in his lot with the Sultan and was duly rewarded with the sheikhdom of the Hirth. He, like his grandfather and great-grandfather before him, is the acknowledged leader of the Hinawis of the Sharquiya, where the

* See pp. 94 et seq. above.

Hinawi concept, in opposition to the Ghafiris, remains today the
most pronounced in Oman. Hinawi tribes outside the Sharquiya,
however, have never owed allegiance to the Hirth and to that
extent the Sharquiya has always tended to have a separatist
feeling about it.

A few miles south east from Qabil the track crosses into the
Wadi Batha, which then leads for sixty miles beneath the edge of
the Wahiba Sands, ending up indeterminately between Bilad
Beni bu Ali and the sea. After one heavy series of rains recently
there was a huge lake in this area formed by the floodwaters of the
Batha. The end nearer Qabil is called Bidiya; its main town is
Mintrub, and it has a clean and fresh atmosphere all of its own
which makes it a particularly attractive corner of Oman. It is the
tribal area of the Hijriyeen, a large tribe whose former influence
has waned into a sort of take-over by the Hirth.

The heyday of the Hijriyeen was the early nineteenth century
when they alone of Omani tribes inflicted defeats upon the invading Wahhabis. In 1813 Mutlaq al Mutairi, one of the most feared
of the Wahhabi governors of Bureimi, was ambushed by the
Hijriyeen near Mintrub, and killed in the battle; his arms and coat
of mail, his head also according to some sources, were taken to
Muscat, so that the Sultan could see for himself that Mutlaq was
dead. In 1835 his son, Saad, took a force to avenge the death of
his father, but the Hijriyeen, warned of its advance, defeated this
too. After this, the power and influence of the Hijriyeen quickly
seemed to wane.

Nothing can be imagined more quiet and relaxed than the
Bidiya today. The Wahiba Sands hang over the edge of the Wadi
Batha in elegant rippling curves, a feast of aesthetically satisfying
geometrical designs; the sand is a soft pastel shade, from pale
apricot to flaming salmon, and curled into the dunes are a few
villages, green palm trees and the firm square lines of mud houses.
Along the wadi the bedu lunge soundlessly on their camels, pro-
viding a picture that is so timeless as to be primeval. Away in the
east is the cone of Jebal Qahwan, handsomely silhouetted behind
Kamil. No wonder there is a lure in the desert; however, safely
grinding along in a Land-Rover, it is as well to spare a thought for
the miles and miles of hot unyielding sand that stretches south
from the edge of the dunes, and also to wonder how long it will

be before they consume first the villages so closely clustered beneath them, then the wadi, and then all the space to the hills. It may be, however, that some geographer will tell me that this will not happen, that wind velocity and directional forces will leave things as they are. I hope so. But assuredly motor cars will oust those camels before a few years are past.

Mintrub itself is tidy, and has an unexpectedly imposing main street with solid houses and a lofty square tower; round a corner is the husn, and the qadi usually seems to be holding his majlis on the sand outside it. The old Sheikh of the Hijriyeen, Hamdan bin Salim, lives in a rustic garden facing on to the dunes. He is quite deaf. He has a hearing aid, but either does not understand the switches, or its batteries are weak—or, perhaps, for he has a twinkle in his eye, he is a deaf diplomat, and chooses not to hear when he does not want to. It does not really matter, for his garden is idyllic, and if you visit him at the right season you sit in the shade of the trees and eat from great plates of grapes and papaya.

Further on down the Wadi Batha is Kamil, which, hidden in the trees and bushes of the plain underneath Jebal Qahwan, has a fort with a tall slender circular tower. One hot morning I stopped there and saw a large gathering some yards away; we advanced towards each other, and solemnly greeted each other; but the Wali, sensible man, had stopped behind, and quietly waited until I had disposed of the first group and crossed into the shade before welcoming me officially.

Often we used to spend a night under the stars near Qabil before returning to Izki, and very pleasant that could be. One occasion we did not stay was after hearing from Sheikh Ahmed's news service about the outbreak of the June war. Having left Sheikh Ahmed we had to go on to Mintrub because we had said we would, and had been given a private escort for the purpose; *en route* there, however, it seemed to me that I ought to get back to Muscat, since anything might be happening there or elsewhere, and, if it were, Muscat was the place where I should be. We mystified the Hijriyeen considerably, therefore, by suddenly announcing at sundown that we would have to leave to get back to the coast. To them this proved, if proof were required, that modern life was mad. On the road back that night we saw one gazelle, two rabbits, one black cat, a lot of mice and camel spiders, and one bedu who had lost his way.

Half-way between Qabil and Izki is the town of Mudhaibi, which is situated in a plain where the Wadi Ethli flattens out, at the end of some large falajs. The Wadi Ethli leads up to Samad and thence to the fork in the road up in the hills where it was necessary to branch left for Qabil. Mudhaibi is a sizeable town, but not one that figures at all in the history books; I suspect it is comparatively newly founded, no doubt whenever the falajs were dug through the plain to provide it with water. Its appearance is a mixture of Sharquiya and true Omani. Outside the main gate of the town is a large square with a gate that is arched, massive and slightly mysterious. Round the corner from the square is a large walled enclosure, and inside that the Wali has built himself (and this in itself is most unusual in Oman in these days) a smart new house complete with verandahs and arches and rather sickly blue paint.

The Wali is Ali bin Zahir, brother—one of them: you may remember there was another in Sumayl as Wali, and there are six more—of Abdulla at Ghafat.* He is a large and regal character, and always carries a revolver in a wooden case. He is also a very good host, and his *haute cuisine* is known throughout Oman. I recall my first morning snack with him, a sort of breakfast, at which we had wafer-thin pancakes (rather thinner than Breton crêpes) with wild honey, pomegranates, bananas, tea, coffee, and dates in a room (this was in his old house) on the walls of which hung one old coal-iron, some mirrors, a few rifles, and, stuck into clefts in the mud by their points, two daggers. His lunches were always delicately spiced, and the huge plate of rice would be surrounded by smaller plates of meat, eggs, fruits, salads, cakes, custard—a sort of Omani rijstafel. It is a peculiarity of Omani eating habits that the nucleus of any meal is rice and goat meat; elsewhere that I have been in the Arab world sheep has always constituted the meat content, sometimes young camel is served as a special delicacy, but goat would be considered a poor alternative. Not so in Oman, where I have never eaten lamb except as a subsidiary, and very excellent, dish, often in the form

* See page 109 above.

of kebab. In fact goat, if it is well cooked, can be delicious, but even more important is the flavouring of the rice, and the admixture with it of raisins, spices and the juice of fresh limes. In all this Ali bin Zahir is an expert, and he supervises a meal with all the care and panache that the chef might expend in a well-starred Michelin restaurant in France. If Arab food is badly cooked, served up with the minimum of extras, or cold, it can be as nasty as any food I know.

Near Mudhaibi is a green and fertile village called Rawdha. In a shaded path there, I once met a man who had lived for years in the Congo. It surprisingly turned out (in elegant French) that he was a sheikh from the village.

Between Mudhaibi and Izki it is another couple of hours jolting in a Land-Rover, mostly through the Buldan Awamir, the territory of the Awamir. They are a very ancient tribe, and a better-known section live near Bureimi in Abu Dhabi territory; some more own some villages on the Batina near Sib. The capital of this group of villages is Qalat al Awamir, not far from Izki, a notable landmark since the old castle was built on a jagged rock that sticks straight up out of the surrounding plain. It is a poor and depressed place now, dusty and with only one sickly falaj to irrigate its few fields. We sat with the sheikhs on carpets under a Suqma tree; they were all tall, and thin and old; all had straggling beards, and one was a greenish mildewed colour. They were an odd lot, but they seemed to be pleased to see us.

One of the pleasures of driving back to Izki from Mudhaibi is watching the Jebal Akhdar draw closer, particularly if you are lucky and the sky is scattered with cool white fleece clouds. The corner of the Jebal above Izki as it swings round from Nizwa down the Gap looks like a bastion or turret of some mountainous castle. Before reaching it you cross the oil pipeline, just to remind you that it is the twentieth century.

A little to the south, not part of the Sharquiya, but not really part of anything else either, are Adam and Izz. Adam is furthest away from the Jebal of all Omani towns, Izz one of the closest to the Jebal of bedu settlements, and they are connected in a surprising way: the Al Mahariq used to live in Izz and were turned out by the Jenaba, the Jenaba used to own Adam and were overcome by the Al Mahariq; that, at any rate, is the satisfyingly neat formula that I was given. Adam is otherwise famous because the Al bu Said come from it.

It is surprising to find a settled town the size of Adam so far into the desert. However, it is laid up against its own hills of Salakh, Huneidala, and Midhmar, and is fed by falajs from them, so this is probably the explanation of its existence there. Its main gate is set in a very deep archway, and its inhabitants treat Land-Rovers (or visitors) as objects of prey, and will steal anything they can lay their hands on. Izz is the complete opposite: a large date grove with practically no permanent settlement, where the Jenaba come in summer for the date harvest but keep well away from in the winter. In a nutshell, the difference between hadhr and bedu; the hadhr are the settled tribes, those who have rooted themselves around the mountains, the bedu those for whom permanent settlement is as irksome as a fly buzzing around your nostrils. Adam and Izz, as improbable a pair of places as you will find anywhere; when they are linked by a motorway, Oman will really be in the twenty-first century.

Dhahira

The district called Dhahira lies to the north and west of Oman province, always on the desert side of the mountain range. Roughly, it extends between Bureimi in the north to Ibri in the south. Ibri has tended to be the fence between the Imamate and the Wahhabi influences; Bureimi the bone between Oman and the Trucial Coast, and behind the coast the sinister aspirations of the Saudis.

If you visit Bureimi it is difficult to imagine it as a forward base of power. That is what it has been, both for Oman and the Wahhabis, or, in their later incarnation, the Saudis. As political commentators have commented *ad nauseam*, and quite correctly, it is an oasis that is strategically situated, both for the Wadi Jizzi and the Batina, Ibri and Oman, and the Trucial Coast. It is one of those places that, if you happen to be the strongest, you will ensure is yours, and that, if you have lost it, you will await the time that you are strong enough to seize it back again.

Bureimi has over the past few years been so much in the news that most people are tired of being told that the oasis is a group of villages, most of which belong to Abu Dhabi, and a couple to Muscat and Oman. This is by now accepted by a majority of persons, although the Saudi claim to the whole oasis is still a diplomatic gauntlet which is, as far as possible, kept out of sight behind the sofas. The ruler of Abu Dhabi and the Sultan of Muscat and Oman have, with the prolonged assistance of the British Foreign Office, staked out an agreed border between their states; that, in a desert area where every depression in the sand is vividly recognised by a hundred Arabs, is at least something. The Omani part of the oasis is in fact referred to as Bureimi, the Abu Dhabi part as Al Ain, each using the name of the largest village within its area. By now there is very little resemblance between them.

Such are the contortions of the border that, to reach Bureimi
from the Ibri direction, you must pass along in the shadow of
Jebal Hafit in Abu Dhabi territory. You then land up in Al Ain,
and turn right half-way down its main street for Bureimi. Coming up from the Wadi Jizzi direction you can, however, reach
it without leaving Sultanate territory. Between Al Ain and
Bureimi there is no obvious indication where that agreed border
runs, and certainly no one to stop you crossing it, so that there
is no difficulty in comparing the two places.

When I first visited Al Ain in 1966, Shakhbut had only a
month before been deposed; the Zaid spending spree was not
yet under way. Al Ain looked like a sleazy mid-West gold-rush
shanty town minus its saloons, from which the prospectors had
long since departed. Its main street was very dusty, because a
week or two before King Hussein had visited, and the mechanical
graders had hurriedly hacked a dual carriage-way in the sand;
down the middle some oleanders were already looking very
tired. A thin line of stores sold Coca-Cola; a workshop announced
'Al Amin Engineering—welding, denting, painting'; a sinister
sign drew attention to a dentist; camels shared the dust with
Land-Rovers, and two banks bravely vied for business. Two
years later it was in many respects the same, except that a number
of prospectors had somewhat unwillingly returned, the dual
carriage-way was now an unedged and highly dangerous slice of
bitumen through the middle of the place, most of the stores had
been torn down at least once and replaced as untidily elsewhere,
and there were no camels to be seen. The two banks, however,
had become three and were beginning to enjoy themselves, and
logarithmic graph paper was needed to measure the Coca-Cola
sales. One day Al Ain may be a memorial to the benefits of
twentieth-century materialism, but it is not yet.

If Al Ain is doing its best to project A.D. 1968 into the desert,
Bureimi is still firmly entrenched in A.H. 1388. The Wali's castle
is no more modernised than any other in Oman (although his
upper majlis is a delightful and breezy apartment, and doubtless
more comfortable than Zaid's modern guest-house in which the
air-conditioning is inconveniently inconsistent); the suq is a
couple of shady tunnels, but there is a bright white house with
a doctor; there is also a rather rusty petrol pump, but no source

of petrol to make it useful. The pace of life in the oasis is like an eccentric machine, one half pounding away to little effect, the other spluttering with no purpose in view. A visit to Bureimi is a wonderland experience, at the end of which you are quite unsure on which side of the looking glass you are standing.

When the Wahhabis from Hasa first marched into Bureimi in 1800, implanted a Governor there, and began to terrorise the surrounding country with a view to imperialistic domination, at least this uncanny schizophrenia was absent; the whole oasis was pure A.H. 1215. Wahhabism was a theoretical puritanical movement, a back-to-first-principles clarion call that appealed, as so many similar movements have appealed throughout history, to a large number of people. Simplicity is an attractive and appealingly simple peg on which to hang a theory; unfortunately it seldom remains simple, and from the peg, in the name of theory, people manage to take down all sorts of peculiar practices. In the name of simplicity it is extremely simple to become intolerant. Certainly this is what the Wahhabis became.

I have no doubt that the germ of Wahhabi belief and doctrine was logically and seriously believed in by its originators as an agent for cleansing and purifying the souls of men who had become impure and unclean. I have equally little doubt that in practice it turned into an excuse, and justification, for conquest, terrorism and quite unprincipled coercion. In south-eastern Arabia Bureimi was the forward base for propagating Wahhabism.

Oman was subject to a series of raids and invasions in varying degrees of force over a period of seventy years. During this time there were a number of Wahhabi governors of invariable rigidity of purpose in Bureimi: Salim al Hariq, Mutlaq al Mutairi, Umar bin Ufaisan, Saad bin Mutlaq, Ahmed al Sudairi, Turki bin Ahmed al Sudairi—a roll-call of names that might even now inject a shiver of fear into the tribes of the Bureimi area, the Dhahira, the Batina coast, and even other further parts of Oman.

Proselytisation should have been their prime purpose, and there was certainly an element of this in their activity. Some of the tribes around Bureimi are to this day Wahhabi, and, as we have seen, way down in the Jaalan the Beni bu Ali were converted and have remained Wahhabi. Their expansion was, however, primarily political with a strong flavour of plain rapacity;

every action, every raid could be, and was, measured in terms of Maria Theresa dollars, and many of them were highly profitable. Payment was enforced, of course, in the name of religion; it was zakat, not plunder. There was, however, another aspect to these Wahhabi raids, which must not be overlooked; many of them were at the request of Omanis. As has been described, the Al bu Said family was anything but a harmonious group even under a powerful Sultan like Said, and splinter groups were, to all intents and purposes, independent rulers of separate city-states, particularly on the Batina. The Wahhabis provided a source of support to these princelets, either when they were threatened with subjection, or when they thought it was time to subject someone else. In earlier times the Persians had often fulfilled the same role. Any opportunity such as this was, of course, tailor made for the Wahhabis, and they never failed to make good use of it. Just occasionally they would make too much use of it, as when the 1865 raid extended to Sur, and Pelly mounted his reprisal upon Dammam.

One should be clear, I think, that the Wahhabis would have undoubtedly conquered Oman if it had not been for the British presence supporting the Sultan. I do not mean that if this had happened Oman would not exist today, for I suspect that the Omanis would have rallied themselves and at some later time (perhaps when the Wahhabis were themselves attacked by the Turks in Hasa in 1871) re-established their independence; nor do I think that in fact the Wahhabis would have ever overrun the Ibadhi strongholds of the Jebal Akhdar; but they would certainly have interrupted, at the very least, the Al bu Said rule. They would never, I am equally sure, have ousted Ibadhism as a religion, and the Ibadhis would have ended up in power again. However, the conditionals of history are not very fruitful. The Al bu Said kept going. Sometimes it was, however, a close thing; for instance, in 1853 at Sohar Sayyid Thwaini (then acting as Regent for his father who was absent in Zanzibar) and Ahmed al Sudairi concluded 'A Treaty of Alliance, Offensive and Defensive, between H. H. Sayyid Thwaini, Governor of Muscat, and Abdulla bin Feisal, Son of the Wahhabi Chief and Commander of the Wahhabi Expedition into Oman'; if it had not ended in this treaty, the Wahhabis would almost certainly have

continued their offensive to Muscat. One might add that the
zakat payable by the Thwaini on this occasion was M.T.D. 60,000
immediately, M.T.D. 20,000 per year subsequently, and 500 bags
of rice, 5 kegs of powder and a quantity of lead for the garrison
at Bureimi. Such was the way of the Wahhabis.

Zakat, in its strict sense and application, is a perfectly respectable religiously ordained payment somewhat akin to the old tithe
in England. Its most common application is to the fruits of the
earth, and in Oman today zakat is payable at the traditional rate
of 5 per cent of value on produce grown on land watered by
wells, 10 per cent of value on produce grown on land watered by
falajs (originally, as with the church tithe, the payment was 5
per cent and 10 per cent of the actual produce). What the
Wahhabis did was to extend to their tribute demands such as
that made on Thwaini in 1853, the term zakat, thus giving it a
spurious spiritual justification.

The example of the Wahhabis in the nineteenth century was
followed with remarkable exactitude by the Saudis in the
twentieth. The Saudi claim to Bureimi, with its long drawn-out
dramatic climax from 31 August 1952 until 26 October 1955, was
intellectually based on an elaborate structure of evidence from
zakat payments and various loyalty documents. J. B. Kelly's[14]
unravelling of the facts behind this façade is, for those who
know anything of the story, a fascinating academic detective
story; even those who do not might become gripped by it. However, even though Kelly has turned the Saudi 'Memorial' inside
out, and Bureimi is basking peacefully beneath a partially Abu
Dhabi and partially Omani sun, the Saudi claim has not yet been
withdrawn. The time bomb is still ticking.

In 1935 the Saudi/Abu Dhabi/Qatar border was all but
settled. But not quite. In 1949 the Saudis presented the claim
that included most of Abu Dhabi and Bureimi; south into Oman
the claim was never actually defined. From circumstantial
evidence it is clear that the claim was made, and the dispute
reactivated, because of the suspected oil reserves in Abu Dhabi
territory (later proved, and now being exported in large quantities). Bureimi, although in popular press mythology it is rather
insecurely anchored upon an underground lake of oil, was picked
on by the Saudis not for this reason at all, but because it is the

only fixed point on which to pick in the area, and because, of course, they had been there before and could weave a handsome historical cobweb of claims around it.

Between 1949 and 1952 inconclusive talks took place, and on 31 August 1952 Turki bin Ataishan drove into the oasis as the appointed Saudi Governor. Soon after, the Sultan gathered his tribal force in Sohar, only to be asked by the Consul General, prompted by the Foreign Office persuaded by the State Department, to lay off;* and it is worth remembering that at this juncture the old Imam, Mohammed bin Abdulla al Khalili, had also gathered a force at Dariz, near Ibri, to assist the Sultan. Further discussions then dragged on, while in Bureimi Turki bribed away in aid of Saudi proof of ownership; finally in 1954 Arbitration Proceedings were agreed upon by the Saudis, and in October 1955 they dramatically fragmented when Sir Reader Bullard, the British delegate, accused the Saudis of trying to subvert the tribunal. Stories of the scale of bribery are legion; many are probably true, but the details and the rumours are not of useful relevance. On 26 October 1955, Turki and the remaining Saudi detachment in Bureimi were evicted by the Trucial Oman Scouts, and they have not yet returned. On that day the British Government declared a frontier which is utilised for all practical purposes to this day.

There can be no doubt that the presence of the Saudis in Bureimi between 1952 and 1955 was one of the main reasons for the Imamate revolt of 1957–9 in Oman. The support of the Saudis for Ghalib and Talib was seen by them to be a legitimate political tactic to gain effective control of Oman. To what extent the Imamate leaders were bought, both morally and financially, in the early days is not clear, but certainly the process was accelerated as time passed. Ghalib bin Ali was elected Imam, allegedly according to traditional methods, in May 1954 on the death of Imam Mohammed bin Abdulla; certainly he had the right qualifications for Imam, but it is hard to believe that there was not an element of manipulation in the election. Ghalib anyway was not, and is not, the significant character in the game; the important, ambitious and varyingly resolute protagonists

* See also page 67 above.

were Talib, his brother, Suleiman bin Himyar, and Salih bin Isa. There is a story that ten years before, in 1944, at a time when the Imam Mohammed was thought to be at the point of death, Isa bin Salih (who did not die until 1946)* and Suleiman bin Himyar agreed to split the country two ways between them, Hinawi and Ghafiri, and offered the Sultan the nominal title of Imam. It is significant mainly as showing the primary interest of Salih and Suleiman, which was simply their own aggrandisement. This is particularly true of Suleiman, who wavered one way and the other throughout the early days of the new Imamate, and only came down firmly on the side of Ghalib in July 1957 at a time when a reading of all the entrails pointed to his imminent victory.

Between May and October 1954, and this was at the height of Saudi activity in Bureimi, the Imamate spread its tentacles north from Nizwa into the Ibri area. In October Sultanate forces re-took Ibri, then Nizwa and other towns of the Interior. In January 1955 the Sultan made his historic trip from Salala with a collection of cars and trucks to Nizwa, Bureimi, Sohar, and thence to Muscat. It was the first, and so far the last, time he has seen the Interior of Oman. Salih bin Isa and Talib fled to Saudi Arabia, Ghalib went, more or less on parole, to Balad Seit near Ghafat, and Suleiman bin Himyar remained under loose surveillance in Muscat, having pledged his loyalty to the Sultan.

The country was at this moment unified for the first time for close on one hundred years, but instead of vigorously consolidating this new situation of potential strength (made even stronger by the final eviction of the Saudis from Bureimi in October), the Sultan returned to Salala and the Sultanate Government slithered back into its usual unimaginative ways. Talib was in the meantime active in Dammam, and in June 1957 was ready for his come-back. In July the revolt started, and Suleiman bin Himyar drove quietly out of Muscat in his car to join it. The situation quickly got out of hand, the Sultan asked for assistance from Britain, and was given it; almost as quickly the situation was recovered, and the rebels retired to the Jebal Akhdar.

Again a partial 1955 situation was allowed to develop, rebel

* See family tree on page 116.

activity and mining increased, until in January 1959 British troops were again asked to assist the Sultanate forces in winkling the rebels out of their last strongholds in the Jebal. Sayq was captured, but the leaders, Ghalib, Talib, Suleiman and Salih all escaped. They are said to have ridden across the desert by camel. They ended up in Dammam, where they are still living to this day. Mining of roads, and other inconvenient terrorist activity continued for a couple of years but then gradually declined and virtually stopped altogether.

If we have strayed geographically from Bureimi in these last paragraphs, we are still nevertheless firmly attached to it politically, for the fuel for the Imamate revolt certainly came from there. For Oman it will be a bad day if the Saudis ever fetch up there again, just as it has always been bad for them when they have been in Bureimi. It is remarkable how strategic considerations can inflate the importance of a place. When you fly over the straggling oasis, dominated by the whaleback ridge of Jebal Hafit, you are unlikely to give it a thought; just shrug, revert to your detective story, and wish the plane would quickly get somewhere it can land.

Down the other end of the Dhahira is Ibri, the largest—the only large—town between Nizwa and Bureimi. Wellsted visited Ibri in 1836, and produced one of the most damnatory and descriptive sentences I have ever read about a town. He wrote:[15] 'The neighbouring Arabs observe that to enter Ibri a man must either go armed to the teeth, or as a beggar with a cloth, and that not of decent quality, round his waist.' When Thesiger was travelling in Oman in 1949 the reputation of Ibri had not improved much, but this was primarily owing to the unsavoury attitude of the Wali, a fanatical Ibadhi appointed by the Imam, towards Christians. The Wali was Mohammed bin Salim al Ruqeishi; I knew one of his sons, and a grandson, in Izki and it would be hard to imagine from meeting them that less than twenty years, hardly a generation, ago, the rigidities of Ibadhi customs held such influence in Oman. Poor old Sheikh Mohammed, whose crime when all was said and done was only to have been an Ibadhi in an Ibadhi society, was put into Jalali by the Sultan after the suppression of the Imamate revolt, and died there, at an advanced age, in January 1968.

Ibri now is a thoroughly genial market town with a thriving suq; being the closest place of any importance to the Oil Company base at Fahud it has almost inevitably benefited in economic terms from this. It has not yet, however, been altered appreciably in character from this proximity (if you accept fifty miles distance as being near), probably because the Oil Company employees, other than Omanis, of course, can only visit it if they have good reason. It has not yet become a tourist centre. The old Imam would appreciate that.

Ibri stands between low hills at the confluence of a large wadi drainage area, one tip of which snakes up into the mountains and forms the Wadi Hawasina watershed. In the other direction it looks out over the desert, and the border between the hadhr and bedu might be drawn with a ruler beyond the date gardens of Ibri. A few miles away is the settlement of Tanam, the Duru 'capital'. There is no similarity, no point of contact between the two; one symbolises the settled town life, the other the small element of permanence that the desert tribes require, a source of dates (and some, the real bedu, do not even have that); it is the same contrast as with Adam and Izz.

The Dhahira is linked to the Batina coast by two main wadi routes, the Jizzi from Bureimi to Sohar, as important a link as the Sumayl Gap, and the Hawasina route from Ibri to Khaboura, of only secondary significance, probably because of its tortuous narrowness. The Jizzi route is broken and slow enough by Land-Rover, but is capable of improvement and could, and no doubt will, turn into an ordinary mountain pass; when that happens it will be a favourite tourist route, for it has many of the right ingredients, fine scenery, wild gorges, water and villages. At the highest village, near the watershed, they have built a small dam of palm logs and have a pleasant pond there; at the lowest village, nearest Sohar, there is one of the best examples of a falaj syphon, where the Falaj al Muleina is carried under the wadi starting from nearly forty feet above it, and ending up the other side forty feet above it. When you come upon it, you can be excused for assuming that an old aqueduct has broken and lost its bridge. But going up the Jizzi I like to think back to Malik bin Fahm and those Persian elephants laboriously walking up the wadi to Nizwa from Sohar; the only animal curiosity that I encountered there was the comparatively domestic sight of a camel leading two cows on a rope.

The Wadi Hawasina route is very narrow and twisting for most of its length, really no more than a cut in the mountains that floodwaters have carved; at the top, before sinking into this ravine there are some fine open views of the mountain range. To be caught in the Wadi Hawasina in a storm would be a most unpleasant and dangerous experience, and for this reason I doubt that it will ever be much more than a track. It is named after the Hawasina tribe, who are the most loyal to the Sultan, and the most trusted by him. Most of his private askars in Salala—a sort of palace guard—are Hawasina, and they also by custom provide many of the askars to Walis; and also, you may remember, the guard for the walls of Muscat. Their senior sheikh is Sultan bin Seif who lives at the end of a falaj leading from the wadi at Hujayri, right on the Batina plain not far from Sahm. Sheikh Sultan acts from time to time as a sort of roving ambassador for the Sultan, and loves to recall the part he played in helping the Oil Company in the early days. Once, after an excellent lunch with Sheikh Sultan, I saw a large thorn bush moving towards me. It was a camel, wholly enveloped in its load; inspiration for an Omani production of *Macbeth*.

The remaining piece of the Dhahira is the Beni Kaab country north-east of Bureimi. As so often happens in Oman this area feels quite different from other parts; you can drive over a pass, past a hill, through a wadi, across a track, and suddenly the whole nature of the country changes. I suppose the same happens in other countries too, but in Oman, where everything is so fundamentally bare and empty, you do not expect it and it can sometimes produce an almost physically jarring sensation, as if one has momentarily lost one's moorings. The road to Mahadha, the Beni Kaab capital, is also the road to Sumayneh, a Sultanate customs post, and thence to Dubai and the Trucial Coast. Much of the country is wild and mountainous, but there is also a potential for agriculture. Sheikh Abdulla bin Salim has begun to tap it, and will produce in Mahadha for you the most delicious vegetables and fruits. Sheikh Abdulla is a surprising character: to begin with, he and his family play a prominent part in the Kelly detective story on Bureimi, but that hardly prepares one for his almost Lebanese appearance when he advances to greet you in suede shoes and a well-cut jacket superimposed on his normal Omani attire; nor do you expect to sit in armchairs and sip tea from a more or less elegant porcelain tea-set, listening to a stream of exquisitely modulated Oxford Arabic. Perhaps it is even more astonishing to discover that this elegant person, having been banished some years ago for sharp practice of one kind or another, mounted a camel and rode all the way to Salala to seek the Sultan's forgiveness. The Sultan was apparently so startled by this feat that he reinstated him.

That brings to an end our trip round the Interior, or at least that part of it which most Muscat residents think of as the Interior. Beyond is the desert.

Desert

For an Englishman the danger of the desert is that he becomes lyrical about it. Such at least has been the tradition amongst English travellers, for whom more than for other nations the desert has provided a sort of spiritual ambrosia. On the whole this was, I think, before the era of the Land-Rover which, enormously useful though it is, is in no way conducive to fulfilment of anything but the journey in hand. My knowledge of the Oman desert, you may be relieved to know, would be nothing if it were not for the Land-Rover.

The desert is never all of a piece, any more than the coast or the mountains; it changes, and with it the characteristics, even the way of life, of those who live in it. Up in the north part, towards Bureimi, it is, not unnaturally, most un-Omani, mixed up with the tribes of Abu Dhabi and with the influences of the outside world of Saudi Arabia. The main tribes are the Naim and Al bu Shamis, whose names will be most familiar to those who have read about the Bureimi dispute; they wavered in every direction, as the magnet seemed stronger one side or the other. They still drift over the border. It would be surprising if they did not, for they are bedu and, for bedu, borders, political borders that is, are a meaningless concept. The Al bu Shamis are, strictly, a chip off the more ancient Naim, but there is little love lost between them now. The senior sheikh of the Al bu Shamis is still Sheikh Mohammed bin Salman, a dark beetling-eyebrowed old rogue, whom I first met in the midst of Bureimi suq; he has done well to last this long. Sheikh Hamad bin Silf of the Naim died last year at the age, it is said, of ninety: practically blind, he would still ride a camel ten miles in a day and think nothing of it. Meeting men like this had a certain glamour, for they had played their part in history and had been recorded for it; not a great part in a world context, but a considerable one in the context of the desert, and they are duly honoured.

The Naim and Al bu Shamis are, in Oman, the only major tribes that use the traditional 'black tents' and practise the sport of hawking. The country up here is sandy but also full of scrub, the sort that bustard like, and bustard are the main prey for hawks. Further south, the country and vegetation changes and the bustard have, if they were there before, been hunted to extinction. Indeed, the number even in the Al bu Shamis country is now much reduced, as are the number of hawks owned. It has become an expensive sport, and the richer sheikhs of the Trucial Coast and the Gulf make it more expensive each year.

If you are looking for the sheikhs you are most likely to find the Naimi ones at a well called Dhaliya, and the Shamsi ones at Sunainah. At Sunainah P.D.(O.) have drilled for, but not so far found, oil. When you sit on carpets spread over a sand ridge, drink coffee, and listen to the evening sounds of a bedu encampment, it is hard to remember that a few hundred yards behind you are the traces of an old drilling location, in the centre of it a piece of concrete with an iron pipe sticking out. And, at that, there might have been more.

Further south, and covering an immense tract of desert, are the Duru. Thesiger quotes[16] one of his companions: 'You cannot trust the Duru. Too many people who travel with them die of snake-bite.' And he certainly had great difficulty with them. But that was twenty or so years ago, when Ruqeishi was Wali in Ibri and the Imam in full power, and no European had been in the area since Cox, who went under the auspices of the Sultan in 1901. Now the Duru are a different proposition; out for what they can get, of course, but the poison has been drawn—because they get a lot more without using it.

The Duru hold such a very large traditional area simply because, I have always assumed, there was so little in it to attract other tribes. It is an irony, or justice if you prefer (or the will of God as they would say), that the oil fields of Oman are right in the middle of it; and that, because it is such a large area, a majority of the Oil Company work takes place, almost by definition, within it. And so the Duru have benefited more than most from the oil era—in terms of employment, that is, for the income from the oil goes directly, of course, to the Sultan.

Fahud, Natih and Yibal, the three oil accumulations that have so far been discovered and are being produced, are about as unattractive as it is possible to imagine places to be. This is more especially the case in summer when the shade temperature (if there were any shade) would be around 130°F. and a miasma of heat covers everything. There is only one piece of drama in Fahud, and that is the sight of the original I.P.C. well, a failure that led to most of the partners withdrawing from the venture, just four hundred yards from another well now steadily producing its few thousand barrels a day. Such are the tribulations and risks of the oil industry. Never mind, it is all one to the Duru.

The Duru area varies significantly, but it is constructed round three main arteries, the Wadis al Ain, Aswad and Amairi. Artery is perhaps a misleading term, for they are normally dry, only filling up furiously for a few hours after a tropical storm; nevertheless, though dry on the surface, the moisture remains underground to nurture grazing for the Duru herds of camels, goats and sheep. More than that, there is also water in quantity underground where the geological formations are right to conserve it; for instance, at Awaifi in the Wadi Amairi, where P.D.(O.) has had a pump for years, which produces water for Fahud and many of the mobile exploration camps in the area at the rate of more than six thousand gallons per day, and has never yet showed any signs of running dry. This provides some evidence that if the water resources of the desert were scientifically assessed and used, much could be done to develop some form of agriculture.

These three large Duru wadis, and indeed all others on the desert side of the mountains, bear few of the characteristics of a valley, the normal English equivalent translation. They are, in fact, depressions in the landscape that carry water if there is any, but not in any consistent sort of way. Through a stony plain they may cut a route that is clearly defined and circumscribed, but in more sandy areas there may be a mass of alternative routes over a wide area, which itself, because of the larger water potential beneath it, will be more luxuriously scattered with trees and bushes than the surrounding blank desert. Down in the Wadi al Ain near Lekhweir it is extremely difficult to pick a way through the sand dunes scattered within the wadi if you happen to have missed the track.

Asa wadi disappears further into the desert so the wadi bed becomes even less distinct. Ultimately it peters out. In the case of the three large Duru wadis, however, the petering out takes place in the area known as the Umm al Samim (the Mother of Poison), a sinister tract which has an almost mythological reputation as a quicksand into which anything from camels to whole cities have at one time or another sunk without trace. It is an extremely unpleasant spot, but its reputation is inflated. It is true that after heavy rains it becomes the cesspit of the three wadis and a slippery, slithery, oozy cesspit at that; to get stuck in the Umm al Samim is in no way difficult, but I think it would take a very long time even for a camel actually to sink right in. Mind you, some parts are worse than others, and all of it is worse after rain, but in 1962 P.D.(O.) managed to get a drilling rig into the northern part of it and drilled a hole there. One day I went to view this desolate site of grey salty mud; in places it has crystallised into a white flaky cover, sometimes it is dark mud, sometimes furrowed like a ploughed field, in places like a bog. I kept severely to what, in 1962 anyway, had been a track. Only the Duru drivers remained cheerful; they were hard at work collecting slabs of very dirty rock-salt.

Salt is about the only thing faintly describable as a Duru industry. Both in the Umm al Samim area, but more particularly from a hill to the south called Qarat al Milh, they cut slabs of rock-salt, carry it off on camels, and sell it in Ibri suq. Also available from Qarat Kibrit nearby is a type of rock-sulphur which is used, after suitable preparation, as a cure for camel mange (though now they have discovered that Gammexane concentrate, sold for quite other purposes, is the most effective antidote).

Beyond the Umm al Samim, which, when you come to think of it, might have been more like Lake Tchad (and full of fish, not mud) if the geology around and underneath it had been different, you come to the sands proper—the edge of Saudi Arabia, and the edge of the Empty Quarter. Down in the Sahma area the dunes can be very beautiful: in winter, at dawn, when it is cool and the air is still, and the edges of the dunes swirl and swing in contours and ripples of symmetry, as if the wind has been for centuries doodling the desert into perfect geometrical curves; but it can also be so hot down there that your eyeballs burn dry, and the shapes of the dunes are hidden in the heat or in the blowing sand. It is then extremely unpleasant.

Not far north of the Umm al Samim is one of those pin-points which modern international diplomacy turns, willy-nilly, into a potential *casus belli*. Saudi Arabia, Abu Dhabi and Oman must meet somewhere and it happens to be at Umm al Zamul (Mother of a special sort of rush matting). I drove there one day, just to say I had been there. It is a well in a bowl of sand dunes, with unpleasant salty water. I was never very clear which block of sand belonged to Saudi Arabia, which to Oman or Abu Dhabi; as far as I can gather none of them would agree anyway, and for practical purposes a *cordon sanitaire* is drawn round the well to form a neutral zone. That could lead to a pretty diplomatic pickle one day, if oil, for instance, came out of that well instead of the tainted water.

Of all their variegated bits of desert the Duru sheikhs seem to prefer the Wadi Aswad, and that is where they tend to migrate so long as the grazing is adequate. Their senior sheikh is Ali bin Hilal who permitted Thesiger to pass through Duru territory in 1949; another sheikh, Huaishil, who was Thesiger's chief Duru helper during his journeys at that time, can also be met without difficulty at Fahud or, if he is not working on behalf of P.D.(O.), wherever his fareeg may be. The Duru, together with most of the other bedu in Oman, live in, if that is the right preposition, fareegs. A fareeg is no more than a halting place, usually a tree, where the family will settle for as long as they want before moving on to another one. Round the tree they may hang pieces of tenting, or build up a burasti hut, put up a pen or thorn thickets to keep camels and goats in at night; it will become a temporary, or in certain circumstances a more or less permanent, home. If they move off, they will inevitably return there later, maybe some months, maybe not for a year, but a right of possession to a certain tree will persist.

Sheikh Ali, one felt, was always happier when in his fareeg in the Wadi Aswad than in his rather more sophisticated piece of burasti at Tanam. Tanam, a few miles from Ibri, is a date grove, and to it, therefore, in season the Duru tend to gravitate; but they get away again, back to the desert, as soon as they can. In Tanam there are now a few water pumps and some cultivation, and even one or two mud buildings, usually store rooms. This is the precise moment for a sociologist to initiate a study into the process of bedu settlement, the transition from bedu to hadhr. It has just started, and it will take a long time, but soon it will be too late to record the whole cycle.

Now, however, before taxi-ranks and tobacconists start up in Tanam, it is still a romantic pleasure, tinged as such pleasures so often are with some discomfort, to sit with Sheikh Ali in his fareeg, sip his coffee, pick a sandy date off his dish, and wonder if you are going to get away without commitment to his some-what basic lunch (none of Ali bin Zahir's *cordon bleu* cookery here). I recall one occasion when Ali spoke of the old days when tribes were tribes and raids were raids; 'and', he said, 'what would you have done with houses in those days? A fareeg could be sacked harmlessly, and replaced as swiftly as the raid was over.' There is something in that. And so saying, he jumped into the Land-Rover for a lift to Ibri. A cry, and we stopped. Out leaped a Duru, picked up from the sand a letter from the Minister of the Interior that I had just delivered to him, handed it to Sheikh Ali, who tucked it back into his head-dress whence it had escaped.

The other major Bedu tribes of Oman are the Jenaba, the Wahiba and the Harasis. Borders between tribes are as hazy as borders between Middle Eastern sheikhdoms or whole countries, but as a general principle the Jenaba live between the Duru and the Wadi Halfayn, and also along much of the coast between the Barr al Hikman and the Dhofar border; the Wahiba live to the east of the Wadi Halfayn towards the coast, including the Wahiba Sands; and the Harasis live in the south-eastern corner of the country, south of the Wahiba and Jenaba and east of the Duru, spread over a large and unsavoury tract of desert called the Jiddat al Harasis.

The Wadi Halfayn and Wadi Andam, running partially parallel until they merge, are two more of the large desert wadis similar to the three Duru ones; the Halfayn, you may recall, started in the main Jebal range, and cut through the middle of Izki before flattening out into the desert. Down near Afar, and further south, the wadi is wide, full of skinny trees, and looks as if it might turn into a thick jungle if the weather suddenly changed and gave it fifty inches of rain a year for a few years. The Wadi Halfayn, together with its tributaries, ends up either in the Barr al Hikman according to one theory or in the sea beyond it according to another; it is a fairly academic point since there is very little water left anyway by the time it has got that far. The Hikman are a small separate tribe who live off the sea; their sheikh, if not to be found on an island called Mahout, will probably be at Jawba, which I once visited shortly after heavy rains, and it was deep in a thick green weed of a pea variety through which the Land-Rover crept, its whole engine completely lost to view.

The effect of rain on the desert is quite startling. The well-used phrase is that it blooms. In Oman it just goes green, given the right amount of rain, and instead of being a glaring expanse of gravel it becomes a sort of African veldt. Indeed, having seen a few gazelle running and jumping across a plain, you look around for the giraffe and zebra. They are not there, and never have been, although a hundred years ago you might have seen a few ostrich. If you are very lucky you might see oryx. I never did, although on one occasion I tried very hard, and with a Harsousi guide nearly succeeded. He found the tracks of six, and some of his colleagues confirmed that a group had been around the area a few days before. We were unlucky, and I never saw anything except oryx droppings. Apparently oryx show up vividly white against the desert gravel, and have an extremely keen sense of smell. I was assured, however, that they have no fear of camels, and that the way to get close is to lie flat on a camel and advance up-wind. The other way, which is why they are nearly extinct, is to chase them from a Land-Rover until they drop. (This barbarous activity will in due course also extinguish gazelle from the desert; it is, I am glad to say, officially banned by the Sultan, although parties from Abu Dhabi and Qatar still engage in it.)

After exceptionally heavy rain you may even get lakes in the desert. I would never have believed this if I had not seen it with my own eyes, and actually gone swimming in one. This was in the area, roughly, of the sands at the edge of Sahma. I was told of these lakes, and assumed an exaggeration; but not a bit of it, precisely two months after the rains I swam in a lake that was still a mile long and half a mile wide and three feet deep in one corner of it. It was, too, as clear as a mirror and a very bright blue and green. Very soon after the storms small creatures, apparently self-generated, began to live in the lakes; they look like one of the links between primeval life and the twentieth century. They will live, it seems, in egg form for up to ten years, preserved in the hot dry sand like the sleeping princess, awaiting the next rains and their particular kiss of life.

Another possible significance of these lakes: not far from this general area, a fairly large number of flint arrow-heads, axe-heads, scrapers and other less obvious tools have been found. They are precisely the same as those found the other side of the Empty Quarter. Finding this elegant evidence of human activity in the midst of the Sahma Sands compelled one to assume that in much earlier days the geography, or climate, of the area must have been so different as to support settled human life in it. Such an assumption seemed an incredible one, until I saw these lakes; if, a thousand years ago, they had formed annually instead of, say, every ten years, then it seems to me that those neolithic Arabs might have been able to live a comfortable enough life near Zauliyah to produce such exciting arrow-heads.

Those were not the only lakes produced by that particular set of storms. When later I made a trip through the Huqf, we found a lake at Ain Thath; almost literally found, for the Harsousi guide with us said he had never seen one there before, and that usually it was only a well. How accurate that was, I do not know (although I never found anyone else who had ever heard of a lake being there), but it was a large expanse of water, about two miles by one mile, and there were a lot of those splendid birds, stilts, standing immobile at its edge. Further on, at Ain Salait, not far from Jawba, there was another lake; beside this one, at the edge of the water, were a flock of flamingoes.

So, not surprisingly, rain has an exhilarating effect upon the desert. Most of the time, however, there has not been any rain for months or years, and then it is a very different affair. Much of the Oman desert, before you reach the sands proper, is flat featureless gravel plain, very often black, though sometimes the stones turn a purplish or greenish colour. Late on a hot summer afternoon, with the sun a burning platinum ball through the windscreen, the stones reflect the light like a shining black ice-rink to 360 degrees of the horizon. You can be there with nothing all round you except that gravel, wherever you look.

P.D.(O.) has a spine road through the desert; it is an old I.P.C. graded track, in some places still quite smooth, in others broken or hidden by fresh dunes. The craziest journey I did was to go from Heima to Sahma, back to Zauliyah and from there to Izki all in one day; it was 375 miles.

Heima, well into Harasis country, has a certain notoriety since there is a P.D.(O.) water well there, not necessarily in use, and it is a landmark for SAF on their long haul from Beit al Falaj to Salala by road. About sixty miles north of Heima through the dunes—past the place where later I had that swim—is Zauliyah. This too was an old P.D.(O.) camp; if it were not, there would be nothing to pin-point on a flat expanse of grey sand. Old drums, a skeleton of a windsock, telegraph poles, blocks of cement, pieces of Land-Rover, all burnt and blistered by an interminable sun, and, in a depressing way, an insult to the desert. Another forty-eight miles further north is a place hopefully marked on maps as Sahma North.

From Zauliyah to Izki is about 250 miles, and the only way to drive this infinitely tedious stretch, particularly in mid summer, is to cut off consciousness and trust to automatic reaction. I find that the desolation of this desert is accentuated by the rusty old drums spaced over the area like disconsolate signposts; in summer they float in a mirage like some shimmering supernatural object, growing, receding, changing shape, until suddenly you are close enough to get them anchored to the sand. A sorry sort of memorial to the oil industry; but they might save your life.

A peculiarity of Heima, and all that area, is that at certain unexpected seasons of the year you may wake up to find a dense fog all round you. The sea is not so far away, and given the right mixture of sea breeze and desert heat, fog is the result. On the one occasion that we seriously looked for oryx, our main apprehension was that the morning might be foggy. Near here I saw a group of fennec foxes, small silvery animals, and a jerboa, which walked into a tent looking for scraps; also some desert hares and monitor lizards. There are two sorts of these lizards, one called a Dhub, which the bedu consider to be a delicacy, and in pursuit of which they will leap from a Land-Rover and charge after the creature until it cowers in terror from the wild shouting that follows it wherever it turns; the other, much larger, is called an

Abu Ruwwal. The Abu Ruwwal can be two or more feet long,
has a vicious scaly tail and hisses like a snake. Wisely, nobody
eats it.

I was told by a seismologist that he had once seen an Omani
sand-cat that looked like a large ginger tom, and on another
occasion had rescued a Terek sandpiper which had flown off-
course in the desert; they took it next day in a Land-Rover to the
coast, but it died *en route*. Apart from mice and camel spiders,
large hairy brutes with lots of long legs, I have not come across
other animals. The fox, incidentally, is a sort of mascot to the
Harasis, who will often leave, in some throw-back of pagan
tradition, a libation of food for a 'Husseini' when they have
finished their own meal. The Harasis are serious about this, but
are prepared also to joke about it; the turtle is a similar Jenaba
mascot, but they become very angry if it is even mentioned.

The road to the coast from the Jiddat al Harasis takes you to
Duqm, another ghost settlement from the old I.P.C. oil-rush era.
In 1954 P.D.(O.) used Duqm as a base for their penetration into
the interior, since the Imamate at that time denied them access
from Azaiba through the mountains. Now only a few Jenaba
fishermen live there; one claims that he still holds the key of the
store, hopeful perhaps for ten years' arrears of wages. The Indian
Ocean slaps down hard on the beach, and a mile or two out into it
stands a squared-off rock-stack, apparently as flat as glass on top.

The coastal area north from here up to the Barr al Hikman is
loosely called the Huqf (which strictly refers to the escarpment
that is its boundary with the Jiddat al Harasis). It is a very broken
area of hills, wadis, inlets of mud salt-flats known as sabkha and
rocky plains. I drove through some time after the storms that had
turned the Jiddat green, and so saw it at its best, led unfalteringly
by a Harsousi who guided us as if he had done the trip weekly for
the past two years (in fact he had only once been in the area in a
Land-Rover, and rather more frequently on a camel twelve years
before).

In my experience, not all bedu have this uncanny sense of
direction, but certainly the Harasis seem to. I suppose that the
more diluted with either settled life or European-type work the
bedu become, the more they lose their traditional aptitudes. Of
all of them, the Harasis are the least diluted. They have no settled

area at all, no date groves, just the Jiddat. And they never feel really satisfied unless they are down there in that inhospitable area; they will work for a bit, but then one day it is all too much for them, and they will resign, and return to the Jiddat. They even have their own language, a version of the South Arabian dialects, quite incomprehensible to any other Arab. They are true individualists, if ever there were any.

Desert, then, can cover a multitude of different sorts of ground. People tend, however, to feel a bit cheated if there is no sand. Oman can produce one large tract of wholly unmitigated sand, enough to satisfy the most unyielding visionary: the Wahiba Sands. This is pure dune country, low in the south, rising to hundreds of feet in height on the northern fringe along the Wadi Batha. The sands run in long parallel valleys north to south, and are practically impassable from west to east. I have only looked at them from the outside; from the Sharquiya, and from an aeroplane going down the coast. The view from the latter showed nothing but sand, and sand, and sand, and left me with no latent wish to plod through them on a camel.

Beyond the Wahiba Sands, the Jiddat al Harasis, Heima and all those remote desert places, and if you continue far enough, say another three hundred miles, you reach Salala, capital of Dhofar.

Dhofar is the land of frankincense and merits a mention in Genesis, according to the scholars, who claim that Sephar (chapter 10, verse 30) should be identified with Dhofar. Said bin Sultan tried to annex it to his empire in 1829, but failed, although subsequently Turki bin Said and Salim bin Thwaini claimed that deputations from Dhofar had visited Muscat and had given their allegiance. During the nineteenth century a number of eccentric characters ruled there, but it was not until 1879 that Muscat could claim any practical responsibility for it. Since then it has remained a possession, almost literally, of the Sultan. There is no link, cultural, tribal, economic, or historic between Dhofar and Oman proper; the only link is geographic, in that Dhofar is contiguous to Oman. On these grounds it might as well belong to the Sultanate; certainly no other country has any better claim.

Nowadays Dhofar* has deep significance to Muscat and Oman,

* See also page 200 below.

in that the Sultan has lived there off and on for thirty-five years, and permanently for the last ten. This is highly inconvenient to everybody except the Sultan himself, and especially to SAF who are committed to holding Dhofar against the so-called Dhofar Liberation Front.

Not far off the coast north-east of Salala is a group of islands which, depending on how you view their status, were very nearly snipped away from Sultanate control.

The Kuria Muria Islands are five unprepossessing pieces of rock called Helaneea, Jibleea, Soda, Haski and Gursond (spelling according to the Aitchison version of the cession). A few fishermen live on the largest, Helaneea, and in 1854 a sharp-eyed British merchant Captain Ord, saw a lot of guano on at least two of the others. In 1854 guano could mean wealth.

The tribulations of Ord and Company, involving the Foreign Office, the India Office, the Colonial Office, the Admiralty, the Bombay Government, the Foreign Secretary (Lord Clarendon), not to mention a supporting cast of solicitors, pirates, labourers and M.P.s, was a mixture of musical comedy and tragedy. Suffice it to say that Ord and Company did manage to extract 26,191 tons of guano in the season 1857/8 and 14,250 tons in 1858/9, before their licence was formally terminated in 1861 because of continued default in royalty payments, but it is improbable that they made much of a profit.

It was Lord Clarendon who had personally been behind the whole project, and who had instigated the cession of the islands to the Crown. Said bin Sultan gave them, with open generosity and complete refusal to accept any payment on 14 July 1854. Clarendon, as I have mentioned elsewhere, in a moment of embarrassment, sent a snuff-box to Said as a return gift.

The guano project collapsed, but Britain still found herself with the islands. She did not get rid of them until 1967. It so happened that they were officially administered from Aden; they were on the Aden books—presumably because the original annexation had been engineered by the British, not the Indian, Government. So, when in 1965 Sir Gawain Bell produced, on behalf of the Government of the Federation of South Arabia, his report on Aden and its future, the Kuria Muria islands were included as part of Aden territory. In 1967, Her Majesty's Government realised that they were in something of a cleft stick; on the one hand, the new Aden Government would take it amiss if they received on Independence Day Aden minus a piece of territory that they had been assured belonged to it; on the other hand, the Sultan of Muscat and Oman would be furious if Britain gave away to a third party (whom he would be unlikely to view favourably under the heading of 'her heirs or successors after her') a piece of the Sultanate which his great-great-grandfather had generously donated to Queen Victoria (after all, when Said had wanted to present to the Nizam of Hyderabad a perfectly useless—to him—state carriage and harness given him by the Queen, he had at least asked permission). The Sultan confirmed he would be furious, and so the British Government gave him back the islands. The Government of South Yemen duly took this amiss, and have said so.

It is possible that the Kuria Muria Islands are not yet lost to the history books.

MUSCAT AND OMAN

✗ Said bin Taimur* ✗

The arbiter of present and future in the Sultanate is the Sultan, Said bin Taimur bin Feisal bin Turki bin Said bin Sultan bin Ahmed bin Said Al bu Said. Of that there is no shadow of doubt. He has also been the arbiter of the past, the last thirty-six years of it.

His father, Taimur, resigned as Sultan in 1932, and retired to Bombay to spend the rest of his life divorced from the worries of ruling. He only died in 1965. The present Sultan was born in 1910, and obtained most of his formal education at a British school in India; when he returned to Muscat he shared in affairs of the State, and was a member of the Council of Ministers.

To understand Oman today it is necessary to understand Said bin Taimur, and this is by no means easy. It is necessary because for thirty-six years he has personally controlled in minute detail everything that has happened in his country, and he continues this rigid centralised form of administration today. He has worked in this way for so long, that it seems most improbable that he can adjust now to something more attuned to the requirements of the 1960s, let alone the 1970s. That is one of the great problems of Oman.

The Sultan, like most of us, is what he is as a result of his own experiences. When he took over Oman in 1932 he assumed responsibility for a pretty unattractive economic mess. In his own words, 'the Sultanate's Treasury was completely empty.' Indeed, for the preceding seventy-five years, really ever since the death of Said bin Sultan and the confirmation of the division of Muscat from Zanzibar by the Canning Award, Oman had been bankrupt,

---

* Before embarking on this part of the book, I would remind you of what I wrote in the 'Explanation' preceding the opening section on Muscat, that I have maintained my description of how Muscat and Oman appeared to me in 1968 in the present tense, even though, to take the example of the very first sentence, Said bin Taimur has not only ceased to be arbiter of anything, but has also died.

or on the verge of bankruptcy. This, as has been seen, was due to a coincidence of a number of factors, of which the most important were: the decline of Omani naval power with the appearance of steam vessels, the campaign waged by the British to suppress the slave trade, the British effort to suppress illegal (to Britain, not to Oman) arms trading, and the increasing need to pay tribal tribute. Apart from some rather erratic exports of dates and fish, the Treasury relied almost entirely on Customs' receipts, the Zanzibar subsidy and, later, the oil concession rental. The amount was pitifully small; in 1931, according to the Sultan, the total budget was only about £50,000.

From the moment that the Sultan entered public life, but even more so from the time he acceded to power, he was circumscribed by economic problems. But he was not, like some of his predecessors, submerged by them; it may well be his proudest claim that he can write, 'from 1933 to this present day there has been no financial deficit in the Government's budget', and indeed this is an achievement which should be credited for what it is. Having duly saluted it, however, one is bound to add that it has had unfortunate effects. The lessons the Sultan learned from his budget-balancing exercises of the thirties and forties have been so deeply imprinted on his mind that he finds it almost impossible to comprehend a situation where such exercises are a total irrelevance.

For the Sultan debts are the ultimate horror. Debts dragged the Sultanate into the mire for fifty years or more, so that each Sultan became wholly dependent on his creditors; Said bin Taimur put an end to that, and whatever else he proposed to do he was not going to fall into that trap again—and besides, there was religion to back him. His words are revealing: '. . . for we did not want to overburden the Sultanate's finances and weigh them down with new debts, after having paid off all the old ones. Doubtless it would have been easy to obtain money in various ways, but this could only have been by a loan with interest at a set percentage rate. This amounts to usury, with which I completely disagree, and the religious prohibition of which is not unknown.' That, and any other quotation attributed personally to the Sultan, is taken from a document[1] he published in Oman in January 1958, the only public statement that, as far as I know, he has ever made; for this reason it deserves to be looked at, and is, I believe, most revealing about his character.

Financial orthodoxy in its strictest definition is, then, one of the Sultan's fundamental principles. From the sorry economic history of Oman, the Sultan learnt two other lessons; the first was that if you are in debt to someone, then that person has a very strong hold upon you and can force you to do things that you would not otherwise dream of doing. In Oman's case the someone was the British Government. The British may have saved the country, but in the process they imposed upon it European disciplines which were neither wanted nor appreciated. The Sultan concluded that the only agreements worth having were those that were without strings, and without hidden implications. Ever since, and frequently to the fury of his would-be advisers, he has upheld this principle.

The other lesson he learnt was that if you wanted to ensure that something was done as you wanted it done then you did it yourself. In other words, delegation was dangerous. He had read of, and seen first-hand, too many of the dangers, and he determined that he would not fall amongst them. He never has. For very many years this was all right, but in 1968 it is not.

The Sultan is a man of principle, but where does principle end and pigheadedness begin. That is a question that many greater men than Said bin Taimur have been puzzled to answer, so he cannot be blamed for not himself succeeding; but what is less certain is that he has ever asked the question, or even noticed that the question exists.

In following his principles he has been consistent, and successful. The greatest crisis that he has had to face during the time he has been Sultan was, without question, the Imamate rebellion. In order to overpower it, he had to call in the British to help him. They came. He was in a potential debt position. It seems to me to be instructive to see how he got out of that one. In the first instance he was lucky, for there was no time for formalities; along came the British troops, disposed of the immediate trouble, and went away again. No commitment except to say thank you. However, it was not to be expected that the British would do nothing, for it was obvious enough to them that unless the Sultan was positively bolstered up, he might well be asking them for repeat performances. At a time when every move in favour of an existing regime against a supposedly liberating opponent produced a babel of activity in the United Nations (it was not very long after the super-folly of Suez), you could not blame the British Government for wanting to get off the hook. They sent out Julian Amery to negotiate something with the Sultan.

Julian Amery negotiated what ended up as an 'Exchange of Letters between the Government of the United Kingdom of Great Britain and Northern Ireland and the Sultan of Muscat and Oman concerning the Sultan's Armed forces, Civil Aviation, Royal Air Force facilities and Economic Development in Muscat and Oman, London July 25th 1958' (Cmnd 507). The letters cover one page, and cost fourpence. This agreement produced SAF, and the promise of seconded officers to help run it; also SOAF; it enabled the R.A.F. to continue to use Salala and Masira; and it foresaw the formation of the Development Department and said Britain would assist the Sultan in carrying out developments. It did not say how British assistance, in money, would be administered, but in fact the arrangement was that an agreed sum would be paid to the Sultan, and he would spend it. He did not commit himself to anything. And subsequently, when British officials urged him to spend it in such and such a way, he firmly pointed out that that was not part of the bargain. Whereas the British Government should have had the whip hand in certain respects, in fact the Sultan had it in all.

This was most evident on the development side rather than the military. Practically all Foreign Office officials who had anything to do with Muscat, and everyone else who knew the country, reckoned that development was the key to solving the Sultan's troubles; development, particularly in agriculture, medicine and education. The Sultan used, with infinite care and minute supervision, the rather meagre sum (£250,000 for most if not all of the years from 1959 to 1967) given him by the British Government, but resolutely refused to add to it from his own revenues (as a matter of fact, there was even some left over in 1968 when payments anyway terminated, and this will be used for the first surveys for the new harbour scheme at Muttrah). In this, as in everything else, the Sultan declined to be bullied. Standing on the letter of his treaties he was in a strong position, particularly with the Foreign Office whose sense of interpretation of official documents tends anyway to be precise, but in the Gulf area to be almost pathological in its insistence on what British relationships are and are not. In this the Sultan is in an impregnable position, and knows it, since Britain has to spend tedious (and in fact fruitless) hours in the U.N. proving that the Sultanate is a sovereign independent state in ordinary treaty relationship with her.

It is worthy of note, in passing, that this theoretical position of moral persuasion (blackmail, if you prefer, when carried through in practice to its logical end) ended in November 1964, when P.D.(O.) announced that it had discovered commercial quantities of oil which it planned to start exporting in 1967. From that moment on the Sultan was worth credit. He never took it, however, not a penny; because of his debt principle. The British subsequently made it clear to the Sultan that from the moment his oil money started coming in, their military and development subsidies would end. Fair enough. But the Sultan would be justified enough in concluding that perhaps other conditions might have led the British to a similar decision; then where would he have been—particularly if he had listened to the siren voices in 1959 and 1960, right up to 1964, persuading him to spend more of his own money too. If you are cautious by nature, you can build up a logical system to persuade yourself to more caution that, because there is logic in it, is difficult to assail. Certainly, no one ever had any success with the Sultan in assailing it.

The Sultan's principle of non-delegation has perhaps led him into what many people believe are his worst and most dangerous attitudes. On one hand the effect has been a complete sterility of decision at any level anywhere in the Sultanate; this hardly mattered, and therefore became an ingrained and ineradicable attribute of all Sultanate officials, in the early days; it was even tolerable, I suppose, up to 1964; but since then, once the Sultanate was guaranteed to become a comparatively rich country, such concentration of decision-making has caused Oman totally unnecessary inefficiency and stagnation. It has been in no way assisted by the Sultan having lived exclusively in Salala for the last ten years, nor by the fact that he himself is not much good at making decisions anyway.

The other effect of this non-delegation syndrome is that over the years the Sultan has ceased to have any trust in people; this is only the obverse of not having given them any responsibility, but it has become a separate positive harm. Indeed, it has become a sort of psychological reaction, so that the people he appoints to posts in the Sultanate need to be persons who themselves are satisfied to do a job in which there are, effectively, no decisions to take. Having opted out of decisions, and, therefore, responsibilities, they can be trusted (if this remains the right word to describe such a state) by the Sultan. This peculiar atmosphere is made even more oppressive by his absence, one might describe it as disembodiment, in Salala. Practically unapproachable (and certainly only approachable by appointment) he is fed by information from all sides and from all levels; some of it may be true, but all of it is weighted. The end result of all this is like a witch's brew.

But, when all is said and done, rural remedies are sometimes more effective than scientific cures. This is what is so maddening to the theorists who legislate for Oman; the Sultan so often just happens, in the end, to be right—or, at least, to be no more wrong than the theorists would have been if they had had their way. Was it luck, or a deep intuition, or what? Whatever it was, there is not much consolation for the theorisers.

So, I think of the Sultan as the epitome of an English Victorian paterfamilias, rigid, upright, uncomplicatedly confident that only he knows what to do at what time in the best interests of his family, steering his people, like children, along the path ordained for them. What worries me, and many other people too, is that in 1968, even if Victoriana is in, the Victorian moral code is way out.

In all fairness I add that those who meet the Sultan, with few exceptions, are quickly won over by his charm and persuasive powers. I have not been to Salala, nor have I ever met him.

There exists a Government—well, a structure that administers Oman, for the process of governing stems wholly from the Sultan.

As an organisation chart, the structure looks reasonably well bolted together, but in practice all the screws are missing. Perhaps it can be best imagined as a mobile; but if that presupposes a degree of flexibility, then the concept of a rigid mobile must be invented to describe it.

There are no Ministers in the Government, only Secretaries, and many of them are missing. External Affairs has not had a Department Head since 1958 (oddly enough this Department used to be a Ministry, first of Foreign Affairs, subsequently altered to External Affairs; the title of the incumbent, if there were one, was modified to Secretary after the last Minister finally departed in 1958); it is run by a clerk who has been signing letters on behalf of the non-existent Secretary for ten years. Customs has not had a Director General since the end of 1966. Even the Ministry of the Interior (the only Ministry) has no confirmed Head, and Sayyid Ahmed bin Ibrahim who has done the job for over thirty years now, is technically no more than 'he who oversees matters pertaining to the Interior'.

Once every year a beam of light is shed on to one aspect of this governmental jumble, when the Table of Official Precedence in Muscat is issued. You then know how to distribute your dinner guests. Way down near the bottom of this Protocol List was one entry that I used to cherish: tucked between Captains above, but with Lieutenants beneath, were 'Other Sultanate Officials in charge of offices (by pay scales)'. Alas, in 1967 they were expunged. Was this a mistake, or have they lost what little rank remained to them? I doubt that we shall ever know.

There is another status symbol of potent value to the holder; the right to speak to the Sultan on his wireless link. Some officials can, others cannot, and that is all there is to it. It is a particularly valuable right if you have it, since the only other method of communication is by letter or telegram (and you can force no one, least of all a Sultan, and still less this Sultan, to answer a letter), or by word of mouth, but you have to obtain permission to visit Salala, which provides a perfect blocking technique to a man who is adept in all forms of stonewalling. Indeed, in a world league Said Cunctator would be right up with those traditional leaders of the field, Fabius and Jackson.

So, in a desultory and rickety fashion, the bureaucracy of Muscat keeps things going and those who live in the country learn to live with the quirks and indecision which newcomers cannot comprehend; then they too learn, and so it goes on. To be fair, there is one aspect of this no-responsibility system which is positive. If the Sultan lays down a rule, this rule will be rigidly observed without any deviation. This means that you know precisely where you are, even if you find it a peculiar position to be in; no grey areas, all is black or white—mostly black, perhaps, but at least you can see the edge, where the white begins again. But to change a piece of black to white, or white to black, is outside the bounds of possibility, beyond the power of imagining—unless the Sultan says so; then the change is immediate and complete. There is a certain elegance, even purity, in such a system, but, even if one can construct a theoretical purity, in practice the Muscat mixture of Sultanate bureaucrats produces an inelegant and indecisive executive arm to Government.

Outside Muscat and Muttrah the country is administered through Walis, local governors. They are appointed by the Sultan (a number are members of his family), and are responsible to him via the Minister of the Interior (henceforth referred to as such even though he technically is not). Each controls all civil matters within his area of jurisdiction, his wilayat. This is the traditional organisation belonging to both Sultanate, and before that, the Imamate. There has been minimal change for a very long time, except that today the Walis are part of a centralised system, whereas, in the nineteenth century, for instance, as we have seen, many of them ran what were in effect their own city-states. They have, too, some of the trappings of the twentieth century now; for instance, a Land-Rover and a wireless set linked to Muscat if they are lucky. What arcane formula is used to determine whether a certain wilayat merits a wireless or a Land-Rover I have no idea, but not all have either or both. Possibly the incumbent himself constitutes part of the formula, although I cannot recall a case where a change of Wali has altered the material status of the wilayat; perhaps it happens. At Izki, for instance, there is no wireless set or Land-Rover; at Ibri there is no wireless set; at Sur, no Land-Rover—and the poor Wali who lives in rural Balad Sur has to travel three miles on a donkey if he wishes to visit anyone in the commercial and social centre of Sur al Sahil.

Indeed, Sur provides the most extreme example of how remote the wilayat system in Oman is from modern life. One day (this was in 1967) a wireless message was received by the operator in the

Wali's husn in Sur summoning the Wali urgently to Muscat. There was no indication what crisis had broken, but it was a top priority urgent recall signal. The Wali happened to be on tour (on his donkey) in his wilayat. The message, with the aid of runners, camels and more donkeys (and, who knows, cleft sticks too) was relayed to him. He hastened back, at top donkey speed, to Sur. He summoned a dhow. Fortunately the sea was calm. Twelve hours later he reached Muscat. Silence. For one whole day nothing happened; for another day nothing, not a word from the Ministry of the Interior. On the third day, a summons. Why did you permit a football team to leave Sur for Muscat on a dhow? No coherent answer forthcoming, or even possible (because not specifically covered in the book of rules i.e. neither not permitted, nor permitted). So, the Wali of Sur backed out, and waited twenty-three more days in Muscat before being told he could return to Sur (by dhow); and the secretary of the Muscat football club was put into gaol for a few days—for what? oh, for having allowed the match to have taken place, perhaps.

That is symptomatic of why the revolutionaries want to get at Muscat; but whether they would make the people of Sur happier is quite another question.

What is more to the point is that this treatment is not abnormal in the eyes of the Omanis. On another occasion the Wali of Bureimi was summoned to Muscat to answer for some suspected misdemeanour and spent the best part of four months away from his post. It was not as if during this time anything was happening, that a dialogue of accusation and defence was being carried on; he just had an interview or two with Sayyid Ahmed, and then retired to his garden at Sib to wait. At the end of four months it so happened that he was told to go back to Bureimi, which by that time was sadly suffering from the lack of any authority. Time seems to be used in this way as a measurement of displeasure. In a different context, sheikhs are sometimes moved to mount a camel and ride to Salala to present a complaint; I know of one man who did this, and had to wait eight months down at Salala until he obtained an audience. For us, brought up in the hustle of the twentieth century, it is the excruciating inefficiency of such a system that pains us. The Omanis are relatively unworried by it. But it is disturbing that the Sultan, the one man who should now be starting to lead a twentieth-century life, has apparently done nothing to change it.

There is another link in the civil control system of the interior, through the sheikhs. Generally speaking, each main tribe has a senior sheikh who is, as it were, ratified by the Sultan as Sheikh. If the tribe misbehaves, he is answerable, and it is he who will be given the traditional tribal tribute by the Sultan. The relationship between such a man and the nearest Wali is variable, and depends largely on the relative power of the tribe and the influence of the Sheikh as compared to the influence of the Wali. There is no rule. Unless the Sheikh is very powerful (or very angry) he will approach the Sultan, if he approaches him at all, via Sayyid Ahmed, the Minister of the Interior, who is, in modern organisational jargon, his line superior.

The tribal system is still a strong and potent force in Oman, one of the last places remaining in the Arab world where this is true. It has many attractions for the romantic, and in the past has been effective enough. It is, however, another target for the revolutionaries, and in the long term they must be right. The transition will inevitably be painful, but will not be less painful if postponed. Again, it is disturbing that the Sultan shows no sign at all of wanting to make that transition. Rather the reverse: he seems to be perpetuating the old system. For instance, in his 1968 statement, he says: 'When we talk about planning we must not forget the oil-bearing area and the Duru tribe who live there. They must be given special attention and must get the projects they need and which suit them.' An excellent sentiment, but when it comes to siting a hospital and school in Tanam (for such in practice are the first projects for the Duru) before anything is planned for Ibri, this is nonsense. I think that, for Oman, it is potentially dangerous nonsense.

That, in a rather fragile nutshell, is the basis of the civil administration of Oman. What very much more effectively glues the country together is the control exercised by the Army. I do not wish to infer by this that the Sultanate is under a military dictatorship. This is very far from the truth. The Army has, however, units throughout most of the country; it has decent communications; it has transport and it is a reasonably efficient and well organised set-up; on most counts it wins over the civil organisation, and hands down overall. It is true to say that the presence of the Army has produced peaceful conditions in the country, but untrue to say that the Army imposes such conditions forcefully. It is important to make this distinction.

SAF, the name by which it is always known, is a relatively efficient and well organised body because it has received a large enough subsidy to equip it tolerably, and because it is largely officered by Englishmen. It is as simple as that. I do not mean by this that Englishmen are the only good officers; SAF would be equally efficient if they were German, French or American, I am sure, but it so happens that most of them are English. Primarily this is the result of the Julian Amery negotiations of 1958.

SAF has grown out of the small force that was lodged in Muscat in 1913*, and moved to Beit al Falaj in 1915, to guarantee the rule of the Sultan against the interior tribes. This was known as the Muscat Levy Corps, and was subsequently reorganised into the Muscat Infantry. Between 1952 and 1954 three other quite separate forces were set up, the Batinah Force, the Muscat and Oman Field Force, and the Dhofar Force. The Dhofar Force has remained to this day a private army (rather surprisingly remained, since it was a group of men from it that tried to assassinate the Sultan in 1966, and it seems hard to credit that a unit that made such a bungle of that would be much use for anything else); the other three were merged in 1957 to form what is now SAF, although subsequently what remained from the Muscat and Oman Field Force was disbanded. What the Amery Agreement did was to provide money for equipment and running costs, and a framework from which serving British officers could be seconded to SAF. SAF has for many years now had an approximately fifty-fifty ratio of seconded to contract officers (many of the contract officers are also British), and has tried to maintain a fifty-fifty ratio of Baluch to Omanis amongst the other ranks.

Between 1958 and 1967 the British subsidy to SAF has run at somewhere between one million and two million pounds per year; it was cut off in March 1967 (the end of the 1966 financial year) when it was considered that the Sultan had sufficient oil revenues to pay for SAF himself, although technically oil money

* See page 97 above.

did not start coming in until the first export went out, in August 1967.

SAF, therefore, is now a self-supporting army. Now that it no longer depends on the subsidy, and the Sultan is confident that money will continue to be earned for the military commitments he has, he is increasing those commitments and improving the material content of SAF. A continuing link with the British Army, particularly in terms of personnel on secondment, is obviously important and useful, since it keeps SAF in touch with modern developments and techniques; but, if all British assistance and contacts were to be cut off tomorrow, SAF could now survive.

As adjuncts to the Army there is a small Air Force (known as SOAF), and the first glimmerings of a Navy in the shape of a motorised dhow. SOAF started life in 1959, as a direct result of the Amery Agreement, and it is now developing into its second phase with the purchase of some jet Provosts. The dhow was bought in 1961, and it is planned to introduce more effective naval craft soon: fast patrol launches which will form the nucleus of a Navy that can patrol the long Oman coastline.

In control of all matters military is the Defence Department, with, at its head, a Military Secretary. The Defence Department was formed in 1958, growing out of its predecessor, the Administrative Headquarters, which was set up in Beit al Falaj in 1955.

A very pertinent question, of course, is what precisely is the purpose of this Army. There is no doubt that its prime purpose is to withstand any revolutionary movement. It is doing that right now, in Dhofar. In Oman proper it has not had to do this since about 1961 when the level of mining and other incidents organised by the Imamate forces slackened off, and then died altogether. As with most armies of this size it is really more of a para-police force than a military machine; and that is what is needed in a large country like Oman full of individualists and tribes whose traditional way of settling quarrels has been more often with bullets than with a formula of phrases. On a reading such as this patrol boats too have their logical place in controlling immigration. Less defensible, it could be argued, is the purchase of expensive new aircraft.

The presence of British troops in Oman has been, and still is, a cause for hysterical propaganda both against the Sultan and the British Government. Such propaganda is not based on any logic, and so it seems to be worth making a few objective and, I hope, cool remarks. The first is that no British soldier, nor any other foreigner for that matter, can enter the Sultanate without the express permission of the Sultan. The second is that every British soldier serving in SAF is under command of the Sultan, who himself pays them (directly if on contract, via the British Government if they are seconded). The third is that, apart from those serving in SAF, no British soldiers are on Sultanate territory unless, with prior permission, they are carrying out some training exercise. I am under no illusions that the third statement is wide open for cynical interpretation. All right, interpret it cynically; but if you do not happen to be a cynic, bear in mind that it can imply what it says.

The British Army did assist the Sultan in 1957 and 1959—at the invitation of the Sultan. Without the assistance given, it is quite possible that the Sultanate would have ceased to exist. Britain gave this help for a number of reasons: her own self-interest in preserving a stable Gulf area, her 1951 Treaty with the Sultan, logical continuation of past support for the Sultanate. Whether such reasons seem persuasive or sufficient depend inevitably on your own perspective.

A legal system provides another form of control within a State. Oman is not quite an exception.

Sharia law is applicable to all persons throughout Oman. To carry it out there are qadis attached to every wilayat in the country, with a Chief Qadi's court in Muscat. In these days one can find in Islamic countries various degrees of modification to the old precepts of this law, which, as most people know, is derived direct from the teachings of the Quran. As a matter of general principle the modifications that have been permitted in Oman are as limited as, I suppose, anywhere in the world. Ibadhism is still strong, and it is a rigid unyielding form of Islam. The Sultan appears—chiefly from the evidence of what he has not done—to be extremely cautious about altering the traditions, or in any way upsetting those who have taken it upon themselves to preserve them.

Up to a point, this is fine; but the fact remains that strict Sharia law was not written for twentieth-century situations, and is often most ill equipped to deal with them. Most Moslem countries have faced this, and made some sort of compromise; usually to appropriate a legal system based either on English law or the Napoleonic code, but to keep Sharia principles for certain classes of activity. In Saudi Arabia, where the puritanical Wahhabis have a certain similarity of outlook to the Ibadhi religious leaders, there has been an impressive and carefully conceived updating of the Sharia system. I hope that one day the Sultan will follow in the steps of the Saudis.

In the meantime the country has to do as best it can with what it has got. Fortunately, the Sharia system is basically most humane; always it looks for a compromise, so that it is at its most successful when it makes no judgement, but merely confirms what the litigants have themselves decided to accept. This may seem a strange statement if you are used to horrific stories of hands being chopped off for theft, and women convicted of adultery being sewn up in a sack and stoned to death. Such things are indeed vile, but qadis today are usually aware that these punishments were legislated for a seventh-century situation, and will strain every nerve to make a settlement out of court which will not involve such judgements. Indeed, such judgements are practically non-existent nowadays in Oman; certainly I never heard of one in the time I was in the country. Sharia principle is very simple, an eye for an eye, but compromise has effectively set a price for the eye.

The actual practice of Sharia law in the Sharia courts is, for a European, startling. Having been on the fringes of rather a lot of it, I can only say that, in a way that seems nearly miraculous, the end result is usually about as just as you can reasonably expect; this is the more so the more potentially serious the case. In minor cases justice seems to me to be pretty erratic, but the effect is seldom disastrous.

What I have tried to say is that justice in Oman is not as bad as it might be thought to be. This is, I believe, generally true. Unfortunately not wholly. It would be less than honest if I were not to mention Jalali, the main Muscat prison in the old Portuguese fort. By any standards the Sultan's treatment of political prisoners in Jalali is absolutely inhuman and inexcusable. He would say (I think) that it is not my business, but that such treatment is the only type understood or even expected in his country. And that is that.

There was a time when, along with all the rest of the Gulf area, Britain had extraterritorial jurisdictional rights over her subjects and protected persons; the type of rights foreshadowed in the Wylde Treaty, and then in the 1833 Treaty with America. Such rights finally came to an end in Oman as from 1 January 1967, and for the previous five years had applied only to consular officials and members of Her Majesty's Armed Forces seconded to SAF or otherwise on duty in the country. Likewise in Kuwait they have ended, but in the Trucial States and Bahrain the fag-end of the system is maintained, soon no doubt to be finally extinguished and relegated to imperial memories.

All foreigners now have every reason to encourage legal reform in Oman, for the Sharia as it is is far too erratic and archaic a vehicle to cope with what is hoped will be a modern developing country. The Sultan has the choice of either following the Kuwait principle, of grafting a modern code on to the remnants of Sharia (Bahrain has done much the same, using an English base instead of a French one), or the Saudi Arabian principle, of modernising the Sharia and training qadis to adapt themselves to the modern mould. There is a long way to go, and the new world is already beginning to trickle in, so I hope he will do something about it soon.

In most respects the Sultan is his own worst enemy, and in no sphere is this more true than in public relations. The trouble is that he appears to consider completely and utterly irrelevant what anyone thinks of him. There is an element which is almost attractive in such wholesale bravado, but in fact it is nothing but plain stupidity. It would be very comforting, perhaps, to be able to be immune from all outside opinion, but it just is not possible. The Sultan's efforts to remain in embattled isolation have been rather successful but have had the predictable result of ensuring that he has a bad press. All the more reason, he says, for having nothing to do with them.

Journalists are anathema; because, one supposes, they say

12

things the Sultan does not like. This is true of many of them, but in most cases they have never been allowed in the country, so can hardly be blamed for a certain waspishness of approach. A few have been in, but even they are condemned for what they have written and probably will not get back again. The irony of it is that those who have had first-hand information have in fact been eminently fair to the Sultan; far too generous, many would say.

Just in case journalists might, for they are creatures of cunning, get in through some back door, and in general to keep out anyone who has no practical reason to come in, there is a rigorous entry visa regime supervised in person by the Sultan. To squeeze through this net is not a simple matter. The Sultan can, of course, rationalise this restriction up to a point by showing that visitors cannot be handled satisfactorily—no hotels, for instance; but if I have space in my house, and want to invite a friend to stay, I can still only do it with the Sultan's permission.

It is, then, very difficult for the outside world to give Oman a good image, since it is not permitted to look at it face-on; what it hears second-hand is almost inevitably somebody's weighted interpretation. It would help if the Sultan himself told people what was going on and why; but there is no newspaper, no wireless station, only those wretched pieces of paper stuck up on the Muscat gate.

There is now one exception: the document from which I have already taken a few quotations. The trouble with this document is that its style and content is about as related to 1968 as Lord Curzon; its title deserves a special publicity award (and tells you more about the Sultan than any journalist, or I, ever will): 'The word of Sultan Said bin Taimur, Sultan of Muscat and Oman, about the history of the financial position of the Sultanate in the past and the hopes for the future, after the export of oil.'

It is an Old Testament document, with the Sultan cast in the role of Jahweh. It is not, however, designed for Europeans, nor is it projected towards public opinion abroad. It is a statement to the people of Oman, and it is the first public statement that the Sultan has ever made. To this extent it is a revolutionary step forward. To which your European, or, even more so, Egyptian journalist can only respond that an awful lot of revolution is needed.

Perhaps this may give some glimmering of an idea of what a chasm of a gap lies between Oman ancient and modern. The point about The Word (as it is fondly called) is that it is a deadly serious document in the Sultan's eyes, and to view it in any other light would provide further evidence of the irresponsibility of third-party criticism and the pointlessness of having anything to do with outside information media. However, the break is slowly coming, for as foreign firms win contracts in Oman under the Development Plan, so publicity follows them, and you certainly see the Sultanate more frequently mentioned in the press now than before.

The Sultan is in some respects unpredictable, and he does genuinely see himself as an innovator. Relatively, as compared for instance to an Ibadhi qadi, he is; and, for them, a dangerous one at that. One modernism that he is said to be in favour of is an Omani wireless station, and an expert has actually visited Muscat to advise on the practicability; even, it is whispered, he would like to have his own television studios so that he could spread primary education through televised teaching. I think it is possible that he has concepts of this kind in his mind, but I very much doubt whether he has any idea at all of what is involved in putting them into practice. When he finds out, I strongly suspect the concepts will melt.

The theme of that biblical apologia, The Word, is money; the lack of it in the past, and what it is hoped to do with it in the future. Development. And that is precisely what the Omanis want to hear about. It is, therefore, unfortunate and unsatisfactory that the document should be so vague. It is also a pity, but not surprising, that its distribution was so erratic.

A Development Department has existed since 1959, formed to administer the subsidy provided by Britain under the terms of the 1958 Exchange of Letters. It has done its best with scant re-sources. It is organised into three divisions, dealing with Health, Agriculture, and Public Works. Health consists of a number of clinics and so-called hospitals scattered throughout the country; roughly, a clinic is in the hands of a male nurse, a hospital has a doctor; all the staff, except for the British Chief Medical Officer, are Indian. One should not denigrate their achievements, but rather sympathise with the appalling conditions under which they must work: lack of funds, and an apparent disinterest by the Sultan in what is being attempted. In spite of this, something has been effected, and the people are better off than they were before. That, however, is about as much as one can say; except to add that if it were not for the Mission Hospital in Muttrah (equally unappreciated by the Sultan) things would be very much worse than they are.

Agricultural development has consisted so far of the establishment of two Experimental Farms, one at Nizwa and the other at Sohar. Again, the story is the same: lack of money, and a disinterest amounting to hostility shown by the Sultan, who, for instance, will not permit any extension work to be done by the staff for the surrounding farmers, and who, for other reasons, has not yet permitted any single individual to purchase a tractor. Not only is the minimum of Governmental assistance forthcoming, but the individual is even hindered from helping himself. This is scarcely credible in a country for which agricultural potential is its greatest asset apart from oil.

The third prong of the Development Department, Public Works, is a rather high sounding title for a road construction and maintenance gang. The Azaiba to Sohar graded road is their achievement, and within its limits a most useful one; but the distance is only one hundred and fifty miles, and it took about six years to complete, so one needs to keep things in perspective. Maintenance is now becoming increasingly difficult because of the age of the machinery, but no new piece of equipment can be ordered unless the Sultan personally permits it.

That is the Development Department, for whose staff I have considerable regard and the greatest sympathy. I remind you that the budget has never exceeded £250,000 per annum.

However circumscribed it is, the Department exists, and could have been used to build a more effective structure ready for the time when more money would be available. Nothing happened; still nothing happens, although at the time I write these words the Sultan is receiving not less than two million pounds per month from his oil revenues. Why did nothing happen? I find a revealing sentence in The Word: 'Yes, only now that we know that revenue from oil will be coming in steadily can we consider and plan and estimate how to put into effect the various projects the country needs.' It is the old story of the Sultan's debt horror. Look at another of his remarks; he has just pointed out that the British subsidy ended in March 1967 and the first oil exports did not take place until August, and goes on: 'During this interim period we depended upon such financial reserves as we had. Had it not been for our economy and for our reserves we would not have been able to bear the burden of expenditure during those months.' Financial orthodoxy, my foot.

However, let us take a deep breath, swallow deeply, and, for a moment, accept the Sultan's bazaar reasoning. Why has nothing happened since August 1967? This is where the Sultan's apologists have to delve deep, and the revolutionaries start waving their rifles, and it is very difficult to be in any way objective. Those who are cynics about the Sultan, and there are plenty, reckon that this is the final proof that he has never really intended to do any proper development; it is all words, and an everlasting postponement. I believe it is more complex than that; that he genuinely wants to engage in some development (and I will come to what he is doing in a moment), but that he is inhibited from using the organisation he has already got because of his inherent mistrust in it. He has saddled himself, as we have already seen, with an ineffective bureaucracy which functions after a fashion without responsibilities being given it, so it would be a complete contradiction to build up part of that bureaucracy for real responsibility and action. I am afraid there is another side to it as well; that he is the arbiter of what the Omani people need and at what speed, and he can see no real urgency to get on with the basics of development other than in the way he has decided is appropriate. In the meantime, the existing Development Department is living in a sort of limbo, barely able to do what it has been doing in the past, and completely ignorant of what role it is to play in the future.

I have stated that I believe the Sultan intends development for Oman. The text for this opinion is available in The Word. 'Firstly we shall begin building offices for various Government Departments; then houses for officials who will come from abroad; then step by step will come various projects such as hospitals, schools, roads, communications, and other necessary

works including the development of fisheries, animal and agricultural resources etc. until modern projects spread over the
whole of the Sultanate, to each area according to its needs.' Then
later, 'We shall reinforce the Government machine by adding to
it a number of experts and technicians. This will ensure that the
Government has a modern administrative machine. The present
situation requires changes in the existing Government set-up.' If
ever a sentence were pregnant, that last one certainly is.

These statements, taken one by one, are unexceptionable; it is
when they are written by the Sultan that they take on a dis-
embodied, wavering significance; it is as if you were reading a
mirage.

However, to get down to the practicalities of the situation, the
Sultan in 1966 appointed a consultant to prepare, and execute, a
regional development plan for Muscat and Muttrah. It has been
prepared in consultation with the Sultan, and it has been accepted
in principle. A deep disadvantage, however, is that it is known in
full only to very few persons, and they are usually sworn to
secrecy. Some parts of it slowly trickle out, of course, when a
tender is called for, or by rumour, but it would be of the greatest
assistance to everyone, and most of all to the Sultan and his
reputation, if it were to be made public. In the meantime, the first
projects under the plan have been initiated: housing for government officials, offices, a new post-office, a girls' school, a hospital
in Muscat, and, most important, a water scheme. All this is in line
with The Word, as one would expect.

Of these, the water scheme is by far the largest, and will cost
about one million pounds; water is to be pumped from the Sib
area to storage tanks for Muttrah and Muscat, and a piped town
supply will gradually be introduced. This is one of the urgent
schemes specifically called for in The Word; the others are
electricity for Muscat and Muttrah (which is well under way, but
is not strictly a Development Plan project at all; it was started
before, and is in effect a private company with majority share-
holding by British interests), the Muttrah port scheme and, at a
slight tangent, a new currency.

Electricity, water and the new port are all of immense importance not only for their practical significance but also because
they provide a visible manifestation of progress. This, as by now

should be appreciated, is very necessary to the Sultan's image. One can only hope that the rest of the plan will soon be divulged, and, what is more important, something will emerge for the improvement of agriculture, health and education in the rest of the country.

As far as I know the only motion towards the development of natural resources, other than oil, has been the granting of a concession for the extraction of minerals in the mountains, and for the fishing of crayfish in certain coastal waters; the terms of such concessions, if indeed they exist, are obscure, and certainly there has so far been no noticeable result. As a matter of passing interest, this is not the first Omani fishing concession to be granted; in 1905 Sultan Feisal bin Turki granted a fifteen-year concession to the Sponge Exploration Syndicate Ltd. to fish for sponges in Oman territorial waters. I wonder if they ever found any.

What Omanis yearn for most of all is the opportunity to educate their children. What the Sultan fears most is education. For it must be true that the more widely educated the people become, the less prepared they will be to accept the rate of development that the Sultan appears to have settled for. Education is at once the weakest link in the Sultan's plans, and the most desired by his people. There are all the elements of a collision course.

The history of education in the Sultanate is a sorry tale. The first State school was started in 1914; this was superseded in 1927 by the Sultaniyya School, which, with a gap of two years when it was shut down, lasted until 1940. In 1940 the Muscat Sayyidiya School was opened, and in 1959 the Muttrah Sayyidiya (with the assistance of the British subsidy). In 1964 a boarding house was built in the grounds of the Muscat school, but it has never housed a single student, ostensibly, I believe, because no suitable boys could be found from the Interior. Each Sayyidiya school has eight classes of forty boys each, and their 'graduation' standard cannot, with the best will in the world, be rated much higher than an English primary. That is the sum total of State education in the Sultanate.

This is bad enough, but what is worse is that the Sultan carries on a sniping campaign at the private schools which have inevitably grown up. His objections to their activities are based on poor teaching methods, overcrowding, or undesirable elements of syllabus. I am sure that education inspectors would agree with him; maybe the people running these schools would too; but they are hamstrung by the restrictions imposed upon them either in the way of building, or of recruiting teachers, so that to hold them responsible for poor quality is a cynical act of injustice. I recall a case from Sur, where some of the local merchants joined together to finance a school for the town, and whose activities were reported to the Sultan in such a way that orders were issued to suppress the school. In this instance, as maybe in some others, the main opposition came from a group of fanatical Ibadhi religionists, a pressure group that still has a potent influence in Oman.

Teachers are at the root of the problem. There are few, if any, Omanis qualified. The only source is the Arab world, either Palestinians or other northern area Arabs for the most part. But such persons are anathema to the Sultan, who views them without exception as a rabid collection of revolutionary socialist nationalists. As a matter of principle, no Arab from outside the Gulf can enter Oman, nor from within it any Kuweiti; so that does not leave a very fruitful source of school-teachers. The few who are in the two State schools are a group of hand-picked Palestinians, whose livelihood in the country depends on their being quite a-political (not an easy thing for any true Palestinian). This utter mistrust and refusal to accept Arabs makes recruitment of anyone for the Sultanate Government a major problem, of teachers a near impossibility. This is one reason why the Sultan's professed wish to develop education is viewed by most people with the deepest mistrust.

Another is his own suspicion of education, his assumption that education leads to trouble. He is, of course, in some ways quite right. He will point to the problems that Arab countries, Gulf countries (Bahrain in particular) and European countries have had from students; 1968 student activities in America, France and indeed practically everywhere else in Europe, will doubtless have confirmed him in his worst fears. What he apparently also believes is that by withholding the possibilities of education from his people he will stop them obtaining it; or if they go somewhere else to obtain it, he can stop them returning to Oman to subvert the rest.

What happens in practice, of course, is that anyone who is able to does go somewhere else to obtain education, or to improve on what he has managed to glean from the Sayyidiya school. Most of them go to Kuweit, where the very generous State system has free places for any persons from the Gulf area. After getting secondary education there, many go on to university; wherever they can get a free place, most often either Cairo or Baghdad, but also in surprising numbers, Russia. Omani graduates in many subjects, from chemical engineering to architecture, can be found scattered round the Arab world; but not one in Oman, and this is the real tragedy.

I have said that Omanis are wanting education more than anything else. This requires a qualification in one direction: that there are, of course, many Omanis, more particularly in the interior, who have not themselves reached the stage of being able to express this desire. For such people the Quranic schools, where the children learn in a plain-song chant great slabs of the Quran by heart, have a temporary sufficiency. I cannot think this will last long.

Education may well turn out to be the most unyielding of the rocks on which the Sultan is likely to stub his toes while leading his people at his speed to the better world he has planned for them. To do anything practical about it he has certainly got to refashion some of his fundamental principles, and that is totally foreign to his nature. As with so many other things in the Sultanate, one can only hope. In the meantime, however, one of the occasions of the Muscat year I find most depressing is the celebration of the Sultan's birthday, at which a concert is put on by the schoolboys of the Muscat Sayyidiya school, and the junior forms sing (in rather charming unison) the praises of their Sultan, from whom all blessings flow. If only a few more did.

The first part of The Word is an explanation, in terms of money, of why the Sultan could do no more than balance his books for the first twenty-five years of his reign. During this time his income was virtually confined to customs duties; other sources of revenue were his Zanzibar subsidy (which is still to this day

paid by the British Government) and a rental for the oil concession, to which was later added, in 1959, the British subsidy.

Customs revenue has been the basis of the Sultanate economy.
In the process it has become a moral duty, in the eyes of the
Sultan, that Omani citizens should pay it. The Sultan's attitude to
the tax is one of almost religious fervour. This is understandable,
but it does not assist towards a more flexible approach now that
customs revenue provides only an insignificant proportion of his
total revenue.

Customs regulations in the Sultanate are, as might be guessed,
peculiar. The oddest thing is that the percentage rate for the
various different categories of imported goods is set not on the
c.i.f. price but the market price of the goods. Admittedly in many
cases, and in all cases where there is doubt, an arbitrary (but
unchanging) percentage mark-up on c.i.f. is used to assess the
market price, but in the case of commodities in common use—
such as rice, coffee, flour, tea, ghee etc.—a price index is established weekly by the customs department for all these items, and
used for assessment of duties of any cargoes imported during that
week. It seems a uselessly complicated way of going about
setting import duties.

The rate of duty is considerably higher than anywhere else
in the Gulf area, where admittedly it is very low. The effect has
been to limit Oman economically to its own borders, and to
attract a smuggling movement through Bureimi from Dubai.
Dubai, that mecca of liberal *laissez-faire* attitudes, has become the
polar opposite of the restrictionist Muscat. The difference between
them is instructive. Dubai is a booming go-ahead developing place
(built up, remember, without oil revenues; oil was not discovered
in commercial quantities until 1967), while Muscat is a dusty and
somnolent town. There seems to me little doubt that if the Sultan
in Muscat had been a character of the type of Sheikh Rashid of
Dubai, Muscat could have captured an enormous proportion of
the Dubai trade. I am not implying by this that, if it had, Muscat
today would necessarily be a better place, although it would be
a very different one, for Dubai's problems are growing the more
prosperous it becomes. But what is true is that the Muscat
merchants know Dubai, and they too realise that, if things had
been arranged differently, Muscat could today be more like Dubai

than it is like Muscat. They, on the other hand, are less likely to think about the problems that Dubai is now collecting, and are inclined to make a comparison between the two which leaves Muscat far behind on every count. They are unimpressed when they are told that the Sultan knows better than they do what is good for them.

The merchants are only one class of citizen, but the word spreads; more people visit the Trucial Coast, and more people become convinced that the Sultan's economic system is a lot worse than those practised by the Gulf sheikhs. They are assisted towards this conviction by a number of particularly irritating import restrictions. The one that has the most retarding effect upon the country and is the most dampening to people's enthusiasm is the order by which no car may be imported without prior permission; from whom? from the Sultan in person. If it seems beyond credibility that a ruler should personally vet every application for a car licence, that is what happens in Oman. Even this might become something of a joke if it were an efficient rubber-stamping exercise, but not a bit of it, there are plenty of people who never do obtain a licence, and some who are left in a limbo state with no answer at all. I know of one person who was intending to start up a new business, was investing a quite large sum of money in this, and who wrote to the Sultan for, amongst other things, a car import permit; six months later he had had no reply at all, and certainly no permit. There is a limit to the number of reminders you can send to a Sultan.

I mentioned elsewhere that there are no tractors in the Sultanate. This is not because there is no one who wants to use one.

The fact that dolls may not be imported is more understandable (this is based on a religious prohibition) than the limitation to ½ kw. for any petrol or diesel engine required for private use. The ban on gas cookers is comprehensible on grounds of safety, even if not, in fact, logical.

It would be misleading if you were to assume that these restrictions, and there are plenty of others which I will come to later, were imposed merely at the whim of the Sultan; that one morning he might wake up and decide over breakfast that it was time for another restriction—though sometimes one is tempted to think this. He is, however, a reasoning man, and behind these bans lie, if one wants to find them, reasons which, at least to the Sultan, are clear signposts to the action he has taken. In the case of the car restriction, for instance, the reason may stem from an amalgamation of concepts: one, that the traditional transportation system of Oman based on camels and donkeys should not, in the interests of the people involved in that system, be ruined overnight; two, that security in the country is still of vital importance and a wholesale invasion of motor transport would be difficult to control; three, that roads are poor and maintenance facilities more or less non-existent. I do not wish to argue about the validity of such reasons, but only to underline that they exist, and that the Sultan, if he felt it necessary to justify some action, would do so on the basis of a rational mental process. This is, in fact, his strength: that his actions are invariably based on a logical structure of reasoning; it may seem crazy logic to someone else, but to undermine even crazy logic you have to dig down deep.

Another of the peculiarities of customs duties in Oman is that a tax is payable on goods bought from one wilayat and sold in another. The symbol of this system is the Rui gate.* The origin of this tax (whether it should be described as a customs tax seems to me dubious, but that is certainly how it is thought of by the Sultan and the Customs Department) is the division of the country between Oman and the coast. In those days the Imamate in the interior, responsible for its own zakat collection, had to pay a tax if it wanted to sell on the coast; this concept was enshrined in the Treaty of Sib, and naturally constitutes one of the main proofs from the Imamate side that interior Oman always has been an independent separate state. Historically the Interior never questioned the justice of the tax, but only objected when it was used by Muscat as a weapon against them, as when in 1920 it was raised from 5 to 25 per cent to force them to come to terms.

To explain this tax in Western terms is not simple, nor probably very profitable. The fact remains that the tax on goods moved from one wilayat and sold in another exists and is applied. All that wood, for instance, which is brought down from the Hajir area on camels and donkeys (what would these men do if three-ton lorries

* See page 69 above.

were unrestrainedly allowed to do the job) is assessed for duty before being sold by the wood brokers in Muttrah; for every donkey load you have to pay half a rupee, for a camel load forty beizas.

It would be a gesture of little economic significance to himself but of considerable value to many of his subjects if the Sultan were now to cancel these internal forms of raising revenue. Unfortunately, this is the sort of gesture he is unlikely to make, because of his deeply held conviction that it is the moral duty of every Omani to pay something towards the upkeep of society. Customs duty has formed one traditional way of ensuring this, and, in order not to risk a weakening of the moral fibres of his people, I do not think he will repeal it. I hope I shall be proved wrong.

Zakat is another form of revenue. This, strictly, is a religious tithe type payment. In Oman today it is assessed in accordance with tradition on the produce of the land; at a rate of 5 per cent if the land is watered by pump or other non-natural means, 10 per cent if from a falaj or stream. Assessment is made on the basis of crop expectation, and the tax is gathered by zakat collectors. Some tribes, or even villagers, may be excused zakat by the Sultan; the Hawasina, for instance, do not pay it, a reward for their long and loyal service to the Sultan; however, even if it is not payable to the Sultan, it may still be gathered by the sheikh of the tribe for his use, as, for instance, is the case with the Beni Ali.

The total income from zakat is a matter for conjecture. I know of one village, neither large nor small, whose assessment for one year was M.T.D. 560; you could multiply this village by many hundreds throughout Oman. It is worth noticing, however, that assessment and collection is still in terms of Maria Theresa dollars. This is, to my mind, a most dishonest application of tradition, in that the official currency of Oman is now supposed to be the rupee and official policy is supposed to be directed towards the removal of the M.T.D. For the Sultan to perpetuate the M.T.D. in this sphere is, to say the least of it, unhelpful. In these days it is more than that, for the M.T.D. value has rocketed upwards; it now stands, in the free market, at about 10 rupees to the M.T.D., although it is officially pegged at 5 rupees to the M.T.D. (the actual rate it was about two years ago); and the import of fresh stocks of M.T.Ds. is not permitted. The result for the Omanis of the interior is that there has been a practical, though not theoretical, price inflation; and the Sultan, in his zakat business, makes a killing.

If customs revenues were the foundation of money past, money present and future comes from oil.

The I.P.C. group obtained the land concession for Oman from the Sultan in 1937. P.D.(O.), in that title, came into being in 1951. For a number of reasons the company got off to a slow start, because of the war, and then because of the internal state of the country. After spending a lot of money, about twelve million pounds, a majority of the partners, in 1960, decided that they did not want to continue. Shell, however, along with the Gulbenkian interests, decided to keep trying, and their resolve was rewarded when on 2 November 1964 they were able to announce that they had discovered commercial quantities of oil in the fields of Fahud, Natih and Yibal, and planned to start commercial exports in mid 1967. And indeed, thirty-three months and £25 million or so of facilities later, this happened.

By Middle East standards the present oil production of Oman is small; but its effect on the Sultanate economy is, of course, enormous. The oil operation itself is simple enough in outline; from Fahud there is a main trunk pipeline 175 miles long, which passes through the mountains down the Sumayl Gap, and ends up at the tanker terminal of Mina al Fahal. At each end are the sort of modern facilities that accompany any oil production project.

Modern technology has been welded to the ancient traditions of the country, and it would be unnatural if problems were not to arise. Most of them are the sociological ones which have already emerged in the later pages of this book; none of them are peculiar to Oman, though the way Oman has so far dealt with them is singular. Oil is the Djinn at the end of the rainbow; plenty of treasure, and plenty of undreamed-of problems uncorked.

Apart from P.D.(O.), which already in 1968 will have produced over two million pounds per month for the Sultan, an off-shore concession has been granted to a group of companies managed by the German Wintershall company. For many years also various combinations of American companies have been searching for oil in Dhofar; in 1967, however, that concession fell vacant after a failure to find any commercially exploitable oil.

Oman may have had to wait for a long time for her oil to be discovered, and the quantities may be comparatively small, but a solid revenue is now assured, and it will not be from want of trying by the oil companies if it is not multiplied as a result of further discoveries.

Oil is the biggest business in Oman, but there are plenty of other smaller ones. There is, however, one looming problem for the Muscat merchant community, which is that there is hardly a single interior tribal Omani who is represented in business. Historically this has been inevitable, and has not mattered very much, but I see it as a great stumbling block for the future. It is, of course, just one illustration of the basic division of the country between Muscat and Oman, but in other countries a similar situation has often led to trouble. One day the 'true' tribal interior Omani may decide that too much economic power is in the hands of the diluted Arab of the coast.

The case of the foreigner is straightforward. He is a foreigner, and must accept the rules laid down for him by the Government; if he does not, he can go, and, since he has the passport of another country, he has (at least theoretically) somewhere else to go. There are many foreign merchants in Muscat: a few European, and a large number of Indians. The latter, whose influence has already withered from the imperial days of the East India Company, the Bombay Government, and Curzon, used to be known, and sometimes still are, as banians; a peculiar word which sounds most disparaging, but has a respectable pedigree from the original sanskrit, and has itself given its name to the Banian tree, under which at Gombroon (now Bander Abbas) a group of banians were, one fine day, found sitting. Their influence has diminished, but there are still many of them, and if every Indian merchant left the country there would be a considerable business vacuum to be filled up.

The people most likely to fill it up would be what I call the diluted Omanis. They have Omani passports and are Omani citizens. The most commercially active of them are Baluch,

Baharina and Khojas (or Hyderabadis as they are sometimes known); their families, originally from Iran, Pakistan, India or Iraq, have been in Oman for many generations, and they have become wholly assimilated into the country. However, when the time comes, I have no doubt at all that they will be graded as second-class citizens. A further trouble is that, as in similar cases elsewhere, they tend to be highly intelligent and progressive and, therefore, successful. In the shorter term, this is no drawback, either to themselves or to Oman, but in the longer term there are many dangers; jealousies are easily generated by success, and at this moment of potential expansion they are ideally placed to seize all the advantages.

It is in no way surprising that this should have happened, for naturally the merchant class has built up in Muscat and Muttrah where trade is centred, and interior Oman has been, until recently, effectively cut off from the coast. The few merchants of any significance in the larger suqs of Bureimi, Ibri, Nizwa and Rustaq purchase their requirements from Muscat and Muttrah (or, in the case of Bureimi, from Dubai); the agencies are held on the coast, and that is where the money comes from. So far, however, the opposite process of expansion by the Muscat merchants through branches into the interior, has not taken place; for the very good reason that there are rigorous restrictions on movements within the country by coastal Omanis, even though they hold Omani passports. The Batina coast is in general free to them, but neither the Khojas nor the Baharina are permitted into the interior at all, and Baluch only with special permission. This, together with the strong limitations on freedom of taxi movements and importation of vehicles has meant that the interior has only the most rudimentary business or commercial activity at all. In that this will have left it free to development by tribal Omanis it may be a good thing; indeed that could, I suppose, if one were feeling generously disposed, be adduced as being a purpose of the rules.

Muscat business is still on a small scale. The merchants are keen, sometimes clever, but have not yet begun to think big; when they do, or are permitted to, there will be some large fortunes made. One typical source of fortunes in the Middle East, as elsewhere, is real estate. That has hardly begun, and the restrictions on purchase and sale of land, and on indiscriminate building, seem to me to be potentially some of the more rational rules. The Development Plan could, and I hope will, lead to an intelligent and controlled development of the two towns. It could even be aesthetically acceptable as well; that indeed would be a triumph. Muscat deserves it.

Muscat and Muttrah are administered by a Municipality, whose offices are in a comparatively new building opposite the Bab al Kebir and just outside the walls of Muscat. As might be expected, the authority belonging to the Municipality is, in general, negative rather than positive. One of its positive achievements, however, is to keep Muscat clean; with such effect that visitors who do not comment on it are the exception. It is the more strange that Muttrah is degrees dirtier. There is probably some subtle interpretation of the responsibilities of the Municipal Adminis- trator to the Wali of Muttrah that is different from those to the Governor of the Capital, which inhibits in Muttrah a full-scale garbage service.

I have never grasped what duties properly belong to the Municipality, nor what is its relationship to Muscat in the person of the Governor, or to Muttrah in the person of the Wali; I doubt that it would have been very useful if I had. Apart from cleaning the place one of its prime functions appears to be maintenance of the road between Muscat and Beit al Falaj, although I daresay that the last mile or so outside the Municipal limits is not its concern. It is a concrete road, but is veneered with bitumen once a year. The operation is primitive in the extreme; one man has a gallon- pot of bitumen and paints it over the road surface with a piece of cardboard, while another sprinkles sand over the tacky bitumen. There is plenty of scope for mechanisation in Muscat.

Another segment of Municipality activity is dealing with hous- ing applications of one sort or another, and the aftermath of fires which annually ravage the brittle burasti huts that so many of the people live in. This is a far more negative side of their business, for restrictions abound and it is difficult to obtain permission to do anything that is new.

The most provocative of these restrictions is that which forbids the rebuilding of a house in any material other than that from

13

which it is already constructed. This means that if you live in a burasti house which is burnt down, you can only rebuild in burasti unless you can obtain special dispensation; such dispensation is normally available only from the Sultan, although I have heard of very few cases where a degree of latitude has been used in interpreting the rule. Likewise, if you have earned some money and want to improve your living conditions with a mud wall, as a matter of principle you cannot do it.

This rule can now be rationalised by reference to the Development Plan, but it would be a good deal easier to stomach if the Plan were published; the rule, too, was in operation long before the Plan was commissioned, so that its earlier rationalisation was either a more remote version of the existing one, or else some abstruse calculation in Salala. One can hardly blame the Municipality who, when there is a fire, at least do their best to organise an appeal fund, which provides some small compensation to the poor people who may well have lost literally all their possessions.

The Municipality is an organisation on to which something more dynamic could easily be grafted. Next door to the Municipality offices a new post-office is about to be built, and in postal affairs the Sultanate has really made progress. In 1966 the first proper Muscat and Oman stamp issue was made, and very attractive it is too with a variety of Omani forts shown on the different denominations. This is a far cry from the time of Sayyid bin Turki Feisal, who also had the idea of issuing his own stamps, but, according to Bent who was visiting Muscat at the time, 'our political agent represented to him that it was beneath the dignity of so great a Sultan to make money in so mean a way, and the stamps have never appeared.'[2] Poor Feisal, he was up to his eyes in debt, harried for this by the British, and then served up with that sort of moralistic nonsense. More recently Oman had to be satisfied with those nasty over-printed stamps supplied by courtesy of and arrangement with the British Government, so one is particularly glad to see them so decidedly philatelically independent at last.

The Police Force has an ill-defined connection with the Municipality, at least in so far as it is responsible for ensuring that Municipal regulations are adhered to. Responsibility for the Police, whose jurisdiction is limited to the Municipal boundary, is

split between the Governor of the Capital and the Wali of
Muttrah, just as the Municipality itself has the same dual master,
so that at this level the duties of the Police are difficult to unravel.
This would matter more if their activities were effective or more
generally beneficial. Their main impingement on Muscat life is
through their rather inert, but necessary, traffic control, but they
could always be counted upon to be lurking in the shadows at
night, ready to apprehend any person who had forgotten his
lantern; moreover, they were, much to the annoyance of the
Muscat garrison troops and their commander, also responsible
for the explosions from Merani fort every evening that signified
that it was time for lanterns to be carried.

Now, a new police force is to be recruited and trained, and will,
it is alleged, be placed under the control of the Minister of the
Interior. Maybe then visitors will again be able to say, as William
Francklin did 182 years ago, that 'the police in Muscat is
excellent.'[3]

Restrictions have been a recurrent word in this text, and it
should be unnecessary to belabour the subject more. It is, however, a subject from which it is impossible to escape in Muscat,
and the Sultan's predilection for rules and regulations is one of the
things that make people so irritated with him and his regime. The
truth is that rules breed rules, and they invariably imply weak
control; it is much easier to tell people not to do things than to
give them the freedom to decide whether or not they should do
something, and then later have to make up your mind whether the
person who has done it should be applauded or punished. As I
have shown, the Sultan's Government is weak, and the result is
that its members encourage him to legislate for situations with
which they themselves would otherwise have to cope. Rules suit
them, and rules suit the Victorian nature of the Sultan, and so, in
a stream of petty restrictions, the rules are propagated. One
should add that they are directed at all levels of society, whether
to order Omanis to wear traditional Omani dress, or to forbid
Europeans to sail a boat east of Muscat harbour.

Petty restrictions are one thing and can be tolerated well
enough by reasonably objective people. It is the vicious ones,
those that retard Omani development, that cannot be forgiven—

like the ban on the import of vehicles or tractors, or, worse still, the rule that forbids a wife to accompany her husband abroad (without permission, of course—permission from the Sultan himself), and, worst of all, the control exercised by the Sultan over Omanis wishing to return from abroad to work in their country—there is no written rule on this, as far as I know, but in practice an Omani who has educated himself abroad will be unable to obtain a job in his home country. Of course, the Sultan can rationalise his regulation, it is for the sake of security. But this type of security is just plugging the holes in the barbed wire round the country's borders; one day the barbed wire will be rolled aside, and none of the Sultan's restrictions will help him one iota.

In spite of his total unconcern for the world at large, for the Arab world of which he is geographically, linguistically and religiously a part, and now too for the oil world to which he is economically attached, the Sultan has realised that he must keep at least one friend outside his own boundaries; and so, following the example of his ancestors and anyway not having had much alternative, he has used Britain as his friend. As I have shown previously, used is the operative word, for he has carefully escaped any too deep involvement and has jealously guarded his independent status. However, when it comes to talking of his foreign affairs you can hardly get away from Britain.

In Muscat there are only two representatives of foreign countries, the British Consul General and the Indian Consul General. Relations with Britain are governed by the Treaty of Friendship, Commerce and Navigation of 1951 which is a direct descendant of the original 1798 Treaty; those with India by a Treaty signed in 1953. The Sultan in practice uses the good offices of the British to represent him and his ideas internationally, in particular at the United Nations, but he has in no way abrogated his right to carry on his own foreign policy. Indeed, if foreign policy is the right phrase, he does himself administer it.

He has diplomatic relations of a sort, but not representation, with America; the original 1833 Treaty* signed by Said bin Sultan

---

* See page 47 above.

with Roberts was renewed in 1958 as a Treaty of Amity, Economic Relations, and Consular Rights, but, although they have frequently considered taking up again the Consular Rights which were last held in 1915, the Americans have not yet returned to Muscat to live; from time to time their representative from Aden drops in to see if anything new has happened.

The Sultan exchanged letters with West Germany in 1967, and the stately hand of protocol seemed, when I left Muscat, to have lighted a fuse which should explode one day in a similar exchange with Holland; the latter, if it succeeds, will be a successor to a Commercial Treaty which the Dutch signed with the Sultan in 1877, but which has since lapsed. I have never been clear as to the exact diplomatic significance of an Exchange of Letters, but clearly some official acknowledgement that the two countries exist is helpful now that there is a commercial link with both through oil; the same link now exists with France, and it is a pleasant conceit to think of de Gaulle thumbing through his Muscat file and carrying on the correspondence from where it was left off by Napoleon.

Whether a treaty legally lapses after some period of years if neither side has made use of it or has not actively renewed it I am not sure, but certainly the Sultan announced in the United Nations (via the tongue of the British representative, of course) that he did not consider treaties made by his predecessors to be binding upon himself unless specifically renewed by him. He said this at the time in order to make it quite clear that as far as he was concerned the Treaty of Sib was a dead duck, but it had the side effect of cancelling those old American, Dutch and French treaties, and ensuring that they, and anyone else who had an ancient treaty in a pigeon hole, must start again.

The Sultan was moved to engineer his pronouncement in the United Nations not because he believes in that body; he does not at all, nor does he have any greater faith in any of its agencies. As far as he is concerned, the U.N. is nothing, but he is willing to allow the British representative once a year to refute the allegations of the 'Special Committee on the Situation with regard to the Implementation of the Declaration on the Granting of Independence to Colonial Countries and Peoples relating to the Territory of Oman.'

The Sultan is so suspicious of and opposed to any outside body interfering in any way with his country, that he would by nature consider membership of the U.N. to be both unnecessary and useless, but he is even more opposed to them because of his experience with them. Oman was first brought up in the U.N. in 1957 after the Sultan had asked for British help against the Imamate rebellion; the British were accused of aggression (and, for that matter, still are). During the following years the British Government finally persuaded the Sultan to invite the U.N. to send a representative to the country to see for himself what the situation really was like. 'On 11th December 1962, at the 1191st meeting of the General Assembly, the representative of the United Kingdom transmitted to the Secretary-General an invitation from the Sultan of Muscat and Oman to send a representative on a personal basis "to visit the Sultanate during the coming year to obtain first-hand information as to the situation there".' The Secretary-General accepted the invitation and appointed as his Special Representative Mr. Herbert de Ribbing. Mr. de Ribbing left New York on 18 May 1963, visited the Sultanate and returned to New York on 1 July 1963.[4] After the de Ribbing report had been presented to the U.N. an *ad hoc* committee was formed to consider the question. The Sultan saw its President in London, but refused to allow its members to visit Oman, and its report was, therefore, rather naturally unfavourable to the Sultan. On 17 December 1965 the U.N. General Assembly passed a resolution recognising the right of Oman's self-determination which was being prevented, it said, by the United Kingdom. This resolution received sixty-one votes for, eighteen against, thirty-two abstentions, with six members not present. And that, as far as the Sultan was concerned, was the final end of any interest he might have had in the United Nations.

The question of Omani independence had earlier been brought up in 1957 by the Arab League States, encouraged by the Imamate Office. There is a story that when the Arab League itself was asked for its support for this demand for independence, their first action was to call for a map in order to be shown where the tract of land was that they were being asked to make into a state. The Imamate Office, of course, was, and still is, the formal political front of Ghalib, Talib, Suleiman bin Himyar and Salih bin Isa, and what they are seeking the independence of is what was earlier described as Oman proper; and part of their legal argument is based on their interpretation of the Treaty of Sib, which, when tabled as part of the data of the case in the United Nations must have had many jurists scratching their wigs. One has some sympathy with the representative of Uruguay, for instance, who carefully explained that his abstentions from voting 'were due in the main to a lack of clarity with regard to the facts'.

As a commentary upon the Sultan himself, the de Ribbing report recorded one paragraph that most characteristically delineated his attitude. The representative of Chile had, before de Ribbing set off for Oman, asked why the Sultan did not send his own representative to the U.N. to defend his case; de Ribbing duly asked the Sultan. 'The Sultan, during the discussion on 24 May 1963, in general emphasised his sovereignty and more specifically stated that (a) his country was not a Member of the United Nations; (b) he had informed the Secretary-General that the discussion by the General Assembly of the question of Oman represented interference in the affairs of his country; and (c) he saw no reason why he should go to court, sit on the "bench for the accused" and be confronted with his own subjects on an equal footing.'

If the Sultan's attitude is uncompromising towards the United Nations as an organisation, it is equally unyielding towards what might in different circumstances be considered his Arab brethren. With very few exceptions he neither likes, nor trusts, them. Brought up in the imperial surroundings of the Chief's College, Ajmer, India, and sensitive to his family traditions of rule, his attitude towards the Egyptians is not far removed from that of the average British tommy of World War Two; a lot of wogs, I am afraid he might refer to them in an unguarded moment (and he would be echoing his great-great-grandfather who referred to the 'fatal consequences' to his rule if his troops were to 'associate with Egyptians'). One reason why he neither likes nor trusts Arabs is that most of them have backed the Imam's case against him, and some of them actually flaunt an Imamate Office in their capitals—Iraq, Syria, Saudi Arabia, Egypt, and even Kuwait. That is why when his people go off in search of education and find it in these places, and above all in Kuwait, he transmits his mistrust to them also and declines to have them back in any responsible function in his country.

It is legitimate to ask whether the anti-Sultan movements have any great potency or following, and I think the answer must be no. The Imam himself is by now, if ever he was not, a purely political pawn in the game, and, what is more, has been seen to be—except by those few rigidly conservative and introspective mountainous Ibadhis who would fervently accept as Imam anyone with the title of Imam. His brother Talib is an unsuccessful (at least so far) revolutionary exile; an awful bore, I suspect, in Baghdad or Cairo by now, and useful only at specific political moments. Suleiman bin Himyar was always an individualist, and only threw in his lot with the others when he was sure it would be to his own advantage; his mistake was that his judgement was at fault, and he has probably regretted it ever since. Salih bin Isa is now an old man who has lost what tribal influence he might once have had.

Apart from the vagaries of the Imamate opposition the Sultan faces also the threats and activities of the Dhofar Liberation Front. This organisation is quite separate from the Imamate organisation and is specifically concerned with the liberation of Dhofar from the Sultan's rule. As I have described, Dhofar is by way of being a sort of personal property of the Sultan; whether the Sultan considers it as part of the Sultanate of Muscat and Oman, or as part of the Sultanate of Muscat and Oman and Dhofar (the latter is included, as you may remember, on the inscription above the main gate of Muscat town) is by no means clear. Its links with Muscat and Oman are confined to the effects of the Sultan himself living there, and the main effect is that because he lives there the Dhofar Liberation Front is trying to seize it, and because of this much of the Sultan's Army is engaged in trying to stop them. It is a peculiar situation.

The Dhofar Liberation Front seems to be organised by Dhofaris; whether dissident or not is a moot point, but certainly dissatisfied. Their support comes mainly from South Arabia, at least to the extent that their members can retreat safely there if under pressure. 'Rebel activity' in Dhofar has been fairly considerable and by no means ineffective, even if success is improbable in the face of the SAF contingent that is tied down there to contain them. As a practical and active organisation, however, there is no doubt that the Dhofar Liberation Front is superior to the Imamate movement.

Now that the Sultan has money from oil, he has plans for some economic development in Dhofar. Like everything else in Dhofar—customs, currency, government, people, climate—development is wholly detached from that of Muscat and Oman. Is it the same country? No; except that the Sultan lives there, and with him his son Qabus, Sandhurst-trained, cooped up in his father's palace like a medieval prisoner, unable to do anything useful either for himself or the country that will theoretically be his one day to rule.

One sees why the opposition exists, and often wishes, in a conspiratorial way, that it were slightly more attractive and efficient.

Even though the Sultan is quite clearly out of harmony with any Arab state that might be described, or wish to be described, as socialist (of whatever variety happens to be in vogue at the moment), he might be expected to be more attuned to the policies and aspirations of the rulers within the Gulf. However, even here, so near at home, he remains distant, supercilious, suspicious and wholly independent. As we have seen, Kuwait is beyond the pale because of its Imamate Office and the sinister propaganda broadcast to Omani students or visitors. Bahrain is not considered evil, nor particularly beneficial; perhaps the Sultan has a hidden feeling that anyway Bahrain should be his, as once it did belong to Oman (but never for very long). Qatar is all that the Sultan disapproves of, although, being uninfluential, is not as bad as Kuwait. As for the Trucial States, fundamentally the Sultan is dubious as to what they are now up to, but he does have a lifeline to Sheikh Zaid of Abu Dhabi.

Zaid was for many years the Governor of Al Ain, Abu Dhabi's part of the Bureimi oasis, including all the dramatic years of the Saudi involvement there. As a result he was close to Oman, knew many of the Omani sheikhs, and also the Sultan himself; when in 1955 the Sultan made his celebrated trip to the interior from Salala he continued his drive right up to Bureimi and met Zaid there. He trusts Zaid as he does not trust any of the others, and Zaid must understand him as much as anyone can understand such a man as the Sultan; mind you, I believe that Zaid finds his attitude towards development and restrictions just as incomprehensible as the next man (he must, for his own attitude is totally the opposite), but still there is an affinity which exists with nobody else.

Indeed, the Sultan's one positive piece of foreign policy for I do not know how many years, probably since 1952 when he was stopped at Sohar from marching on Bureimi, occurred in 1968 when he invited Zaid to visit him in Salala. What is more, Zaid went. One of the results of the meeting is that the lifeline is being strengthened into a hot line—with, who knows, a scrambler built into it.

What should happen, geographically and economically, is that the Sultan should join a Trucial States Federation (which should never anyway have become involved with Qatar and Bahrain) and history would neatly repeat itself with a Greater Oman. It will not happen, certainly while the Sultan is in power, but it would make more basic sense than anything else in the area, including what is happening now. Oman, with its potential for agriculture, its population (small enough at 750,000 but a welcome multiplication to the Trucial Coast), and its relatively small oil production would complement the enormous oil production of Abu Dhabi and the commercial acumen of Dubai, and in theory the result could be a viable state—which is what everybody badly needs in that part of the world. I exclude, of course, the question of personalities, because this is merely a pipe-dream composed of geographical and economic smoke-rings.

In the meantime Oman goes its own inimitable way, and it is, of course, extremely difficult for the Sultan to find anyone, except the British, to help him. Practically everybody else is ruled out for one reason or another, and in particular all those who would theoretically be of most benefit, the people who talk the same language, the Arabs.

Apart from the British, who, it should be repeated, are all there as mercenaries, civilian or military, recruited and paid for by the Sultan, only the Indians are really considered to be suitable for jobs in the Sultanate; and, preferably, Indians who are not Moslems, just to be sure there will not be any influence through religion.

There is the tragedy, a collision course set between an old way of life and rule and the new requirements of modern democracy. It is plain for all to see, and everyone sees it, except for old Said bin Taimur bin Feisal bin Turki bin Said bin Sultan bin Ahmed bin Said Al bu Said sitting in his decrepit castle by the sea in Salala.

Postscript

I have been true to my promise, and have resolutely declined to burden my text with anything that happened post-Said bin Taimur. Nor is it the purpose of this book to make judgements on what he did in the light of what has happened since. That is another story.

I must now make my ritual remark on the transliteration of Arabic words, but it will not take long. I have attempted to be consistent; I have tried to produce a word that sounds in English approximately similar to the Arabic sound; anyone who puts his mind to it will be able to criticise the result.

Finally, I should like to say that I should probably not have visited Muscat and Oman, and would certainly never have written this book, if I had not been employed by Petroleum Development (Oman) Ltd. To them, to the people of Muscat and Oman, and to others who were connected with the country, many of whom were in some way, and often quite unwittingly, of assistance to me in writing this book, I record my grateful thanks.

1974

✶ Sultanate of Oman ✶

I went back to Oman, for a few days only, in 1983. I was right to record impressions of Said bin Taimur's pre-1970 Muscat and Oman. It has been transformed. The Sultanate of Oman is a different country set in the same surroundings.

The forts of Muscat, Merani and Jalali, are still there. They still release their daily whiff of history, but less pervasively, into the town. Unless you make a special diversion up the old road and over the pass you will unexpectedly arrive in the middle of Muscat on a motorway through what used to be a hill and, failing to find the old gateway and its Hawasina guards and seduced by the Sultan's new and overpowering palace, may entirely miss the sensation of history. Not everything in Muscat, however, has been knocked down; indeed, many of the old houses have been preserved and stand in a sleek splendour that they can never before have known.

I am not so sure about Ottavi. Fifteen years ago he would, as I suggested then, have felt at home even though I and my family were living in his house. Now Beit Fransawi is back with the French government as their embassy; but, when I looked in on it, I could see only a chaos of rebuilding. I do not know, and hesitated to find out, whether the old stairway to the roof will be preserved, whether a new flagpole will be erected and whether the iron ring will be left embedded in the stone. But even if the tricolor flies again I suspect that Ottavi would now find himself disoriented amongst too much that was unfamiliar. No doubt I should too, if deposited here after another seventy-five years.

Change in Oman is deep and pervasive; even physical, to the extent that hunks of hill and slabs of skyline have been forcibly removed to allow roads or buildings to be constructed. None of this is surprising given that in the years before 1970 practically nothing changed and that in the years after 1970, but particularly those since 1973, the dollar revenue to the country from oil has been counted in billions rather than millions. I sometimes wonder what Said bin Taimur would have done, or failed to do, with such riches, what new version of The Word he might have composed, how long he could have maintained his remote methods of rule. The answer is, of course, in what happened. He was removed in 1970 precisely because he was incapable of dealing with the changes implicit in his increasing oil revenues, and Qabus emerged from his palace prison in Salala to provide the social and economic change and development that his father was unable to handle.

So, the new Oman has fizzed into the 1970s and 1980s under the tutelage of Qabus, rocketing through statistical sound barriers and hurtling past slower moving competitors on the GNP growth ladder. Not everything has been for the best all the time but the people of Oman have every reason to be grateful to Qabus for what has been achieved and Qabus satisfied for having achieved it. There are few people who visit Oman today who do not find it a friendly, unflamboyant, uncomplicated country and that is not something that can be said for most countries of the Middle East or, for that matter, of the world in general.

One thing that remains the same is the line of the Jebal Akhdar seen from the Sumayl Gap or, still tilted in slabs at, presumably, the same same angle, from Nizwa. You look at it, however, from an airconditioned car speeding along a sweeping highway unaccompanied by dust or sweat. At the turning to Sumayl village I could have bought tennis balls at a supermarket, eaten at the Sumayl restaurant or filled the car at a petrol station. I could have spent a couple of hours at the new Izki cinema. I could have posted a letter at the Birkat al Mauz postbox instead of rushing past on the bypass. At the Firq roundabout I had the choice of following Route 15 to Ibri or Route 31 to Salala. I could have telexed the Nizwa Motel for a room. I did, however, stay there for a night and ate a Nizwaburger for lunch, but it was too cold for a swim in the pool.

Next morning we stopped in Nizwa and were able to climb up the great circular tower only because we had the correct permit (as we also had in our pockets for Jibrin). The suq beneath is not so much changed except that the silver is modern and very expensive, but a large Ibadhi mosque has been built beside it and on the opposite side of the main road is a group of shops overshadowed by a branch of the Oman Bank for Agriculture and Fisheries. However, the old tree by the suq entrance is still there and so is the Friday market of sheep and goats, each one led round a dusty path to the accompaniment of unchanged yells of encouragement.

Jibrin was a joy, apart from the date palms which were dying either from disinterest or lack of water. The Ministry of National Heritage has been given encouragement and resource to preserve Omani history and art and a marvellous result is being achieved in restoring the exquisite painted ceilings and walls of Jibrin castle. And that tamarind tree is still there.

Back at Bahla, just under the shadow of the castle, a group of Omani travellers was waiting for the next Ibri–Muttrah bus, whose timing was exhibited on a smart bus information board beside the stop. Behind, every house, mud or concrete, in Bahla town was crowned with its television aerial. We then went on to Tanuf where the ruined town seemed even more desolate after fifteen more years of sun, wind and crumbling. Round the corner, however, at the entrance to the tumbling crags of the wadi, there was a real Himyarific surprise — the Tanuf water bottling plant. Who would have imagined that there was any life left in the place after all that RAF rocketing, and that, for the diners in the Musandam coffee shop, the Qurm restaurant, Sur night-club and Jibrin ballroom of the Muscat Intercontinental, Tanuf spring water would compete with Evian in satisfying their thirsts?

It only took a couple of hours or so to drive back to Qurm where the Intercontinental faces the beach and the sea. The mangrove swamp at the end of the Wadi Adai is now a wildlife reserve and the crabs have to share that part of the beach with the hotel's fitter clients who make use of the Qurm joggers' trail. At the weekend the beach is also a favourite place for ball games and for elderly strollers out for some light exercise with the dog, as if it were Weston-super-Mare or East-bourne. A few hundred yards back is the main motorway into Muttrah and Muscat, thick with traffic jams half the day, cars slowly circling immaculate lawned and flowered roundabouts, lorries grinding gears past what used to be, but has long since vanished beneath concrete, the Rui gate and customs post.

All this outward change is straightforward and expected. It would be surprising only if it had not occurred, but even so it succeeds in startling anyone with a memory of the absolute, extreme contrast of Said bin Taimur's Muscat and Oman. And, apart from the Indian de-signed palace in Muscat, there is a further pleasure in the surprise of finding that the result is unobtrusive and altogether natural.

External change is one thing, visible, even tangible. It is self-evident that all these billions of dollars must also have done something for the Omani way of life and character.

As you emerge from what until now has been the last section of this book, the most striking elements of transformation in the lives of Omanis relate to communications, education and health. All that de-pressing miasma of 1960 constraint and restriction has evaporated into an atmosphere of activity, noise, movement and money-making. It is not so much a changed country as a new one.

In the preceding paragraphs I have been travelling at speed around part of Oman, but there are hundreds more miles of road open to cars, trucks and anything moving on any number of wheels. There is even an internal airline. Television and radio, broadcast from studios just outside Muttrah, are available all over the country. Roads lead to schools, to hospitals, to clinics. A university is being planned. In little more than ten years Oman has become an oil-powered market economy welfare state.

All this change and development has catapulted the Sultanate into the world. It still remains a bit secretive as a country, so that a visitor, for instance, must obtain sponsorship before being issued with a visa. This prevents tourism, for which the country is not yet provided with sufficient facilities, but means that the marginal touristic activities of residents and visitors are all the more pleasant and enjoyable. But the isolationism of Said bin Taimur is a thing of the past. Oman is a member of the United Nations; it has embassies in thirty-five countries; it has twenty-six foreign representatives in Muscat; it is a member of the Arab League and many other Arab organisations; it is a member of the Gulf Cooperation Council. It is even at peace with South Yemen, having won its border war with the Dhofar Liberation Front long since.

Fifteen years ago it did not seem a task beyond achievement to sit down and write about Muscat and Oman in two hundred pages and within that length to cover most of what ought to have been covered. A very large volume would today be needed to do equivalent justice to the Sultanate of Oman. However, as I drove out to Seeb International Airport past the old Beit al Falaj airfield, now covered with the houses, shops and streets of a township, and past Azaiba, where the old P.D.(O.) airstrip is still distinguishable on a ridge above the motorway, I determined to tag on to my original postscript this brief addendum. It is nice to do what I had never intended to do as a sort of additional salute to a country and a people who are so genial. I hope that it will be time, after another fifteen years, to do it again.

1984

Notes and Sources

MUSCAT

1. William Francklin: *Observations Made on a Tour from Bengal to Persia in the Years 1786-7* (T. Cadell, London 1790)
2. J. T. Bent: 'Muscat', *Contemporary Review* Vol. 68 (1895)
3. J. R. Wellsted: 'Narrative of a Journey into the Interior of Oman', *Journal of the Royal Geographical Society* (1837)
4. J. T. Bent: op. cit.
5. J. T. Bent: op. cit.
6. *History of the Imams and Seyyids of Oman by Salil ibn Razik*—translated by G. P. Badger (Hakluyt Society 1871)
7. J. T. Bent: op. cit.
8. *Kashf al Ghummah*: 'An Anonymous History of Oman Probably Written in about 1728'; translated by E. C. Ross in 1874 (*Journal of the Asiatic Society of Bengal* Vol. XLIII)
9. G. P. Badger: op. cit.
10. A. Auzoux: 'La France et Muscate aux 18e et 19e siècles', *Revue d'Histoire Diplomatique* XXIII (1909), XXIV (1910)
    H. Prentout: *L'Ile de France sous Decaen, 1803–1810* (Paris 1901)
11. C. V. Aitchison: *A Collection of Treaties, Engagements and Sanads Relating to India and the Neighbouring Countries* in twelve volumes
12. Quoted in S. M. Zwemer, *Arabia, the Cradle of Islam* (Edinburgh 1900)
13. *An Account of the Monies Weights and Measures in General Use in Persia, Arabia, East India and China . . . the Whole Alphabetically Arranged on a New and Useful Plan for Business* (London 1789)
14. J. B. Fraser: *Narrative of a Journey into Khorasan in 1821–22* (London 1825)
15. *The Arabia Mission.* Quarterly letters, Annual Reports. 1890–1899 (New York)
16. P. Z. Cox: 'Some Excursions in Oman', *Geographical Journal* (1925)
17. Ibn Hawqal: *The Oriental Geography of Ibn Hawqal*
18. Eugene Stock: *An Heroic Bishop* (Hodder and Stoughton 1914)
19. William Francklin: op. cit.
20. S. B. Miles: 'Journal of an Excursion in Oman', *Geographical Journal* (1896)
21. Marco Polo: *The Book of Marco Polo, the Venetian*
22. Albuquerque: *The Commentaries of the Great Afonso d'Albuquerque*

23. S. B. Miles: *The Countries and Tribes of the Persian Gulf* (1919; Second Edition with introduction by J. B. Kelly, Frank Cass 1966)
24. Albuquerque: op. cit.
25. Bertram Thomas: 'The Musandam Peninsula and its Inhabitants— The Shihuh', *Journal of the Royal Central Asian Society* XV (1928)
26. For details of this episode see Briton Cooper Busch: *Britain and the Persian Gulf 1894-1914* (University of California Press 1967)

OMAN

 1. Quoted in J. B. Kelly: *Britain and the Persian Gulf 1795-1880* (Oxford University Press 1968)
 2. Quoted in S. M. Zwemer: op. cit.
 3. Described in Al Salimi: *Tuhfat al Ayan* (Cairo 1931)
 4. E. C. Ross: op. cit.
 5. S. M. Zwemer: op. cit.
 6. J. T. Bent: op. cit.
 7. Ibn Batuta: *The Travels of Ibn Batuta*
 8. S. B. Miles: 'On the Border of the Great Desert', *Geographical Journal* (1910)
 9. J. R. Wellsted: op. cit.
10. S. B. Miles: 'Across the Green Mountains', *Geographical Journal* (1901)
11. Justin Perkins: *A Residence of Eight Years in Persia, among the Nestorian Christians; with Notices of the Muhammadans* (Andover U.S. 1843)
12. E. C. Ross: op. cit.
13. Quoted in J. B. Kelly: op. cit.
14. J. B. Kelly: *Eastern Arabian Frontiers* (Faber and Faber 1964)
15. J. R. Wellsted: op. cit.
16. Wilfred Thesiger: *Arabian Sands* (Longmans 1959)

MUSCAT AND OMAN

 1. *The Word of Sultan Said bin Taimur, Sultan of Muscat and Oman, about the History of the Financial Position of the Sultanate in the Past and the Hopes for the Future, after the Export of Oil* (January 1968)
 2. J. T. Bent: op. cit.
 3. William Francklin: op. cit.
 4. U.N. Document A/5562 (8/10/63)

Apart from the works mentioned above, many of which have been of far wider general value than the few references quoted, I have made particular use of the following:

C. F. Beckingham: 'Reign of Ahmed bin Said', *Journal of the Royal Asiatic Society* (1941)

C. S. D. Cole: 'Account of an Overland Journey to Meskat and the Green Mountains of Oman', *Transactions of the Bombay Geographical Society* (1858)

R. Coupland: *East Africa and its Invaders* (Oxford University Press 1938)

Encyclopaedia of Islam

Paul W. Harrison: *Doctor in Arabia* (Robert Hale 1943)

David Holden: *Farewell to Arabia* (Faber and Faber 1967)

G. F. Hourani: *Arab Seafaring* (Khayats, Beirut 1963)

J. B. Kelly: 'Sultanate and Imamate in Oman', *Chatham House Memorandum* (1959)

R. G. Landen: *Oman since 1856* (Princeton University Press 1967)

L. Lockhart: 'The Menace of Muscat', *Asiatic Review* (1946)

John Marlowe: *Persian Gulf in the Twentieth Century* (Cresset Press 1962)

James Morris: *Sultan in Oman* (Faber and Faber 1957)

H. Moyse-Bartlett: *The Pirates of Trucial Oman* (Macdonald 1966)

Harold Peake: 'The Copper Mountain of Magan', *Antiquity* (1928)

A. W. Stiffe: 'Visit to the Hot Springs of Bosher near Muscat', *Transactions of the Bombay Geographical Society* (1859)

Bertram Thomas: 'Arab Rule under the Al bu Said Dynasty 1741–1937', *Proceedings of the British Academy* (1938)

Sir Arnold Wilson: *The Persian Gulf* (George Allen and Unwin 1928)

Fuller bibliographies can be found in a number of the books referred to above.

☙ Appendix 1 ❧

THE WYLDE TREATY

Philip Wylde was the representative of the East India Company from Surat, who was sent, at the request of the Imam Nasir in 1645, to Sohar to negotiate a treaty with him. He signed it in February 1646, and its terms are quoted in the letter he forthwith dispatched, from the pinnace *Lannaret*, to Surat on February 19th.

It is a notable document in that it embodies, albeit in a tentative form: in clause one, the concept of currency convertibility; in clause three, the concept of exemption from customs duty; in clause four, the concepts of Anti-Trust and Retail Price Maintenance; in clause five, that of religious toleration; and in clause six, of extraterritorial jurisdiction:

'Agreement and conditions of peace propounded by Philip Wylde . . . to the people of Sohar, for them to keep, and observe, without breach.
1. That we may be granted and permitted free trade within the dominions of this kingdom, without prohibition of any commodity to be brought, bought, or exported out of the kingdom: neither limitation, confining to a certain quality of merchandise: in lieu of which, being sold, to receive such coins as may stand with our liking;—carrying it where and whither we please.
2. That if any of our goods shall be stolen, the King shall be liable to make satisfaction.
3. That we shall pay no Custom for any Goods or Merchandise brought or imported out of the kingdom.
4. That no man shall engross to himself, in the way of merchandising such commodities as the English bring:— but that all Merchants, without exception, may have free liberty to buy, at such rates as they can agree for.
5. That we may have licence to exercise our own Religion.
6. That if any, it should so happen, broils and offences betwixt the English and these Country people:—the

Governor of the same place shall punish the Mussulmen; and the Chief of the English shall do justice among his own people.

7. That the English shall be tolerated to wear the Arms ashore.

8. That no Christian shall have license, in any part of this kingdom, besides the English:—on which performance, they enjoin themselves to supply this Port, yearly, with Ship, or Ships, bringing such Commodities as India, etc., adjacent ports, afford, suitable to what be demanded.'

Appendix 2

THE 1798 AND 1800 TREATIES*

The treaty of 1798 was the first treaty proper that was signed with Oman, and confirmed that Britain, not France, was the most significant influence in the area.

Translation of the Cowlnamah, or Written Engagement from the Imam of Muscat—1798

Deed of Agreement from the State of the Omanian Asylum, under the approbation of the Imam, the Director, Syud Sultan, whose grandeur be eternal! to the High and Potent English Company, whose greatness be perpetuated! as comprehended in the following Articles:—

Article 1

From the intervention of the Nawab Etmandi Edowla Mirza Mehedy Ally Khan Bahadoor Hurhmut Jung never shall there by any deviation from this Cowlnamah.

Article 2

From the recital of the said Nawab my heart has become disposed to an increase of the friendship with that state, and from this day forth the friend of that Sircar is the friend of this, and the friend of the Sircar is to be the friend of that; and, in like manner, the enemy of that Sircar is the enemy of this, and the enemy of this is to be the enemy of that.

Article 3

Whereas frequent applications have been made, and are still making, by the French and Dutch people for a Factory, i.e. to seat themselves in either at Maskat or Goombroom, or at the other ports of this Sircar, it is therefore written that, whilst warfare shall continue between the English Company and them, never shall, from respect to the Company's friendship, be given to them throughout all my territories a place to fix or seat themselves in, nor shall they even get ground to stand upon within this State.

* The texts are quoted from C. V. Aitchison.

Article 4

As there is a person of the French nation, who has been for these several years in my service, and who hath now gone in command of one of my vessels to the Mauritius, I shall, immediately on his return, dismiss him from my service and expel him.

Article 5

In the event of any French vessel coming to water at Muscat, she shall not be allowed to enter the cove into which the English vessels are admitted, but remain without; and in case of hostilities ensuing here between the French and English ships, the force of this State by land and by sea, and my people, shall take part in hostility with the English, but on the high seas I am not to interfere.

Article 6

On the occurrence of any shipwreck of a vessel or vessels appertaining to the English, there shall certainly be aid and comfort afforded on the part of this Government, nor shall the property be seized on.

Article 7

In the port of Abassy (Goombroom) whenever the English shall be disposed to establish a Factory, I have no objection to their fortifying the same and mounting guns thereon, as many as they list, and to forty or fifty English gentlemen residing there, with seven or eight hundred English Sepoys, and for the rest, the rate of duties on goods on buying and selling will be on the same footing as at Bussora and Abushehr.

Dated 1st of Jemmadee-ul-Awul 1213 Hegira, or 12th of October 1798

Not content with his Treaty, and afraid that perhaps the French might still have a trick up their sinister sleeve, a further confirmation was signed in 1800:

'Agreement entered into by the Imam of the State of Omam with Captain John Malcolm Bahadoor, Envoy from the Right Honourable the Governor-General, dated the 21st of Shaban 1213 Hegira, or 18th January 1800.

Article 1

The Cowlnamah entered into by the Imam of Oman with Mehedy Ally Khan Bahadoor remains fixed and in full force.

Article 2

As improper reports of a tendency to interrupt the existing harmony and create misunderstanding between the States have gone abroad, and have been communicated to the Right Honourable the Governor-General, the Earl of Mornington, K.P., with a view to prevent such evils in future, we, actuated by sentiments of reciprocal friendship, agree that an English gentleman of respectability, on the part of the Honourable Company, shall always reside at the port of Muscat, and be an Agent through whom all intercourse between the States shall be conducted, in order that the actions of each government may be fairly and justly stated, and that no opportunity may be offered to designing men, who are ever eager to promote dissensions, and that the friendship of the two States may remain unshook till the end of time, and till the sun and moon have finished their revolving career.

Sealed in my presence.

John Malcolm,

Envoy.

Approved by the Governor-General in Council on 26th April 1800.'

Appendix 3

AL BU SAID DYNASTY, 1749–

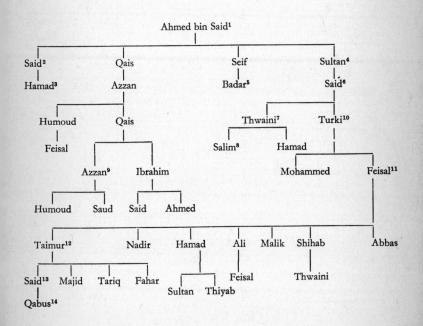

1868–1871	Azzan bin Qais (also Imam)
1871–1888	Turki bin Said
1888–1913	Feisal bin Turki
1913–1932	Taimur bin Feisal
1932–1970	Said bin Taimur
1970–	Qabus bin Said

Index